NE

ZULU FOUR

NEW SAS 3

ZULU FOUR

David Monnery

First published in Great Britain 1997
22 Books, Invicta House, Sir Thomas Longley Road,
Rochester, Kent

A CIP catalogue record for this book
is available from the British Library

ISBN 1 86238 009 0

10 9 8 7 6 5 4 3 2 1

Typeset by Hewer Text Composition Services, Edinburgh
Printed in Great Britain by
Clays Ltd, St Ives plc

1

I thought I could hear rain splattering the forest canopy way above us, but only a few drops were reaching the ground, and for all I knew they were the leftovers from some earlier downpour. There was no way of knowing, no way of seeing beyond the tunnel we were in. It did seem even darker than usual, more claustrophobic than ever, and I had to keep reminding myself that all the vegetation around and above me wasn't really pressing in on my head. Of course it was hot, the sort of sticky, skin-crawling hot you only ever get in a rain forest. I felt like I was walking through an endless darkened greenhouse without ventilation. Sweat was stinging my eyes, almost gushing from my armpits, pouring down my sides. I could feel panic rising somewhere deep inside me. I wanted out.

And then we were in the village and the Cambodian soldiers were starting to push the locals around. The more the villagers protested their innocence the harsher the soldiers' voices grew and then the first shots were fired and the old man's head exploded in blood and brain. Everything was moving now, with people running in all directions as the gunfire solidified into a wall of sound which I thought no one could possibly break through. But at the end of it, as the wall gradually undid itself and only stray shots remained, there were enough women left breathing for the soldiers to throw themselves on.

No one was taking any notice of me. I just stood there as the world whirled around me, paralysed as much by disbelief as fear, half hearing the screams of children fighting to save their mothers, watching them stabbed with bayonets, seeing the mothers raped by as many as were able and then shot, their half-naked bodies left sprawling in the dust. I saw the soldiers grinning at each other, the trace of uncertainty in their eyes all that remained of their humanity. I heard a baby crying in one of the huts, and I started walking towards it. A dead woman lay on the dirt floor inside; the baby beside her had been shot through the head at close range.

I stood there beside them, the crying still loud in my head, trying to work out what direction it was coming from. Someone poked me in the side and I spun round, waking myself up.

'It's your turn,' Ellen said groggily.

'Right.' I swung myself out of bed and reached for the dressing-gown, feeling the cold air bite on my jungle-hot skin. Twelve years, I thought, and that day was still coming back to haunt me.

Our daughter, Louise, stopped crying almost as soon as I gathered her up, and though she agreed to take some nourishment from the bottle, I think it was company she really wanted. I cradled her in my arms and sat by the window in the old rocking chair Uncle Stanley had left me, the one which used to sit in his window overlooking the Thames. Here it looked out over our garden – a wilderness in wait for my retirement from active duty in just under a year's time – and, in the distance, the dark silhouette of the Black Mountains. It wasn't yet one in the morning and the slim crescent moon disappearing behind them was lovely enough to warrant the pointing of a pudgy finger and a little squeak of pleasure from my daughter.

Louise Fullagar, now five weeks old, and hopefully one of the lucky ones. Both Ellen and I were naturally convinced of her beauty and intelligence, and, like most couples in love, we fully expected to be the exceptions, a couple who actually stayed together long enough to watch their child grow up.

At least in England she would probably get the chance. If you believed what you read in the tabloids you'd think we lived in the most dangerous country on earth, chock-full of vicious murderers, berserk road-ragers and God only knows what else, but in reality there are very few places in the world which are even half as safe to live in. And, in part, that's because you can usually count on the forces of law and order in England. The police may be dab hands at forging the odd confession, and many an Irishman will be pleased to tell you that the Army's hands aren't exactly spotless these last few decades, but at least weapon-bearing forces of the Crown don't make a habit of going on murderous rampages through the English countryside.

The baby in my dream might not have been crying, but it had been real enough, and sitting there wide awake I could still conjure up every detail of what I'd seen inside that hut all those years before. I'd been the junior member of a small SAS team sent to Cambodia to help train the Khmer People's National Liberation Force, and although we'd been assured by the usual Foreign Office smoothies that this army had no meaningful relationship with the notoriously genocidal Khmer Rouge – they were simply allies in the struggle against the current Vietnamese occupation! – it soon became apparent that, like the Khmer Rouge, the KPNLF was much more interested in fighting its own people than any foreign army. The destruction of the village was the worst atrocity I witnessed but by no means the only one, and eventually it became apparent to even the morons in Whitehall that this wasn't the sort of endeavour they wanted British soldiers to be associated with.

That wasn't the worst of it though. I still dreamt about that day quite often, but never once had I dreamt that any other SAS men were with me. And yet I knew they had been – it was as if some part of my mind still refused to accept that they'd behaved in the way they had, not only letting it all happen but actually participating in the mayhem.

An internal inquiry had been held when we got

back to Hereford, and both men left the SAS soon afterwards, but there was not one dishonourable discharge, much less a court martial. I wanted to quit myself, but was dissuaded from doing so, partly by other lads in my troop, partly by the realization that there was nothing else I really wanted to do with the next ten years of my life. Soon after that I was sent as part of another team to West Africa, one that managed to save a lot of lives, and I suppose I learnt to accept that the business in Cambodia had been enough of an aberration for me to let it go. I hardly ever thought about it in waking life, but the dream still came back to torment me every now and then.

It wasn't always the same version though, and tonight's had been a case in point. Cambodia has no true rain forest, and the one in the dream was in Brunei, where, like every other SAS wannabe, I'd undergone a month of training and testing before being badged. That had been a nightmare of rather a different kind, much more of a struggle for me than the UK-based part of Selection, but I'd managed to come through it all right. I'd arrived out there full of the usual hype about the jungle – how vibrant and beautiful it all is, how it's got more species in a square centimetre than the rest of the planet put together – but I just plain hated the place. It was dark, it was hot and humid, and it was full of things which wanted to bite or sting you. Everything was confused and indistinct – the place was a mess. I learnt to live with it, to do all the things you needed to do to survive in it, but I sure as hell never learnt to like it. Give me the mountains any day, preferably above the mosquito line, where you can see what you're doing, where the air's clear and the colours are bright. That feels like life to me, whereas the jungle feels like a huge, dripping coffin, dark green and dank, a place where things rot.

I smiled at my own vehemence and looked down at Louise, now sleeping peacefully in my arms. 'No jungles for you,' I murmured, then gave her a wry smile. The way things were going they'd all be gone by the time she grew up.

I looked out at the moon again and sighed. The last vestiges of the dream were fading away, turning the events it re-created back into history, bringing me back to the present. I just sat there for a while cradling my daughter, staring out at the faint glow which hung above the vanished moon, feeling pleased with how my life had turned out.

After all, there was no way I could have known that this time round the dream had also been a portent.

The following morning I arrived late for the class I was giving, and the scant sleep I'd been getting must have shown in my eyes, because even the Continuation trainees looked sorry for me. I was reviving myself with whatever it was the canteen called coffee when one of the duty adjutants delivered an invitation to an audience with the CO. There'd been no rumours of foreign jobs brewing, and I was pretty sure I'd have heard if an embassy had been seized or the royal family kidnapped, so I assumed that the old man just wanted an update on how the reorganization of Training Wing was going.

I walked across the parade-ground to his office, noticing the promised rain clouds gathering in the western sky, and reminded myself to ring Ellen and find out how her postnatal appointment had gone. The CO greeted me with a smile and put aside what he'd been reading – a piece on one of the Spice Girls entitled 'I'm no slapper'. Hardly the sort of reading matter a commanding officer turns to before sending out one of his men on a death-defying mission, I thought, and inwardly breathed a sigh of relief.

We went through the usual niceties as we waited for the tea and biscuits to arrive, with him enquiring after Ellen and Louise, and me wondering whether to ask about his wife, whose framed photo had mysteriously reappeared on his desk after several months' absence. I decided against it, and instead looked round the familiar office, thinking that in a year from now the battered desk and the photographs from Malaya, the antique filing cabinet and view of the parade-ground, would all have been relegated to the rank of memories.

'Have you been following what's going on in Zaire?' the CO asked, moving us abruptly into the professional realm.

'Vaguely,' I replied, my mouth half full of chocolate digestive.

'Well, you'll be getting a full briefing on the local

situation tomorrow,' he said, shattering my illusion that we were embarking on a cosy chat about Regimental affairs. 'As far as I can tell,' he went on, 'it's basically a civil war between Mobutu and everyone else, but there also seems to be some sort of tie-up with the Rwandan business.' He shrugged. 'Either way, civil wars in that area tend to be rather uncivil affairs, and there's the usual concern for all the foreigners – white foreigners, that is – who are likely to get caught in the middle. Most of them are French, Belgian or American, and the fear is that they'll end up paying for the fact that their governments have helped keep Mobutu in power for the last twenty years. French and US troops are already setting up camp in Brazzaville – across the river from Kinshasa – and getting ready to pull their people out if the shit hits the fan.' The old man paused for a sip of tea before continuing. 'There's only a few Brits involved – fifty-something that the Foreign Office know about – but for reasons best known to the politicos one particular group seems to be getting all the attention.'

I raised an eyebrow.

'It's a medical research team. Two doctors, two nurses and a technical jack of all trades. Three women and two men. According to the Foreign Office they're doing vital research – my caller didn't specify into what – and also running a clinic for the locals.' He reached behind him for the somewhat worn *Times Atlas* which leant against the wall and heaved it on to the desk, narrowly avoiding both mugs of tea in the process. 'They're somewhere in here,' he murmured, running a finger across the relevant map. 'Here,' he said, jabbing with his finger. 'Kima itself isn't marked, but it's about halfway between Punia and Mangombe.'

It seemed a long way from Brazzaville.

'About twelve hundred and fifty kilometres,' the CO said, as if he'd read my mind. 'It's just inside the Super-Stallion's range. The Americans have agreed to loan us one for the exfil. As usual, they've got twice as many as they need.'

'And when are we planning to take them up on their generous offer?' I asked.

'That's still up for grabs. The Government doesn't want these people brought out unnecessarily, but it does want a team in place which can pull them out at a moment's notice.'

'If the French and Americans go in for their own people, then ours will be left pretty exposed,' I thought out loud.

'True,' the CO agreed. 'This lot are right in the middle of the jungle, of course, and the war may just pass them by. Either way, you'll have an all-expenses-paid holiday in the sun,' he went on cheerfully. 'With maybe one taxi ride thrown in.'

'Yeah, right.' I'd heard that one before.

'I thought I'd give you Sheffield and Crawford again. You all seemed to work well as a team in Central Asia.' He gave me a questioning look.

'Yeah, we did.' I'd also grown pretty fond of them both.

'Good. For a fourth I thought I'd give you Paul Mowatt.'

I smiled. 'Any particular reason?' I asked sardonically. Mowatt was one of the few – the very few – black members of the Regiment.

'The fact that he's black won't hurt,' the CO admitted. 'But if he wasn't good enough in his own right I wouldn't be sending him.'

I nodded. I didn't like it much, but then I suppose I would have found it hard warming to anyone filling the spot previously occupied by the late 'Lulu' Llewellyn, who'd been killed in Afghanistan during our last sojourn abroad. And I didn't much like the idea of someone being selected for a mission on the grounds of skin colour, but then I didn't suppose Mowatt would either.

'When are we leaving?' I asked, trying to sound more enthusiastic than I felt.

'Day after tomorrow,' the CO told me. 'Air Afrique from Paris.'

The airline food would be crap, I thought sourly. And Brazzaville would probably turn out to be a Class-A dump, full of locals wanting your clothes as proof of friendship and eager young Americans bursting with naivety, depressingly empty of those things which made life bearable, like a decent breeze or a wife and child. And it sounded like we could be stuck there for weeks.

'I'd better get the others together then,' I said.

On the way back across the parade-ground I suddenly remembered telling Ellen I'd make sure last year's Central Asian job would be my last lengthy foreign assignment. My three-month captivity in Afghanistan during her pregnancy had given her a bad scare, and I hoped she wasn't going to be too pissed off. I began rehearsing my pitch – Brazzaville might be boring, but at least it wouldn't be dangerous . . . just one more chore to get through before retirement.

I'd just about convinced myself when the familiar voice of Uncle Stanley started up inside my head. Brazzaville probably was a dump, he said, but it was a dump I'd never seen, and it sat beside one of the world's great rivers, the one his namesake had explored, the one which Conrad had sailed up before writing *Heart of Darkness*. Where's your sense of adventure gone? he asked me indignantly. Don't you want to see one of the last great stretches of rain forest on earth?

Not really, I thought, but I couldn't tell him that.

It took me the best part of the day to run the other three to ground, but eventually we were all ensconced behind a bolted door in an unused rec room. I laid out the minimal info which the CO had given me, and watched the others' reactions, paying particular attention to Paul Mowatt, the only one I didn't know.

He was a good-looking guy, tall and obviously very fit. His accent fooled me for a few moments until I

11

realized it was just more middle-class than most of those I was used to listening to at work, whether white or black. I later found out he'd grown up in Bristol with a lawyer for a dad, but for the moment all I saw was an easygoing exterior which could be hiding something or nothing. I suspected the former – he seemed like someone who kept his thoughts pretty much to himself, which, in the predominantly white world of the Regiment, wasn't surprising.

'Gonzo,' as Brian Crawford was universally known, seemed the same as ever. His resemblance to the famous Muppet was as hard to pin down as it was to deny – there was just something there. As usual he was bursting with encyclopaedic information about our intended destination – the Congo, he informed us, might be only the fifth-longest river in the world, but it ranked second behind the Amazon in the volume of water it carried. I found myself looking forward to seeing him practise his Tai Chi exercises in the most ludicrous places, and wondered if he'd find anyone to sing Abba songs with now that Lulu was gone. I rather hoped not.

Pearson Sheffield, or 'Sheff' as he was known to everyone but his mother, was the youngest of the other three. He'd been born in Manchester and raised not far away in Northwich, losing his father in a fishing accident when he was seven. He had no siblings and was obviously close to his mother, who now ran a successful hairdressing business. Sheff's exterior was all hip cynicism, but he hadn't fooled me since we spent time together on secondment to the Det, and during our three months in Central Asia he'd let his guard down more than once. If he'd only stop killing people with the amount of secondhand smoke he generated he'd be the perfect companion.

All three of them took turns studying the atlas I'd borrowed from the library. It wasn't as good as the CO's, and the only sign of the medical research clinic was the pencil mark I'd made in what I hoped was the appropriate place. Not that it would have mattered for the moment – the only thing the map told us was that beaten tracks were thin on the ground in eastern Zaire, and that our research clinic wasn't on one of them.

'What are they researching?' Sheff asked.

'No idea,' I said.

'Zaire's the place they had the Ebola outbreak,' Gonzo offered encouragingly. 'I read a book about these lethal viruses, and that was one of the worst. It just melts your innards, reduces everything to mush in a few days.'

'Oh, brilliant,' Sheff said. 'That's all we need.'

'The good news is that it kills so fast that the victims don't have much time to pass it on – the virus is too efficient for its own good. But they reckon that eventually it'll mutate into what they call a "slow burner", like AIDS.'

'Didn't AIDS come from that part of the world?' I asked, interested despite myself.

'Probably,' Gonzo agreed. 'They definitely think it

first appeared in the rain forest, and a lot of people think that building the trans-Africa highway – he scoured the map and found it a couple of hundred kilometres north of our target – was what let it loose on the world.'

'Maybe our people are looking for a clue to the common cold,' Sheff said hopefully.

Paul Mowatt smiled at this, which I took to be a good sign. 'How many of them are there?' he asked.

'Five,' I said, and repeated what the CO had told me.

'Why us?' Gonzo asked. 'Seems like a funny place to send a squad from Mountain Troop.'

'We don't have a Jungle Troop,' I said.

'Yeah, but . . .'

'It's because we're beautiful when we're angry,' Sheff suggested.

'Or because we all speak French,' Gonzo guessed.

It turned out we could. I told the others that an expert from the FO would be briefing us the next morning on the local situation, and that we could make whatever plans we needed to make after hearing what he had to say. The job looked pretty straightforward to me, and my only real concern at this point was how I was going to convince Ellen that it was.

The first hour back at home was spent fussing over Louise, and then there was supper, the washing-up, and *The Archers* to get through. It looked as though I'd be out of the country when the Grundys' fate was decided, but maybe the World Service would carry news of the tribunal's decision.

When I did finally get round to telling Ellen about the job she took it better than I expected. 'Only a few weeks?' she asked, and when I nodded hopefully she refrained from bringing up the other times I'd misled her with my over-optimism. Nor did she seem worried by what diseases might be lying in wait for me at the research clinic; on the contrary, she seemed to expect we'd find a cranky Scotsman with a pony-tail who'd just found a cure for cancer. This, apparently, was the plot of a film called *Medicine Man* which she'd seen on a plane the previous year. Personally I wasn't anticipating meeting Sean Connery in darkest Africa, but it certainly seemed a nicer mental image for her to hold on to than Gonzo's innards turning to mush.

'And don't forget we've already got our tickets for visiting your sister,' she told me. 'Eighteenth of June.'

'Months to spare,' I said. I was looking forward to seeing Maureen myself, not to mention exploring the area around where she lived in northern New Mexico. She'd emigrated when I was still at school, so we weren't exactly close, but I did feel much better disposed towards her than my upwardly mobile brother and his alcoholic wife in leafy Chingford. My mother, father and Uncle Stanley were all dead, and the Docklands I'd grown up in had been concreted over and sold to yuppies. The last time I'd visited Wapping even the Thames had looked different. Maybe it was

15

just me, but it no longer seemed like the river Uncle Stanley used to think of as a gateway to the rest of the world. Just step aboard when the tide's ebbing, he'd say, and see where the water takes you.

These days it took you as far as a row of metal nuns called the Thames Barrage.

'So how long do you think you'll be gone?' Ellen asked, interrupting my reverie.

'Two or three weeks,' I said, erring as usual on the hopeful side.

The item on the *Nine O'Clock News* that evening was encouraging. The rebel forces still seemed to be advancing, and most of the eastern part of Zaire seemed to be in their hands. The front line on the BBC's map didn't look that far from the research clinic, so the chances looked good that we'd be ordered in sooner rather than later. Of course, I knew from experience that a line on a map was anything but a line on the ground, and there was always the chance that the clinic would be bypassed by the advancing rebels. If so, we might have a long wait, but maybe, just this once, my optimism would be justified.

I fervently hoped so. At that moment in time I really liked my life in Hereford.

Next morning the four of us were gathered in the 'Kremlin's' briefing room, under the baleful glare of the stuffed water-buffalo's head which was mounted on the wall. It was a memento of the Regiment's rebirth in Malaya in the fifties, and seemed to look a bit grumpier each time I saw it. Feeling its age, I supposed.

Martin Denison, the expert from the Foreign Office's Africa Desk, was about a quarter of an hour late – a victim of British Rail, he claimed, or whoever it was ran the trains from London in these enlightened days of private snouts in the public trough. He looked younger than me, and seemed in good spirits despite his run-in with raildom, but then I suppose for him this was a nice day out in the country.

After introducing himself and shaking us all by the hand he unrolled a map of Zaire which was much better than anything we'd yet seen – Central Africa wasn't high on the British Army's list of priorities – and fixed it with some difficulty to the easel. 'The geography's sort of self-explanatory,' he began. 'Where you're going there's rain forest in every direction for at least three hundred kilometres, lots of big, sluggish rivers and not much in the way of roads. This one from Kisangani to Bukavu' – he ran his finger down it on the map – 'has been paved fairly recently and should be passable. All the others will be difficult at best.'

I listened, hoping this was all academic as far as we were concerned. This was a contingency briefing, a 'just in case we got stranded in the middle of Zaire' briefing. A Sod's Law briefing, I thought pessimistically.

'To the west and north,' he went on, 'the forest stretches a lot further, but about three hundred kilometres to the south and east it turns to tropical grassland, a wide swathe in the south and a narrow strip here in the shadow of the mountains which line the western edge of the Great Rift Valley. The climate where you're going is about as equatorial as it gets – there's no discernible dry season and you can expect a heavy downpour at least once a day.'

'Put down umbrellas,' Sheff told Gonzo, who, as usual, was taking notes.

Denison then ran through the various tribal and linguistic groupings – which, I'm afraid, went in one ear and out the other – before offering us a précis of the country's history. And a sad history it was. Apparently King Leopold of Belgium had scooped up this last piece of Africa in the general European land-grab at the end of the nineteenth century and proceeded to run it as a private fiefdom for his personal enrichment. Rubber was the way to get rich, but the locals' reluctance to do all the work necessitated a system of virtual slavery. Every native was given a quota to fill, and those who failed had their hands chopped off by the local overseers, who duly presented grisly baskets full of the smoke-cured limbs as proof of their dedication to Leopold.

Denison sighed. 'Eventually there was an outcry,' he went on, 'Leopold was forced to hand his private domain over to the Belgian Government, and its policies, though much the same in essence, were at least implemented with some degree of lip-service to the notion of a common humanity. But in more than half a century the Belgians did nothing to prepare the country for an independent existence. Education was left to missionaries and the usual divide-and-rule policies ensured that all the political parties were either regionally or tribally based. When independence was suddenly granted in 1960 the number of native graduates was barely into double figures and the country as a whole was ready to fall apart.

'There was one politician who looked like he could hold it together – his name was Patrice Lumumba – but he was too left-wing for the foreign business interests, and he was killed in mysterious circumstances. That ushered in five years or so of civil war, at the end of which one Joseph Mobutu emerged triumphant. He's been in charge ever since, and he's been an unequivocal disaster for the country. The country's earnings – most of them from copper sales – have either been spent on national monuments to himself or simply been paid into his and his cronies' European bank accounts. Ninety-nine per cent of Zaire's foreign aid has gone the same way. Mobutu himself probably has about $8 billion stashed away.'

'Christ,' Sheff murmured. 'Why's no one tried to off him before now?'

'Oh, they have. In the late seventies there was a major attempt to overthrow him by local guerrillas with Angolan assistance, but the French, Belgians and Americans bailed him out with both military and financial help. Since then the economy and the regime's human rights record have both taken a turn for the worse. What should be one of the richest countries in Africa is one of the poorest.'

'What's made the Americans and the others change their minds?' Paul asked. 'I mean, why aren't they helping the bastard out this time?'

Denison smiled. 'The Cold War's over. The French would still like to keep the devil they know in power, but the Americans have lost interest, particularly in Africa.'

'So what started this particular war off?' I asked.

'That's hard to say. The rebellion in the east officially got going last autumn, but its roots go back to 1994 and the Rwandan civil war. After the Hutus in Rwanda turned on the Tutsis and butchered several hundred thousand of them, the Tutsis made a major comeback and drove a huge number of Hutus over the border into eastern Zaire, where they lived in refugee camps for a couple of years before the two conflicts coalesced, so to speak. The Hutu refugees in Zaire have sided with the Zairean Government, and the Zairean rebels, many of whom are Zairean Tutsis, with the Rwandan Tutsis.

'Two wars for the price of one,' Gonzo said with mock amazement.

'That way, you only need to pay rent on one battlefield,' Sheff put in.

The FO man smiled. 'And there's one more complication. I said the Hutu refugees sided with the Zairean Government, but really it's only a small number of them – mostly young men still wanted for genocide in Rwanda – who are fighting alongside Mobutu's troops. Most of the refugees are just that, and this war is just one more disaster for them.'

Denison was quite human for the Foreign Office,

I thought, but then he was a civil servant, not a politician. After he'd finished and we'd sadistically pointed him in the direction of the canteen, the four of us got down to the real business in hand – deciding what we needed to take to this particular party.

I began by stating the obvious, that what we were going to need would depend on what we ended up having to do. 'In the best-case scenario we're just a particularly attractive bunch of flight attendants,' I said. 'In the worst case . . .' I began, and stopped. What was the worst case?

'Are we assuming the chopper can land on the doorstep?' Gonzo asked.

It was a good question, and I spent most of the next twenty minutes on the phone looking for the answer. By the time I got back to the briefing room the other three were all laughing at some joke of Sheff's, which I took to be a good sign. Already I found myself liking Paul, though I wouldn't have been able to say why.

'Yes,' I told them. 'There's a football pitch.'

'So, what can go wrong?' Gonzo asked, and proceeded to tick off potential answers to his own question. 'One, the chopper could crash-land, or just fail on the ground. Two, the place could be under fire . . .'

'Three, they could have all gone shopping,' Sheff suggested. 'Or for a picnic.'

I shook my head. 'They'll know we're coming.'

'Four,' Paul added, 'we might have to hold off visitors while we load up whatever needs to be loaded up.'

'Either way, we'll need to protect the chopper while it's on the ground,' Sheff said.

'I'll look into it,' I said, 'but I don't imagine anyone out there'll be carrying anything more than an automatic rifle. Not off the main roads anyway. So MP5s should do the job, together with whatever handguns we fancy.'

'I'd like to take an M72,' Paul said, almost apologetically. 'It makes me feel lucky,' he added, 'and you never know.'

I glanced at him, wondering if he'd known that Lulu had always carried one of the light anti-tank weapons for much the same reason. 'Whatever turns you on,' I told him.

'What about basic supplies?' Gonzo asked.

I shrugged. 'The usual jungle stuff. We shouldn't be on the ground for more than an hour, so there won't be time for a three-course meal.'

'And if the chopper crashes?'

'I'm sure the clinic will feed us,' I replied automatically, but he was right. 'OK,' I said. 'We'll take enough for a few days.'

'If we don't need it we can always leave it for the locals,' Sheff suggested. 'They've probably never seen a Mars bar in wherever it is we're going.'

'What *do* they eat in Zaire?' I wondered out loud. Africa was one of the few places on earth which didn't seem to export restaurants.

'Each other,' Gonzo said drily. 'Cannibalism's still the done thing in parts of Zaire.'

* * *

My last evening at home was a pretty sombre affair. I suppose part of me was already *en route* for Africa, because although there was no lack of effort or goodwill on either of our parts, Ellen and I didn't seem able to connect in the way we were used to. We tried talking about our plans for life after the SAS, but none of it seemed real, and we ended up watching TV most of the evening, settling for the sort of closeness which doesn't involve active communication. Ellen could easily have been angry with my self-absorption, but she wasn't, and I thanked God I'd found someone like her to share my life with.

Louise woke me again in the early hours, this time out of an apparently dreamless sleep. I sat with her in the window once more, gently rocking her back to sleep as I stared out at the night. It was a beautiful moonless sky, with legions of clouds sweeping out of Wales across the starry backdrop, and I found it difficult to believe that in less than thirty-six hours I would be stepping out into a tropical steam bath. Sitting there, my daughter in my lap, I felt as content as I could remember, and the prospect of a few hours in the jungle seemed no more than an irritating hiatus, after which my real life could happily resume.

2

We flew to Paris the following afternoon, and then endured a six-hour wait for the Air Afrique overnight flight to Brazzaville. Gonzo and Sheff took a cab into the city, where Gonzo sought out and found our best map yet of the Kima area and Sheff did a rough survey of the local talent. Paul and I spent the time cooped up in the small room which the French authorities had set aside for us, him reading some detective story set in postwar Berlin, me listening to Otis Redding on the new Discman Ellen had bought me for my birthday. Four meals were delivered to our cell, and working on the assumption that Gonzo and Sheff were dining at some slick restaurant in town we consumed two each, complete with the accompanying quarter-bottles of wine. This proved an unpopular move, but after much eyeball-rolling at the ceiling – 'What can you do with the English?' we could almost hear him say – our local keeper managed to find two more.

The flight was as boring as night flights usually are – the only exceptions, in my experience, have been those through so much turbulence that terror takes over from boredom. There was a film, but I soon lost interest – twenty-something angst, whether in music or films, seems to leave me cold these days. Been there, done that, I thought – I'll be back for more when my daughter comes of age.

We were served another meal, but all I could manage was the dessert and wine. Never drink on a night flight, I remembered Ellen saying, and as a travel consultant she'd done enough flying to know. It dehydrates you, stops you sleeping, gives you a headache, she'd warned me. And she was right. The lights went out and I felt anything but sleepy. On the contrary, I could feel a headache coming on.

The hours went slowly by, punctuated only by the cries of babies and the snores of SAS men. I pictured the Sahara beneath us giving way to open savannah, and that to the fringes of the forest which lay at the continent's heart. I pictured Ellen sitting in the window with Louise, and as strips of light brightened around the blinds I told myself to start living in the here and now. The job waiting for us might be a complete doddle, but it still had to be done, and done well. This might well be my last time abroad for the Regiment and I wanted to make absolutely sure I didn't let my standards slip during the final run-in. 'You can do anything well, anything badly,' Uncle Stanley used to say. 'From rolling a cigarette to choosing a partner. And though sometimes you can't choose what you do, you can nearly always choose how well you do it.' It was about the only piece of adult wisdom I'd consciously carried with me from childhood, and sometimes I wished I had it written out on a dog-eared piece of paper which I could pull from my pocket and look at.

The flight attendants – I still couldn't help thinking of them as air hostesses – brought round a parody of a continental breakfast and pretty soon after that the plane began its descent, bouncing its way down through the cloud layers until the sea of greenery was visible below. As the plane turned I caught a glimpse, above the wing, of a vast river, two cities clustered on either side, their tallest buildings still dwarfed by the immensity of green which surrounded them. The larger of these was Kinshasa, capital of Zaire; the smaller was our destination, Brazzaville, capital of the Republic of the Congo.

As we came into land a few minutes later I had the impression of a few very tall buildings marooned in a sea of trees. One of the skyscrapers reached a lot higher than the others, and from the seat in front of me I could hear Gonzo telling Paul that it was the tallest building in Central Africa – vital information if ever I heard any. Overall though, I was pleasantly surprised – from the air at least, Brazzaville looked a much nicer place to be marooned in than I'd expected.

The airport was a modest affair about five kilometres from the city centre. There were no movable exit corridors, so we were treated to steps and a hundred-metre walk across the tarmac, quite far enough to appreciate the heat and humidity. It was only about eight in the morning, so God only knew what it would be like in a few hours' time.

Someone from the British Embassy in Kinshasa was supposed to be there to meet us – we don't have an embassy in Brazzaville – but for several minutes we scoured the air-conditioned arrivals hall in vain for a friendly face. He finally appeared with a uniformed Congolese in tow, introduced himself as Mark Pressman and his colleague as Pele – 'just like the footballer' – and set about the business of finessing us through the various formalities which heavily armed groups of foreigners have to endure on entering the Congo Republic.

It took about ten minutes in all – our fellow-passengers were still queuing – and then we were piling ourselves and our weaponry into two jeeps for a short trip across the tarmac to a part of the airport which was obviously reserved for military use. Several US Marine Corps helicopters were visible in the distance, most of them Sikorsky CH-53 Super-Stallions of the type earmarked for our possible rescue mission. More unusually, on the waste ground behind them, two Russian MiGs and at least four tanks had been left out to rust.

Pele noticed what I was looking at. 'They are from the bad old days,' he told me in immaculate French. 'When our friends the Americans arrived last week they were taken out of the hangars to make more room.'

The Americans had certainly arrived. Several hangars had been turned into a makeshift base, complete with generators, radios, computers, showers, offices, and even a full-scale medical unit with several surgeons on hand. There weren't many actual Marines in evidence, but according to Pele most of them were out rehearsing their evacuation drills for the day when the shit hit the fan across the river in Kinshasa.

Our British mini-contingent had been allotted one solidly partitioned-off corner of a hangar. The furniture consisted of four bunk-beds, each with its own mosquito netting, and a huge wooden table. On the latter, which was set back against the hangar wall proper, sat a cardboard box full of pagers and a telephone.

'OK?' Pele asked.

'Yes, thank you,' Pressman said. 'If we need anything we'll come and find you,' he added, as the smiling Congolese hovered in the doorway. Once he'd reluctantly absented himself, Pressman wiped his brow with his handkerchief and perched himself on the edge of the table like a schoolmaster. He was quite a tall man, with thinning blond hair and a skin which looked as though he'd spent too much time in the tropics.

'Is this how we get room service?' Sheff asked, looking at the phone.

Pressman didn't smile. 'I'm afraid there's no international calling from here, so unless you have friends in Brazzaville that's pretty much redundant,' he said.

'We can always call out for a Chinese take-away,' Sheff decided.

'Arrangements have been made for you to share the Americans' facilities,' Pressman said. 'I believe they have an excellent mess here.'

'And the pagers?' I asked.

'A gift from the Yanks. We've managed to rig up a comm link between our embassy in Kinshasa and the Marine radio room here, so if you're needed in a hurry they can page you anywhere in the city.' He smiled for the first time. 'We didn't want you stuck in this room for weeks on end waiting for the word to go.'

'So who decides when the word gets spoken?' I asked.

'We do,' he said. 'Our intelligence people are constantly monitoring the situation in the East, and we talk to Dr Moir on the radio at a fixed time each day. He's very reluctant to abandon the clinic at this stage of the work, but I don't get the feeling – how should I put this . . .? I don't believe he's interested in heroic gestures. If their situation deteriorates I'm sure he'll take the appropriate decisions. After all, he does have three women to consider.'

'I should be so lucky,' Sheff murmured.

I hesitated. Moir might be the most practical man on earth, but in a place like Kima the first signs of a deteriorating situation were likely to be armed men coming out of the trees. As for Pressman's 'intelligence people,' they were probably relaxing in smart expat cafés across the river, 'monitoring the situation' by reading the local newspapers. I said as much, but a little more tactfully.

Pressman shrugged. 'Short of having a man with the local rebels, I don't see what else we can do,' he said.

'You could put us in immediately,' I suggested, somewhat impulsively. 'Then, if there's a major drama, we'll be on hand to offer protection for however many hours it takes for the exfil chopper to arrive.'

Pressman opened his mouth to say something, but apparently thought better of it. 'It's a thought,' he said eventually. 'But I'll have to talk it over with London. Zaire is still a sovereign country, after all, and spending an hour on the ground to rescue some of our nationals is a different proposition from setting up camp on their territory for an indefinite period.'

I nodded. 'There wouldn't be any medical reasons why we couldn't stay on-site?' I asked.

'Not that I'm aware of.'

'Do you know what they're doing research into?' I asked bluntly. 'No one else seems to.'

'No,' he said curtly. 'All I know is that London is convinced of its vital importance.'

I felt he was telling the truth, which only made the whole business more mystifying. What sort of research would require that level of secrecy? Or was there no secret at all? The effort, ingenuity and taxpayers' money being devoted to the Moirs' evacuation might simply mean that they had family or friends in high places. 'The nobs,' as my shop-steward dad used to tell me, 'look after their own.' But Pressman didn't seem like the sort to put much stock in class as the motor force of history, so I kept that thought to myself. We could always ask the Moirs in person once we reached Kima.

Pressman then took me to meet the American base commander, a Marine colonel whose haircut seemed designed to make his head look square. But despite this unfortunate resemblance to Kryton in *Red Dwarf*, Matt Liebowicz seemed a nice enough American of the old school, instinctively open and more than willing to give you the shirt off his back, always assuming you weren't bent on burning his flag or insulting his womenfolk.

He took us on a tour of the still-burgeoning base, which was now home to more than a thousand Marines, more than twice the number of American civilians in Zaire whom they were supposed to evacuate. There were another thousand on the aircraft carrier *Nassau*, which was apparently anchored three hundred kilometres off the Zairean coast, and no doubt a Coca-Cola pipeline was being laid across the floor of the Atlantic even as we spoke. Of course they had a Super-Stallion to lend us – they probably had a chopper for anyone who wanted one.

Tour over, Pressman announced he was returning to Kinshasa. He'd talk to us on the comm link next morning, after the embassy had received its daily report from the research clinic. 'And I'll put your suggestion to London,' he added.

Back in our quarters, my suggestion had not been seen in quite such a positive light. As Sheff put it: 'We've no sooner set foot in Hamburger Heaven here, where they probably serve about five meals a day and take you on day-trips, than you get up and volunteer us for a stint in the middle of the fucking jungle . . .'

'Think about the nurses,' I reminded him.

'There'll be nurses here,' he retorted. 'American nurses. And probably pool halls and bowling allies and computer games. In the jungle we'll just be sitting there watching the rain dry.'

I laughed. 'It probably won't happen,' I told him. 'The whole idea's much too sensible for Whitehall to go along with.'

'So what's the programme?' Gonzo asked.

'We're just on call,' I said, 'and as long as we're carrying these' – I started distributing the pagers – 'I reckon we can do what the hell we want.'

'Well, let's get hold of some transport and take a trip into town then,' he suggested.

After finishing our unpacking, which must have taken all of two minutes, the four of us trooped across to see the quartermaster sergeant, who, Colonel Liebowicz had told me, would fulfil our every reasonable desire. Five minutes later we were barrelling down the road in a brand-new jeep, which Sheff seemed to be aiming in the general direction of the tallest building in Central Africa.

The city – population 700,000, according to Gonzo – seemed as pleasant from the ground as it had from the air. It was certainly hot and steamy, but the long lines of mango trees offered almost continuous shade, and not surprisingly the whole atmosphere seemed much more relaxed than the only other African city I'd ever seen – Monrovia at the height of the Liberian civil war. We left the jeep in what looked like a parking place, hoping it would still be there when we got back, and wandered round the centre like any group of tourists. A bookshop supplied Gonzo with the extra guidebooks he would need to bombard us with useless information, and a music store gave Sheff the chance to buy some cassettes of the local music. Listening to it thundering out of the shop's speakers, I thanked God for the personal stereo.

Paul, meanwhile, seemed to be quietly taking it all in – the sights and sounds and smells of a foreign country. I wondered what it was like for him, returning to the continent from which his distant ancestors had been bloodily prised. American blacks – African-Americans as they like to be called these days – seemed to put much more store by their African past than their British counterparts, but according to Africans I met in Liberia that was mostly because they had more to be angry with at home. I had no idea how angry Paul was, or how deep he might have buried that anger, but I knew he had to have a pretty thick skin, or he'd never have lasted, or wanted to last, in the SAS. Maybe we'd get to talk about it before long, but I wasn't counting on it.

Gonzo dragged us into the National Museum next, Sheff moaning away about how much he hated places like that. But it was beautifully cool inside, and even he seemed fascinated by the striking Congolese masks on display. There were two groups of neatly uniformed schoolchildren doing the rounds, each with a female teacher who didn't look much more than sixteen. The children gawped at all us clod-hopping great foreigners, but particularly at Gonzo, while their teachers flashed great big friendly smiles of the sort you hardly ever seem to see in England.

Gonzo's guidebook claimed the interior of the cathedral wasn't a patch on the exterior, so instead of going in we took over a bench and just stared at it for a few minutes. A crowd soon began to gather around us, and we moved on in search of lunch. Gonzo was all for diving in at the deep end, culinarily speaking, but the rest of us thought we'd hold off on the monkey and porcupine for a day or so more. A restaurant recommended in the guidebook supplied grilled chicken sandwiches which weren't that far removed from what our stomachs were used to, and a small bar farther up the street enabled us to get acquainted with both the local beer and sundry members of the local population. They were surprised to find we were English rather than American, and even more surprised to find us fluent in French. We covered the usual global topics – football and the sex life of the Spice Girls – before venturing into the situation in Zaire. As far as our new Congolese friends were concerned the main preoccupation was whether or not Brazzaville was going to be invaded by Mobutu's fleeing supporters, many of whom were no better than violent criminals. On the wider issues, they were more than a little cynical. The rebel leaders might do more for Zaire's people than Mobutu had done – they could hardly do less – but no one was holding their breath. And as for the Americans now turning against the man they'd kept in power for thirty years, and calling for more democracy . . . well, that was just a joke. At least the French never pretended to be anything but self-interested bastards.

While we were in the bar the sky darkened, unleashed a downpour, then brightened again, all in the space of a couple of beers. Deciding to complete our round of sightseeing by visiting the zoo, we walked back through the dripping trees, reclaimed our borrowed jeep from the children who were playing in it, and headed across town. After paying the paltry entrance fee we wandered round the various enclosures, most of which were small enough to send an Animal Liberation Front member into hysterics. There really wasn't much to see, with one magnificent exception – the gorillas. Sheff tried to engage one in a sign-language conversation, but the gorilla turned out to be too fluent for him.

We made our way back to the airport base and crashed out for a couple of hours with a book or tape before our thoughts turned to dinner. The Marine canteen was as good as we'd expected, and between fending off questions from our hosts – 'What are you Limeys doing here, anyway?' – we all ate too much ice-cream. Back in our own square of hangar we decided that the military life wasn't that bad after all. By about ten o'clock we were cocooned away under our mozzie nets, looking for all the world like four enormous insects about to hatch. I lay there and found it hard to believe that it was only thirty-six hours since I'd kissed Ellen goodbye.

Next morning dawned bright as the one before, and in those few minutes before the humidity caught you by the neck it felt really pleasant. We made our way to the Marines' mess, and piled our trays high with pancakes and maple syrup, bacon and 'eggs-over-easy', toast and grape jelly, and mugs of 'regular' coffee. If an army marches on its stomach, I should think the US Army moves pretty slowly.

Breakfast over, we walked across to the hangar which housed the radio room, just in time to receive Pressman's early-morning bulletin. According to Dr Moir, there were reports of rebel troops in Obokete and Mahulu, which were both about a hundred kilometres away, to the north-east and north-west respectively. The only Government troops still in the vicinity seemed to be a band of Serb mercenaries – they had been reported as going through the small town of Kasese, some eighty-five kilometres to the west.

I was studying our map while Pressman told us this, and the geography seemed to bear out Moir's feeling that the war was going to miss the clinic. Each of the places mentioned was on a major road – whatever that meant in the jungle at the height of the rainy season – and the doctor might well be right in his supposition that movement on those roads would be so difficult as to render the clinic almost unassailable.

On the other hand, warring troops often needed medicines and Europeans made good hostages. I still thought my notion of stationing our four-man team at the clinic made more sense than waiting for trouble twelve hundred kilometres away, and I told Pressman so.

'I'm beginning to agree with you,' he said, surprising me. 'And I submitted your proposal to London last night. We should be getting a decision sometime today.'

Which left us with nothing to do but carry on playing tourists. Gonzo had already decided that he wanted to take a look at the Congo's famous white- water rapids a few kilometres downstream, and the news that you could watch them with beer in hand from the terrace of a scenically sited restaurant was enough to convince the rest of us. We drove out in the jeep, ordered our drinks and feasted our eyes.

It was impressive, even before we knew – courtesy of our indefatigable guide – that we were watching thirteen per cent of the world's untapped hydroelectric energy tumble past. The book also recommended a closer look, so after downing several bottles of the local brew we dutifully went down to the river in search of a boat. There were several flat-bottomed pirogues for hire, and a few minutes later we were being paddled out in the direction of a sandbar. I glanced across at Sheff and Gonzo in the other boat, and decided they only needed pith helmets to look like Livingstone and Stanley.

We were just stepping out on to the sand when all our four pagers started beeping furiously in our pockets, first alarming and then vastly amusing our paddlers. The four of us stared at each other, took one look at the rapids and indicated that we wanted to be taken back to shore. The two Congolese looked at us as if we were mad, shook their heads in wonderment, shrugged, then did as we asked them. As we hurtled back into town I idly imagined them later that day, telling their friends in the local bar what had happened and inviting suggestions as to what made foreigners such inexplicable people.

Back at the radio room a friendly Marine with a shaven head connected us up with Pressman, who wasted no time on preliminaries. 'We've lost contact with the clinic,' he began. 'The radio may be down, or something more serious may have happened. Either way, Whitehall OK'd your plan, so we're sending you in now. I've already talked to Liebowicz, and there's a helicopter standing by. He also suggested sending half a dozen Marines along to help out, just in case you do walk into real trouble, and I gratefully accepted. Separate commands, I'm afraid – you'll just have to get on with each other. And one last thing – one of our people will be coming along for the ride. His name's Knox-Brown, and he should be with you sometime in the next half-hour.'

'MI6?' I asked.

'Did I say that?'

It was the first time I'd heard amusement in Pressman's voice. 'What authority does he have?' I asked. I was beginning to get the distinct feeling there was more to all this than met the eye, and the last thing I needed in such a situation was someone from 'Six' staring over my shoulder and 'advising me' that Her Majesty's Government would 'prefer' I did in some other way whatever it was I was doing.

'He can fill you in on that,' Pressman said evasively. 'Good luck,' he added, and cut the contact.

'Christ,' I muttered. I didn't like the sound of any of this.

I filled the others in on what had happened.

'So we don't know whether we're staying or coming straight back out?' Gonzo asked, rather too cheerfully for my liking.

'Looks that way,' I agreed reluctantly. 'If it's just their radio on the blink we'll stay and look after them. If there are Indians circling the cabin then we'll have to bring everyone out.'

'If there are Indians circling the cabin the Yank pilots may not fancy putting down.'

'Right,' I agreed. 'But we'll deal with that problem when it comes up. There's no way we can know what's going on out there without taking a look for ourselves.'

'If it looks too dangerous to land we can always ask the Yanks to drop us off somewhere nearby,' Paul suggested.

'And then give them a buzz when we want to be picked up again,' Sheff added.

I stared at them both, suddenly feeling my age. Being dropped off into the middle of a jungle civil war wasn't something I really wanted to contemplate. If the clinic had been invaded by a few drunken soldiers we could probably see them off without too much difficulty, but anything more than that and we'd be talking real drama. I didn't fancy having to choose between abandoning the clinic staff and taking on a battalion of local troops on their own terrain.

'So when are we leaving?' Gonzo asked.

'When the local James Bond gets here.'

I explained about Knox-Brown and they laughed, no more impressed by the sound of him than I'd been.

'I think I've got it now,' Sheff said. 'The clinic's just a cover. Maggie Thatcher has set herself up as a female Dr No in the middle of the wrong jungle, and all her old friends in the Government have been persuaded to bail her out.'

'She probably has photos of them all in compromising positions,' Gonzo agreed.

'Mostly on their knees,' Paul added, getting into the swing of things.

'Well, I'm glad that's sorted,' I said. 'Now let's get our bags packed. We'll take everything we brought with us, plus whatever we can scrounge from the Americans in the next half-hour. Sheff, get hold of as many of their Meals Ready to Eat as you can. And don't forget the tiny bottles of Tabasco sauce and the

M&Ms. If we're stuck out in the jungle for days we'll need our treats.'

We scattered, Sheff on his begging mission, Gonzo and Paul to get our gear together, me to liaise with Liebowicz and check the helicopter. Fifteen minutes later we were standing out on the tarmac, gear loaded, watching the sky darken in preparation for another downpour. Sheff had just learnt to his disgust that Marine helicopter flights were designated 'no smoking', and was trying to get as much nicotine into his bloodstream as possible before we took off.

He wasn't alone – several of the Marines who had been detailed to accompany us were puffing away nearby in their own little circle. Their OC was a young lieutenant named Singer, who spoke with a Southern drawl and looked like he belonged on a farm. The six boys under his command seemed even younger, just as earnest, and perhaps a bit scared, which was a pretty sensible way to feel. After all, we were about to head out on a very long limb, with no assurance that it wasn't already broken.

The jokes had dried up among our little group – we were undergoing our usual pre-op metamorphosis from four lads out on the town to a quartet of Britain's finest. I went over in my mind what Pressman had said, and wondered again what business a medical research clinic in the jungle was of MI6's. And then there were the Serb mercenaries, who no doubt had plenty of experience when it came to mistreating civilians. I had the feeling that over the next few years the world was going to see quite a few repeats of *Serbs Behaving Badly*.

The rain was just beginning to fall when the small helicopter bringing Knox-Brown came into view, and by the time it landed raindrops the size of tennis balls – well, almost – were plummeting to earth. He raced across the tarmac to join us in the belly of the Super-Stallion, but still suffered a major soaking.

My first impression was of a man in his early thirties with silver-rimmed glasses, who could have passed for a smooth young executive from the forehead down. But whether by design or accident, his hair, short on the sides and tufty on the top, gave him the air of a bespectacled Tintin. He seemed amiable enough as we introduced ourselves, but I couldn't see his eyes, and I had no desire to find myself playing the role of Captain Haddock in this particular venture. Though, having said that, I could definitely see a future for Sheff and Gonzo as the bumbling Thompson Twins.

Knox-Brown was full of apologies for keeping us waiting, which I took as an opening to ask the obvious question – what was it about this research clinic that required his presence on our little jaunt?

'They're British nationals in danger,' he said glibly.

'There are a lot of British nationals in Zaire,' I said. 'Don't tell me they've each been assigned a saviour from Six.'

He smiled at that. 'The clinic's funded by Overseas Development,' he said, as if that explained anything.

But then again, maybe it did. I still hadn't quite

got used to the idea of government as no more than the servant of business, but given that mind-set, I suppose the clinic might represent an investment worth saving. If so, then why not send representatives of the intelligences services, not to mention the SAS, to save it? As the roar of the rotor blades strained toward a higher pitch I idly wondered whether the expected Labour government would be any different. I thought not, but maybe I was just getting too cynical in my old age.

The eleven of us occupying the chopper's belly didn't have much of a view of the outside world, and the noise of the engines put paid to any hopes of conversation, so we were all left to our own devices for the duration of the flight. I tried reading my paperback – a novel called *Birdsong* about an Englishman's experiences in love and the First World War – but it needed more concentration than I could muster. I remembered Uncle Stanley's theory about the twentieth century – that belief in God had died in the trenches, pulling the moral rug out from under us all, and that the only real story after that was communism's failure to provide a working alternative. I didn't know enough history to know if he was right, but there didn't seem much doubt that the moral rug was pretty frayed and tattered, and much as I wanted to, I found it hard to imagine that the century my daughter was about to inherit would be kinder than the last.

So much for philosophy. I did a round of the American faces opposite, and realized that they really didn't fit in with my preconceptions any longer. I suppose I was too used to watching Vietnam films like *Platoon* or *Apocalypse Now*, in which all the American troops are either burnt-out psychos or drugged up rock 'n' rollers wearing headbands. This bunch looked like college jocks, fresh-faced and muscular, without a thought between them. They knew why they were here in the practical sense – to watch the Limeys' butts for a couple of hours – but I didn't think they had a clue as to what it was all about. And worse than that, I didn't think they cared.

To my left Knox-Brown was sitting back, eyes closed, looking older than he had before. His skin colour didn't suggest that he was permanently stationed in the tropics, but neither did he look like the usual caricature of the British visitor, overdressed and perpetually mopping his brow with a white handkerchief. Maybe he'd be OK, maybe he wouldn't. With any luck we'd all be back in Brazzaville for a late supper and I'd never have to find out.

To his left Paul was staring into space, an almost dreamy expression on his face, and beyond him, wedged in the corner, Gonzo had his head in a book, as if this was just another holiday flight. Sheff had his Walkman on, and I dreaded to think how loud he was playing the music to override the roar of the engines. All three of them looked pretty relaxed, but there was an almost visible tension in the way they sat, turned a page, fiddled with a tape. They might have shoved it to the back of their minds, but their bodies knew they were going into danger, and they were buzzing with anticipation, bracing themselves against whatever surprises fate had in store. This, after all, was one of the reasons why we'd all joined the SAS, because we liked adventure holidays which really were an adventure.

There were other reasons too, of course – some of them not so noble. I'd joined the Army because a friend I'd been accompanying to the recruiting office had dared me to, which was a pretty stupid reason to do anything. But I like to think I wouldn't have accepted the dare if I hadn't already been looking for something more adventurous than my brother's bank career. Who knows? I hadn't regretted the decision very often, either that one or the one to try for the SAS. The business in Cambodia had got me thinking seriously about packing it in, but that was the only time I'd felt like doing something so dramatic. I suppose the last couple of years had been less than inspiring, but that was mostly because for the first time in my adult life I actually had a life outside the Army.

Overall, I reckoned the SAS had made pretty good use of what I had to offer, and we'd come out just about even. They'd had seventeen years of my time; I'd seen a lot of the world, worked most of that young man's anger out of my system, learnt a little about the way things were, and hopefully grown up a bit. And now I was ready to move on, always assuming the jungle would let me go home. I tried to look on the bright side – if there'd been trees to hide behind in Afghanistan I probably wouldn't have spent three months in captivity.

There were certainly lots of trees below. Ten minutes before our ETA at Kima the pilots invited Singer and I forward for a better look, and there was the jungle – a green sea stretching to every horizon. We were flying a couple of hundred metres above the canopy but I felt as though I could smell it and hear it – the damp odours of decay, the monkeys and birds howling out lead lines above the insect rhythm section.

And then we saw the break in the unending sea which we were looking for. The red streak of a road was now visible to our left, and where it snaked to cross a medium-sized brown river an area about two hundred metres square had been hacked out of the jungle. A trio of longish, one-storey buildings lined one side of the road, and on the other was the promised football pitch, which amounted to no more than a bulldozed piece of land littered with tree stumps which sloped gently down to the river. At its other end several smaller buildings had been erected.

The pilot flew the Super-Stallion along the imaginary touch-line farthest from the road at about a hundred metres, and we all craned our necks for signs of a hostile reception.

No one fired at us, but no one waved at us either. The whole settlement seemed deserted, at least by the living.

The pilot swung the chopper round and did another fly-past, this time following the line of the road. 'That looks like a body,' the co-pilot said calmly, and sure enough, on the ground in front of the buildings behind the pitch an African was lying face down in the mud.

'Oh shit,' someone muttered. It was me.

The pilot was turning the helicopter again. 'Are we going down?' he wanted to know.

There didn't seem to be any choice. We'd not been fired on, we'd not seen any evidence of an enemy presence, and we had to find out if our compatriots were lying dead in their clinic.

'Yes,' Knox-Brown said, beating me to it. 'Let's go down and take a look.'

3

Africa rose up to meet us, and the Super-Stallion touched down with only the slightest of jolts. The roar of the engines and rotors would have covered the sound of any gunfire, but crouching in the open doorway we could see no sign of movement in the buildings on either side of the road. Instinct told me that there was no ambush waiting to happen, but my instincts had been wrong before, and like all the others I took a deep breath before leaping down on to the soft ground and heading at a run for the nearest of the three large buildings across the road. The doors were open but there was no movement there, nor in the slatted windows or the tangled weeds which grew between the stilts on which the building was raised.

We had decided the division of labour on the way down – us Brits would take the large structures to the east of the road, while the Marines guarded the chopper and took those on the other side. They were also responsible for the road to Punia which plunged into the jungle to our left; we for the one which headed out across the rickety-looking log bridge in the direction of Mangombe. Paul and Gonzo would look after that chore while Sheff and I went through the buildings.

We took the steps on to the terrace at a run, ending up with our backs to the wall on either side of the open doors like any decent pair of American TV detectives. I was irritated to find that Knox-Brown was right behind me, but it didn't seem like a good time to debate our overlapping spheres of responsibility.

'Just keep behind us,' I hissed.

'Of course,' he said mildly.

Sheff and I went in, MP5s at the ready, but the only thing moving inside was a fluttering curtain in a back window. We were in the clinic, and the last group of out-patients had obviously been severely pissed off about something. Chairs and magazines – which included a year-old *Private Eye* – were scattered across the floor, and those few medical supplies which hadn't been stolen were lying beneath empty wall cabinets. On one wall a large Amnesty International calendar had been slashed with a sharp instrument.

We went through the two small consultation rooms at the back, and a mini-ward of four beds which had been built on behind. There was a large patch of blood in one of the beds, and a single sandal, which looked decidedly European in origin, lay in the middle of the floor.

From the main clinic a side door led, via a corrugated-iron covered walkway, to the next building. This clearly housed the research facility, and here the intruders had allowed their destructive impulses a freer rein. In one room each of three monitors had been stoved in, most likely with a rifle butt, and the meat of the computers had been given similar treatment – no one would be accessing those hard drives in a hurry. Trays of what had probably been plant samples had been randomly distributed over the floor and walls. There was broken glass everywhere, and the building was pervaded by a sour smell I didn't recognize, but which I hoped had nothing to do with Gonzo's tales of organ-mushing viruses.

'Oh, bugger,' Knox-Brown said quietly behind me.

The other main room was lined with around a hundred cages, and there seemed to be a live monkey in each, though most of them seemed sunk in various degrees of torpor. Even the few that had the energy to rattle their cages looked like they'd already exhausted themselves. It was all a little too reminiscent of those pictures which opponents of animal testing liked to parade, and I turned away feeling more disgusted than I would have expected.

There was a one-room annexe behind the research facility, and here nothing much seemed to have been disturbed. The unmade double bed contained only one pillow, and all the clothes hanging on the makeshift drying rack were women's, suggesting that the room was one woman's living quarters.

Sheff and I took another covered walkway to the third building, which was divided into three bedrooms and one communal living room. One of the bedrooms was clearly occupied by two women, the other two by single men, which didn't say much for the state of the Moirs' marriage. The radio in the living room had been been left for dead, but there was no blood on the floor, no sign that any of the occupants had put up a violent struggle. And that seemed to sum up the whole place – it wasn't the *Marie Celeste*, but it didn't reek of murder and mayhem either.

We retraced our steps and checked out the shack beside the clinic which housed the generator. This wasn't working, but as far as I could see no deliberate effort had been made to disable it.

We emerged to see a couple of Marines escorting an African towards the helicopter. I got an OK signal from Gonzo up the road and walked across, Knox-Brown trotting at my heels like an eager bloodhound.

'We found three more bodies inside,' Singer told me. 'Two men and a woman. The woman was naked,' he added, and ran a hand through the stubble on his head which passed for hair, looking even younger than before. 'This guy was hiding under a bed,' he said, gesturing in the direction of the prisoner, a slim Congolese with hair shorn almost as short as his own and prominent cheek-bones. 'But he doesn't speak English.'

I refrained from asking Singer why in hell's name he should, and asked the African in French what his name was. 'Nyembo,' he said, flashing me a gap-toothed smile.

'At least three four-wheel-drives, and two eight-wheel trucks,' one of the Marines interjected, having presumably been reading the runes in the muddy road.

'Which way did they go?' I asked Nyembo.

He pointed to the left, in the direction of Punia.

'When?'

He shrugged. 'Early this afternoon. Maybe two o'clock.'

I supposed that was good news – so far they were only about five hours ahead of us. Whoever 'they' were. I asked.

'They were mostly white men,' Nyembo said. 'But no French or American. They spoke a language which I have never heard before.'

Serbs, I thought. Shit. 'How many?' I asked.

He thought about it. 'Fifteen?' he said eventually. 'Fifteen white men, I mean. There were also some Mobutu soldiers and a few Hutus – maybe twenty-five altogether.'

A psychopath's UN, I thought. 'The Genocide Brothers,' I murmured to myself.

'And they took the doctors and nurses?'

'Yes.'

I stared at the wall of brooding jungle sixty metres away across the pitch, thinking that it could hardly have been worse. This was just the dilemma I'd dreaded, except that of course it wasn't really a dilemma at all.

Even Singer knew that. 'I guess you won't be coming back with us,' he said. 'Though I don't see how you're going to go after them without any transport.'

I looked at Knox-Brown, who so far had said nothing. 'Forgive me for asking the obvious,' I said, 'but have any arrangements been made for someone to come and get us?'

'No problem,' he said, rather too easily for my peace of mind.

I probably sighed. 'OK, let's get our stuff off the chopper,' I told Sheff.

A few minutes later the five of us were watching the CH-53 disappear above the treetops, heading home for Brazzaville and the sort of supper we wouldn't be seeing for a while. Looking round at my three SAS companions, I saw their faces mirroring the look on my own – we were suddenly a very long way from home.

Knox-Brown, on the other hand, looked more Tintin-ish than ever, but then he probably didn't know any better.

The tropical sky was darkening with its usual swiftness, and we had decisions to take. If we were going to spend the night in the immediate vicinity, it might be more advisable to set up camp in the relative safety of the jungle. But I reckoned we could afford the luxury of wooden floors and a real roof for the time it took us to plan where we were going from here, so I sent Gonzo after a couple of kerosene lamps I'd noticed in the clinic stores cupboard and told Sheff to start a brew-up in the communal living room.

Five minutes later we were all sitting in easy chairs,

lacking only a TV, a few six-packs and a reproachful wife to complete the impression of a lads' evening at home. I'd thought about leaving someone on watch outside, but decided that (a) we'd hear any approaching vehicles and (b) the chances of a visit from armed pedestrians in the next half-hour were too slim to worry about.

Gonzo and Paul hadn't heard the whole question-and-answer session with Nyembo, so we went through it again, this time in more detail. The Congolese described the sudden appearance of the Serb-led group late that morning. Dr Barry, as he called Moir, had been arguing with the group's leader, a tall man with a scar on his neck – Nyembo drew a finger down his own to indicate its position – when there was gunfire from the houses across the road, first from inside and then outside, where one of the cook's assistants had been shot dead trying to escape across the football pitch. Dr Barry had gone even whiter in the face, and Dr Rachel had grabbed hold of his arm and said something in English – probably that they must go with the soldiers or all the Africans would be killed. Dr Rachel was a very kind woman.

And they had gone an hour or so later, the two doctors and the nurses and Andy. Another man had been bayoneted when he tried to save his wife from the soldiers, and after they had raped her she had been killed too, but everyone else had either run away the moment the soldiers arrived or had been spared when they left. The survivors had all gone back to their village up the road, but he, Nyembo, had returned to pick up some belongings he had left behind in his rush to get away. He had just been gathering these together when the helicopter landed.

I asked him what sort of weapons the Serbs and their allies had been carrying, but the word 'guns,' together with hands held about half a metre apart, was as precise an answer as the Congolese could offer.

'At least we know they don't have any artillery,' Sheff said.

'I wish we'd brought a mortar along,' Gonzo murmured.

'Well, we didn't,' I said flatly, as I spread out our map on the floor between us. Its scale of twenty kilometres to the inch wasn't ideal, but it was the best we had. 'So where are they now?' I muttered, as we all dropped to our knees like a cabal of war gamers.

'The road to Punia is bad,' Nyembo volunteered, 'and they may not have reached the town by dark, but if they have, then the road north to Yumbi is better.'

'What about the one south to Isambe?' I asked.

'Not good.'

Punia was only about thirty kilometres to the west, a distance we could probably cover on foot by dawn, but there was no guarantee they'd have stopped there, and we might well run into other forces.

'If we knew where they were headed . . .' Sheff wondered out loud.

'They will try to cross the Congo,' Nyembo said

authoritatively. 'Nearly all the area to the east of the river is now held by the rebels.'

'Where can they cross?' I asked, hoping he really knew what he was talking about. In much of the Third World it's considered more polite to make up an answer than admit your ignorance.

'Here is the nearest place,' he said, pointing out a settlement called Poma on the Congo's right bank. 'There are boats there, but they may all be on the other side of the river – no one will want to ferry these people, because they know it will mean trouble for them from somebody. And the river here is more than a kilometre wide, so they will have no other way to get across.'

I stared at the map for a while, thinking it was probably more important to keep ourselves on the board than make great speed across it. If the research team had been taken as potential hostages or bargaining counters – and I couldn't see any other good reason for taking the men along – they were probably in no immediate danger. But if we were removed from the board, and the clear trail which I was quite confident the Serbs would now be leaving was given a chance to grow muddy, then the chances of anyone else being sent in to look for them seemed remote. We needed to find out more about the relationship between the Serbs and the Government forces; we also needed to find out more about this particular Serb commander, if that was possible. And I really didn't want to walk the whole hundred kilometres to the Congo, through territory that Nyembo claimed was now occupied by rebel troops. Somehow I didn't think they'd take too kindly to our presence on their newly conquered soil.

'Is there anywhere round here we can get hold of some transport?' I asked Nyembo.

He looked doubtful. 'There is only the mission up the road, and their only vehicle has been broken down for months. There are trucks in Mangombe, but . . .'

'The vehicle at the mission – what is it, and what's wrong with it?' I asked.

Nyembo shrugged. 'It's an American four-wheel-drive – a Dodge, I think. And no one knows what's wrong with it.'

'How far away is the mission?'

'Seven kilometres on the road, maybe three through the jungle.'

'We could take a look,' I said, and turned to Paul. 'I've been told you're an ace mechanic.'

'Not bad,' he admitted.

'I think we should talk to Kinshasa before we do anything else,' Knox-Brown said suddenly.

It sounded like a good idea, if only to check out the exfil arrangements should we successfully recover the captives. I told the others to get us ready for the road and went in search of our radio. The PRC320 Clansman which had been supplied to us for this mission was heavier, less adaptable and generally less state-of-the-art than the PRC319 which we'd been using in recent years, but it was still capable of sky-wave transmissions, in which the operator's signals are bounced off the planet's outer atmosphere. The Regiment had normally used the PRC320 as a Morse transmitter, but Pressman had insisted that on this mission we use the set's voice/speech capability. The help in Kinshasa probably thought Morse was a TV detective.

I carried the set across the road and out on to the dark expanse of open ground, Knox-Brown trotting at my heels. Squatting down on my haunches, I aligned the antennae, opened a voice channel and told the embassy, a thousand kilometres to the west, that I was calling. It was only a few seconds before Pressman's voice was booming in my ear; the Marine pilots had obviously radioed ahead with the news of what had happened at Kima.

I gave him the whole story anyway, complete with an explanation of our decision to miss the return trip, and then gave him the space he needed to get the obligatory Foreign Office response – annoyance with anyone for doing anything which might embarrass anyone else – off his chest. But, rather to my surprise, he simply asked what we intended to do next. 'Go after them,' I told him, adding that we needed all the intelligence he could gather about our quarry.

He promised to do what he could, and asked to talk to Knox-Brown. I handed over the headphones and hovered for a few seconds, until the MI6 man pointedly told me he could pack up the set and bring it back across the road. I took the hint and walked away, ignoring the boy inside my head who wanted to be difficult. The darkness was almost total now, but we'd been blessed with a clear sky and the thinnest of crescent moons, at least for the first part of the night. I swatted a mozzie on my bare arm, became suddenly aware of the thousand others buzzing in my vicinity, and hurried back into the relative safety of the clinic.

Once inside, I made straight for the research lab, hoping I might find something which would explain Her Majesty's Government's need to keep me in the dark. There were a lot of papers, most of them statistical printouts, littering the floor, but none of them had the sort of explanatory headings – something on the lines of 'Ebola viruses per square millimetre of monkey shit' – which I needed to make me any the wiser. I was just standing there feeling frustrated, conscious of the scrabbling noises from the monkey room, when it occurred to me that Nyembo might know what sort of research the Moirs had been doing.

As it turned out, I didn't have to ask him. I came in through the clinic's back door just as Knox-Brown carried the radio in through the front. He set it down gently on an upright chair, beamed at us all and proudly announced that he'd been given clearance to put us fully in the picture.

'Hallelujah,' I muttered.

'There's a good chance the Moirs have developed an effective vaccine for AIDS,' he told us. 'They've been testing it for several months, and reporting good results – not conclusive results, but good ones.' He paused and looked round, as if to make sure we'd understood the importance of what he was saying.

'Maybe the Serbs are working for a condom company,' Sheff suggested with a deadpan face.

Knox-Brown couldn't quite repress a smile at that, so there was probably still hope for him. Meanwhile I was wondering why the Government had decided to offer such unprecedented protection to a couple of doctors. Surely not because it cared a fig for the well-being of AIDS sufferers?

It took only a few seconds for the penny to drop once I'd performed my new trick of recasting government decisions as corporate calculations. An AIDS vaccine would be worth a fortune to whichever pharmaceutical giant owned the rights, and to the country of origin of that corporation. Who wouldn't pay through the nose for such a vaccine, which would offer not only protection from the disease but also the promise of good old, casual, condom-less sex?

For a couple of seconds I entertained the notion that the Serbs were working for a rival pharmaceutical company, but then dismissed it. They were just a bunch of homeless thugs trying to make a dishonest crust, and they had no idea they'd just kidnapped the UK's best potential earners since the Beatles.

'Are they carrying the formula in their heads?' I asked Knox-Brown.

'I don't know. There are no floppy discs with the computers, which makes me think they either took them with them or managed to hide them when the Serbs arrived.'

'Either way we've got five lives to save,' I said. 'And seven kilometres to walk.'

'Yes, but only three through the jungle,' Nyembo interjected helpfully.

'You know the way in the dark?' I asked doubtfully. Getting lost in the jungle wasn't among my plans for the night.

'No problem,' the Congolese said, displaying his gap-toothed grin again.

Why was he being so helpful? I wondered.

'Dr Rachel has been very good to my family,' he said, as if he'd heard the question. 'She and Nurse Nell cured my brother when he was ill.'

I looked at my watch. It was seven-fifteen – five-fifteen in England – and my daughter would just be waking from her afternoon nap. I wished I was there to watch her demolish another mini-jar of baby food and burp her way through a video.

Instead I joined the others in slurping mosquito repellent all over myself, wondering as usual whether enduring a few bites didn't make more sense than coating myself with stuff which was known to melt plastic. We then did our Vincent Van Gogh act with the camouflage cream.

'Is this really necessary?' Knox-Brown wanted to know, holding the proffered tube as if it was a stick of dynamite.

'It won't help us to be invisible if your face

is shining out like a beacon,' I told him bluntly.

We took time to move all the corpses into one building, laying them out side by side on the floor. In this heat they would soon begin to decompose, but the living's need of our time was greater than the dead's need of burial, and Nyembo assured me that relatives would come to collect the bodies once they knew the killers were gone.

A few minutes later we were on our way, heading out along the road in the direction of Mangombe. Once across the almost silent river, we left the open sky behind. Ahead of us the road ran off into darkness through a tunnel of overarching foliage, and to the left, where Nyembo led us, our path led through a few metres of thick vegetation before emerging into a different kind of openness, that of a primary jungle floor. And even as I steeled myself against the claustrophobic damp I had to admit the grandeur of it all, the slivers of moonlit piercing the canopy roof way above us, the tree trunks and hanging lianas like pillars in a vast hall.

It was easy walking. The foliage was nearly all above us, the light just bright enough to see by. Every now and then we could hear animals making waves in the canopy above, and occasionally the sound of a floor creature shuffling hurriedly away from our line of march. Insects buzzed around us with a determination which didn't say much for the efficacy of the mozzie rep, but that was nothing new either. I swatted at them for a while, but eventually gave up in disgust and just concentrated on keeping pace with Nyembo.

It didn't feel particularly hot, but sweat was pouring off me just the same. A swishing sound in the canopy caught my attention, and I realized it must have started raining in the world outside. As if to prove the point, large drops of water began falling like miniature depth-charges from the roof above.

A little more than half an hour after leaving Kima we became aware of a faint yellow glow in the distance. After gleefully pointing out this evidence of his navigational skills, Nyembo rapidly increased his pace, and I almost sent myself sprawling across an outflung root in my haste to catch him. We had to be sure that there were no other soldiers at the mission, I explained, before we made our grand entrance. He obviously didn't think this likely, but allowed himself to be hamstrung by our caution, and we all advanced carefully to a vantage point some ten metres in from the jungle's edge.

The cleared area in front of us seemed about three times the size of the one at Kima, though in the gloom it was hard to judge distances. The yellow glow came from a lamp which hung above the walled compound of the Catholic mission away to our left, and fainter glows were emanating from a couple of the rounded silhouettes dead ahead, but none offered much in the way of general illumination, not with rain falling heavily from a cloud-blanketed night sky.

'There are no soldiers,' Nyembo said confidently,

and it looked as if he was right. There were no rowdy noises, no sign of transport – the place looked deader than Southend in winter. And only mad dogs and Englishmen would be out on a night like this.

We trotted across the open space in the direction of the mission, drawing not so much as a dog's bark but getting thoroughly drenched in the space of fifty metres. I didn't mind so much for us as I did for the radio – it was the PRC320's notorious vulnerability to damp which had induced the boffins to produce such excellent waterproofing for the PRC319.

Nyembo pulled the rope which rang the bell, and a minute or so later a middle-aged man in an oilskin cape opened the gate. He had short, dark hair, dark eyes and five o'clock shadow. He didn't look too well fed, and the Gallic cheek-bones almost jutted from his face.

He also looked for a moment like he was expecting the worst, but when he saw Nyembo's face his whole posture seemed to relax.

'This is Father Laurent,' Nyembo said. 'These are English soldiers,' he explained to the priest.

The man's eyes took in the guns slung from our shoulders and after a short moment's hesitation he ushered us in through the gate and across to the veranda of what I took to be the mission house. Two kerosene lamps hung from the rafters, spreading their dim light across the compound's courtyard and the walls of the buildings which surrounded it – various sheds, one of them used as a garage, the chapel.

Through the open windows of the priest's house I could see a table piled with books and a profusion of locally made furniture.

He seemed uncertain whether to ask us in, and, looking at the water dripping off the others, I could understand why.

'They have come to find the doctors at the clinic,' Nyembo began, before I had the chance to say anything.

'They are not here,' the priest said, removing the oilskin to reveal jeans and an open shirt. He was doing a good job of not saying so, but he obviously didn't want us there. Probably because we were soldiers, but maybe because he didn't like Englishmen – such vile prejudices have been known among the French.

'We know that,' I said. I introduced myself and the others, then told him why we'd come to Kima and what we'd found.

'I know what has happened,' he said sadly. 'Those who were killed have family here, and others arrived here this afternoon with the story of what happened. But I didn't know that the men responsible had left Kima – in fact I've been on the radio trying to alert the local authorities. Who were they, these men? And why have they taken your countrymen away?'

'They seem to be a mixture of Serb mercenaries, Government troops and Rwandan Hutus. We don't know what their reasons were for taking the doctors and nurses, but they can't have been good, and in order to get after them we need some transport . . .'

'They want to borrow the pick-up,' Nyembo interjected.

The priest looked surprised. 'It is not working,' he said.

'Maybe we can repair it,' I suggested. 'One of my men is pretty good with engines.'

'Well . . .'

'What's the matter with it?' I asked.

'I don't know. Kombo . . . our driver . . . his father's been sick and he's been helping his mother in Kisangani for more than a month, and no one else knows anything about engines. If your man here can fix it . . . Though I don't know how I'll explain to my Order . . .'

'Her Majesty's Government will naturally provide full compensation for the vehicle,' Knox-Brown said pompously.

'Well . . .' Father Laurent turned and called out the name 'Gérard', whereupon an African boy of around ten suddenly materialized from inside the house. 'Show this man the pick-up,' he told him, and after looking the rest of us over with obvious interest the boy led Paul across the rainswept courtyard and into one of the sheds. 'Please, sit down,' the priest said, indicating the wooden bench which lined the inner wall of the veranda. 'I . . .' he began, but stopped himself, then suddenly smiled for the first time. 'I'm sorry,' he said. 'I'm not being very hospitable, but . . . well, our ability to offer hospitality is somewhat diminished of late. We have some thirty Hutu refugees staying here, and feeding them has put a big strain on our resources, as I . . .'

'We have our own food,' I interrupted him.

He smiled again, looking relieved. 'These are bad times for this area,' he said, 'and though part of me knows that we need an upheaval if there's to be any hope of real change, well, the upheaval has to be endured nevertheless. I'm sorry for what happened at the clinic. I know that their work was mostly research, but they have been a great help to the people in this area.'

'They never say no when people ask,' Nyembo added.

'Do you know which way their abductors went?' the priest asked.

'West,' I said. 'But once they reached Punia they could have turned north or south, or just continued on to the river.'

'To the river, we think,' Nyembo offered.

'I don't think they will have gone north,' Father Laurent said thoughtfully. 'There are rebel troops in Obokote – I spoke to our mission there earlier this evening. The missions have their own network,' he explained. 'We talk to each other quite a lot.'

I wasn't surprised – it must be a lonely life. 'Are there other missions between here and the Congo?' I asked.

'There's one near Yumbi, and another south of Isambe.'

'Could you talk to them tonight, and find out the

situation in their areas? Whether they've seen the Serbs, of course, but also whether they know of any soldiers in their area, Government or rebel.'

'Yes, of course.'

He seemed to be warming to us a bit. 'I'll go and check how Paul's doing,' I told the others. 'Why don't you lot get the stove going? A potful of the Americans' freeze-dried gourmet meals and cups of tea all round.'

The rain seemed to be lessening as I crossed the courtyard. Inside the garage Paul was bent over the engine of a pretty ancient-looking half-ton Dodge pick-up – late-seventies or early-eighties vintage, I guessed. Gérard was holding up a kerosene lamp for him, making an almost biblical picture of their haloed heads. 'Any joy?' I asked.

Paul straightened up. 'There's nothing that can't be fixed. It's not sparking properly, so I'll have to adjust the timing. It shouldn't take more than fifteen minutes, but the carburettor's clogged solid as well, and cleaning that out will take a couple of hours. Once that's done . . .'

'How about fuel?' Knox-Brown asked from behind me.

'Apparently there's a drum of the stuff some-where.'

'Do you need any help?' I asked.

'Gérard here's doing a fine job.'

The boy grinned at the sound of his name. It was probably his bedtime but I decided to let him stay up a bit longer. 'Food's on the way,' I told them both in French, and walked back across the courtyard. It had stopped raining during the last few minutes, and already gaps were appearing in the cloud cover. On the veranda Sheff and Gonzo had emptied several pots of freeze-dried MRE delights into a saucepan of water and were hard at work watching it boil. Inside the house Father Laurent was talking to someone, presumably on the radio.

He came out in time to watch us eat, bringing news that there were rebel troops in both Obokote and Isambe – the Serbs' only obvious way out lay down the road to Poma and across the river. I looked at my watch and discovered it was almost nine o'clock. If Paul got the pick-up going in the next couple of hours we could hit the road at once. But should we?

I thought about it for a few moments, and decided against it. At night we'd either have to drive with our lights on, thereby giving any hostile forces ample warning of our approach, or risk ending up in one of those mud holes which could swallow a whole vehicle on a rainy-season road. The seven hours we would theoretically save – theoretically because we'd probably be able to move faster by day in any case – weren't worth the risks of wrecking the vehicle or driving it into an ambush. Also, we'd all function better after a few hours' sleep.

When I shared this with the others, they all relaxed and started yawning. Father Laurent went in search of the hammocks he kept for unexpected guests, and

I went to tell Paul that there'd be one waiting for him on the veranda when he'd finished. He and Gérard were still eating their meals, the boy with rather more enjoyment than the man. 'Another hour, I should think,' Paul said, and Gérard nodded his agreement.

When I got back to the house Sheff and Gonzo were stringing up the last of five hammocks, and after a few minutes of desultory conversation Father Laurent, who seemed singularly uninterested in news of the outside world, wished us goodnight and disappeared inside the house. A few minutes later the mournful strains of a female singer came wafting out. I had a feeling it was Edith Piaf, but that was probably because the only other French singer I'd heard of was Charles Aznavour. I was still waiting for 'Je ne regrette rien' when I fell asleep for the first time.

A little later I was woken by the sound of an engine firing, and I slipped back into sleep with a smile on my face. At least we had a working vehicle for the next day.

4

The inner clocks of the mission cockerels were obviously a bit off because it still seemed pitch-dark when they roused us all the next morning. It was almost five-thirty though, and as I lay there in the hammock I could hear sounds of activity coming from both inside the mission house and the clearing beyond the compound walls.

We would breakfast on the move, but a quick brew-up seemed in order while we went through our ablutions and tried to get our morning craps out of the way. Paul had brought the pick-up out of the garage and the tea was just being poured when Nyembo put in an appearance.

'I come with you,' he said.

I hesitated, partly because Father Laurent had just walked through the door. He was wearing his professional outfit this time, and looking none too happy.

'I know the roads between here and the river,' Nyembo said. 'And I wish to help Dr Rachel.'

I looked at the priest, expecting opposition, but he offered none. 'Nyembo can bring back the pick-up,' was all he said, which on first hearing sounded more mercenary than it was. You only had to look around the compound to realize that even a vehicle like the one in front of us represented a huge outlay.

'We'd be grateful for your help,' I told Nyembo, and received one of his best gappy grins in reply. 'And yours,' I told Father Laurent, offering my hand.

The sky was swiftly lightening now. We piled our gear aboard, and then ourselves – Paul, Nyembo and me in the cab, the other three in the open back. The priest opened the gates and stood there watching anxiously as Paul carefully inched the Dodge through the narrow gap. In the clearing outside there was even more activity than I'd expected. A long line of women with jugs had already formed by a standpipe, and a crowd of people were sitting around freshly kindled fires beside a long, rectangular hut with a plaited-grass roof. I guessed it was a school, and Nyembo confirmed as much. 'The Rwandans sleep there at night, and the children have their lessons there in the daytime,' he explained.

'Good luck,' Father Laurent shouted after us, and several small children took up the refrain as we bounced past them along the muddy track which bifurcated the clearing. Mist was already rising from the grass and I could feel the sweat gathering on my skin as Paul aimed the pick-up down the tunnel through the trees and headed for the slightly grander road from Mangombe to Punia.

He took the track slowly, hoping to minimize the

chances of the wheels slipping on one of the numerous patches of glistening mud and sending us into one of the trees which arched across the track. The making of the road had created a hole in the canopy above, encouraging a flurry of secondary growth on either verge which threatened to overwhelm the track itself and blocked off any view into the jungle beyond. Would-be ambushers could hardly have wished for a better set-up, and I only hoped that any forces in the vicinity had better things to do with their time than sit around waiting for a pick-up full of SAS men to come by.

We reached the main road – a slightly wider river of mud – and turned west. Kima would be our first stop, Knox-Brown having persuaded me to sanction a ten-minute search by daylight for the computer discs he had failed to find in the dark. We arrived at the clinic about a quarter of an hour later, and Paul pulled the Dodge to a halt just inside the jungle while we watched for any signs of movement. There were none – the place seemed as bereft of life as it had the previous evening.

Paul drove forward, and while he and Gonzo stood guard over the vehicle the rest of us quickly went through all the obvious hiding-places in the three main buildings. But we found none of the missing discs, if indeed any such existed. Back outside, the expanse of grass across the road was gently steaming in the early-morning sun, giving the whole scene a feeling of other-worldliness. I decided to raise Pressman on the radio while I had the chance. It was a bit on the early side for a diplomat, but I was afraid conditions farther down the road might not be so conducive to a private chat.

He did sound a bit the worse for lack of sleep, but the information I'd requested had obviously arrived during the night, and he read through the report for me. The Serb commander's name was Stojan Mejahic; in December, along with fifteen of his countrymen, he had been hired by the Mobutu family to defend the town of Shabunda, in eastern Zaire, against the rebels. He called himself a colonel, but there was no record of anyone of that name holding that rank in the army of the former Yugoslavia. There were, however, intelligence reports of a Serb militia leader in the Krajina region of Croatia bearing the name and assumed rank. This man had disappeared from public view early the previous year, soon after it was announced that the UN War Crimes Tribunal was about to start investigating the mass killings which had taken place in that area in 1994. If the two men were one and the same – and it seemed odds-on that they were – he was probably accompanied by his son Dragan, whom the UN investigators also wished to question.

It got worse. In Shabunda the self-styled colonel had apparently set himself up as a local Kurtz – he of *Heart of Darkness/Apocalypse Now* fame. Mejahic had sentenced more than thirty people to death for travelling without documents, had personally shot two priests whom he wrongly branded impostors, and had casually murdered five teenage boys who annoyed him in a market. He was known to have personally tortured several prisoners – leads from a car generator attached to the genitals were his favourite method – and there were reports that he had slashed the throats of twenty still-officially-missing prisoners with a bayonet. 'He's described as "a very deranged individual",' Pressman concluded, which definitely sounded like something of an understatement. I could hardly wait to catch up with him.

I filled the embassy man in on our last twelve hours, and what we were hoping to accomplish in the next twelve. His 'good luck', like Father Laurent's, didn't exactly overwhelm me with optimism.

Still, according to the map, the Congo was only about a hundred and seventy kilometres away, which meant that we needed to average only about fifteen kilometres an hour to reach the river by nightfall. Not a hugely ambitious programme, I thought, if only for the first fifteen minutes of our journey.

That was how long it took us to reach our first serious mud. The going was tricky from the beginning, but with each hard-won kilometre it got trickier, as the puddles of red-brown ooze gave way to mud baths of ever-increasing depth. Eventually we reached one that was fifteen metres long, spanned the road from jungle edge to jungle edge and was deep enough to cover the pick-up's axles. It took the six of us about half an hour to manhandle the vehicle from one end of it to the other, after which time we were all encased in gunk from head to foot. Half a kilometre down the road we encountered a similar patch, the first of four more, all of which seemed a little deeper and clingier than the one before. The sun beat down on our endeavours, and the sweat flowed off us in streams, mingling with the blood-coloured mud. In the trees which leant out across the road monkeys gathered to take the piss, and even Nyembo's beaming smile seemed to be in danger of going out.

And then our luck changed. One kilometre went by without a hold-up, then another. We came to our first village since leaving Kima, a few round huts planted in a clearing hewn from the jungle. Naked children ran after the pick-up, hands held out for anything we had to give, while women perched on discarded tyres around cooking fires stared at us with apparent indifference. Outside a small church of mud and wood a hub-cap had been hung for use as a gong.

The road led back into the partial shade of the giant trees. I reckoned we'd travelled about ten kilometres in four hours, which wasn't quite the schedule I'd had in mind. Still, the mud holes hadn't been new, and according to Nyembo the Serbs had five vehicles to wrestle through each one. They wouldn't be pulling away from us – not yet at least.

Not that I had any idea of what we would do if we caught them. As the jungle floated by, sometimes awash with brightness and vividly coloured flowers, sometimes turned a pale, luminescent green by the thin beams of a canopy-filtered sun, I found myself marvelling at the collective insanity – I didn't want to take all the credit for myself – which sent four SAS men charging after about twenty-five psychopaths of assorted nationality led by a deranged Serb. We were going to have to be either very cunning or very lucky, and I didn't much like the idea that Louise's continued possession of a full set of parents would be down to chance.

These thoughts were interrupted by another mud hole, this one some thirty metres long, which depressed us all no end. It took most of an hour to negotiate, but the muddiest hour proved to be the one before the dawn, metaphorically speaking, because the remaining twenty kilometres to Punia, though continually difficult, didn't oblige us to take any more baths in the stuff.

As we neared the town the land cleared for agriculture on either side of the road first became a continuous strip, then widened out, giving us an horizon more than fifty metres distant for the first time that day. On the outskirts we crossed a river on a long, narrow bridge, drawing stares from a bunch of women who were doing their washing in the Coca-Cola-coloured water, then drove up a gentle, curving incline between serried mud houses. After a few hundred metres the road suddenly widened, and a large, brick-built church appeared in the distance. There was now a line of palms running down the centre of the street, and white-stucco buildings with wide verandas on either side. Once they'd probably paid host to gin-sipping colonialists, but now they looked down at heel, with paint peeling from the woodwork, cracks gaping in the walls and pillars.

There seemed to be hardly anybody about: a couple of men looked up from a mattress they were lying on, two more were sitting with their backs against a wall drinking beer. The only garage we saw was closed, and the few shops we saw might just as well have been – the shelves visible beneath the awnings were mostly bare. Between two of the houses I noticed an old Studebaker that had been stripped of its wheels; the chassis rested on wooden blocks, and in the front seat a young boy was gripping the steering wheel with great concentration. I was just coming to the conclusion that he was the only source of energy in the town when I spotted the roadblock up ahead.

On what was presumably the crossroads at the centre of town two vehicles had been parked nose to nose in the classic fashion, one a jeep, the other a pick-up of rather more recent vintage than our own. As we motored slowly towards them I counted eleven men in and around the two vehicles, most of them toting Kalashnikovs. I rapped three times on the cab's rear window to alert those in the back and asked Nyembo if he could identify the men up ahead.

'I think they are Government troops,' he said hesitantly.

One of the men was walking towards us, palm upraised.

'Stop us here,' I told Paul, who duly obliged. We were about twenty metres from the man, who was now standing still and staring anxiously in our direction, trying to work out who we could be and whether we posed a threat.

'Just you and me,' I suggested to Nyembo, half expecting him to refuse.

'OK,' he said with a nervous giggle.

'If the shit hits the fan,' I told Paul, 'that gap on the left looks just about negotiable. We can RV further down the road, on the edge of town.'

He nodded, looking as nervous as I felt. If the shit did hit the fan Nyembo and I were going to need good running shoes, always assuming we didn't get dropped in the first exchange of fire.

I climbed slowly down from the cab, leaving my MP5 on the seat and making sure to keep both my hands out in the open. Nyembo dropped down nimbly beside me, and we walked slowly towards the man standing in front of the roadblock. He wore no insignia, but there was intelligence in his face and I assumed he was the officer in charge. The AK47 was held loosely in his hands, the barrel waving in our general direction rather than pointing right between my eyes.

Someone in my head was telling me he'd never felt scareder, but I silently told him to shut up. 'Good afternoon,' I said clearly in French, and smiled my biggest smile.

The officer wasn't impressed. 'Who are you?' he asked curtly. 'And where have you come from?'

'From Kima,' I said instinctively. 'We're with Colonel Mejahic.'

The expression on his face was one of surprise, but there was something else there too – something which looked like fear. I pressed what I hoped was an advantage. 'We were left behind to take care of some prisoners, and then we had some trouble on the road,' I explained. 'How many hours are we behind him?'

The man glanced at his watch, which looked from a distance like one of the *Star Wars* watches an American burger chain had been giving away in England the previous Christmas. 'About twelve hours,' he said. 'They came through at about two in the morning.'

'Heading for Poma, right?'

He shrugged, but one of the men behind him said something which made the others laugh, and I began to relax. 'Aren't you and your men heading east?' I asked, feeling pretty confident that this lot wouldn't share a road with friends of Mejahic even if their lives depended on it, which they probably did.

'Maybe tonight,' the man said carefully, then turned to give the men behind him an order. One of them climbed into the cab of the jeep, engaged the engine and reversed it out of our way. I gestured to Paul to bring the pick-up forward and tried not to let my body sag with the relief it was feeling. Nyembo scuttled aboard and I climbed in after him. 'Good luck,' I told the officer as we pulled past him, and I even meant it.

We turned on to the main road which ran beside

the church, and once out of earshot and rifle range, began whooping like demented savages.

The road to Yumbi followed a river for a couple of kilometres, but then dived back into the jungle, albeit with rather more confidence than our original track from Kima. This was a wider thoroughfare, in Zairean terms probably a main road, and in normal circumstances I would have felt confident of us reaching the turn-off just before Yumbi in not much more than half an hour. But the complete lack of traffic in either direction didn't seem normal, and neither of the two obvious explanations – more roadblocks or more mud – seemed very appealing.

Still, the kilometres rumbled by and I was just beginning to pin my hopes on a block beyond our intended turn-off as the reason for the empty road when we found ourselves running parallel to the river once more. The difference this time was the people camped alongside it. There were hundreds of them, maybe even thousands, arranged in groups large and small, listlessly sitting or lying on the ground between river and road.

'They are Rwandan Hutus,' Nyembo explained. 'Some of their young men fight with the Government troops against the rebels, most of whom are Tutsis, and so they are afraid that the rebels will punish them all. That is why they are here.'

'But where do they think they're going?' Paul asked.

Nyembo shrugged. 'They don't know. Away from the rebels, that's all.'

We drove on by, the sky darkening above us, and within a few seconds the rain was beginning to fall, first in drops, then in what seemed like a sheet of water solid enough to surf on. The refugees disappeared from view, along with the road ahead, and Paul was forced to reduce our speed to little more than a walking pace.

This went on for about twenty minutes, during which time we can't have covered more than a couple of kilometres. The rain then slackened, though even at a quarter of its previous power it seemed heavy by English standards. The verges were now empty, as if the refugees had been swept away by the torrent, and by my reckoning we were about five kilometres from Yumbi.

According to our map the town was on the other side of the Lowa, which looked a pretty hefty river for a mere tributary, albeit of the mighty Congo. The turn-off to Poma was on this side, just short of the bridge which carried our current road into the town. I asked Nyembo to describe the topography, but apart from asserting that the jungle ran right down to the river he couldn't add very much to what the map indicated. The turn-off was just a turn-off, maybe thirty metres from the end of the bridge.

I was coming to the reluctant conclusion that a CTR, a close-target recce, was in order when a pair of headlights suddenly brightened in the gloom ahead – we had wheeled company for the first time in about seventy kilometres. It was a smaller vehicle than ours, which boded well, and it soon became apparent that the driver was intending to pass us rather than block our way, which boded even better. 'Block the road,' I told Paul, who obligingly slewed the pick-up at an angle which could hardly be misinterpreted.

I got down, taking the MP5 with me this time, and called to Sheff to join me. After he'd leapt down from the rear we both splashed our way through the waterlogged road to opposite sides of the car. A European face full of anger looked out at me from the open side window, but the voice which went with it was eager to placate. This man had obviously been in Africa long enough to know that you don't lose your temper with armed men, whatever their colour.

'How can I help you?' he asked, looking from me to Sheff and back again.

'Have you just come from Yumbi?' I asked.

'Yes. I run the mission there.'

Another priest – the place was overrun with them. 'Are there roadblocks between here and the town?' I asked.

He hesitated, as if he was wondering whether to tell me the truth or not. 'There's one at this end of the bridge,' he said eventually. 'But I don't think they're letting anyone through.'

'They let *you* through.'

'I'm visiting the Rwandan refugees. There's a camp down the road which you probably saw. They want the world to think they're behaving properly,' he added cynically.

'How many men are manning the roadblock?' I asked.

'I didn't count them.'

I could understand his point of view – he didn't know us from Adam, so why should he take sides? 'OK,' I said. 'Thank you.'

He gave me an ironic smile, and I signalled to Paul to let him by. His car was already disappearing down the road, sending up fountains of water, as Sheff and I climbed back into the Dodge. 'Will you know when we're getting close to the bridge?' I asked Nyembo.

'I think so,' he said, in a tone which didn't give me much confidence.

'Take it slowly,' I told Paul, and for the next ten minutes or so we swished through the light rain, Nyembo leaning forward with his nose almost against the windscreen, trying to distinguish between apparently identical pieces of jungle road. We had just approached a tighter than usual turn in the road when he suddenly cried, 'Stop!'

Paul obliged.

'Round that corner the road begins to go downhill,' Nyembo said. 'Not steep, but steady, all the way to the river. It is half a kilometre perhaps, or a little more.'

'Let's have a conference,' I told Paul, and the two of us got out. The other three, who'd spent most of the last hour supporting a tarpaulin with their heads, clambered damply down beside us. I explained the situation, and the two immediate options available to us: a CTR or a CLB – 'Charge of the Light Brigade'.

'We might be lucky,' Sheff said, 'and if it was raining like it was half an hour ago . . .'

'It's tailing off,' Paul noted.

'I think we should try cunning first,' Gonzo said. 'We can always go in with all guns blazing as a last resort.'

He was right, of course, and I forced myself to accept the hour or more such caution would inevitably cost us.

'How about Nyembo driving it through on his own, and picking us up down the road a way?' Paul asked.

It seemed like a reasonable idea, but the expression on Nyembo's face didn't look too encouraging, and the more I thought about it the less I liked it. 'He's bound to be stopped,' I said. 'Which means he'll need a good reason for being there. They'll probably confiscate the pick-up anyway and if they're at all suspicious they might well shoot him into the bargain.'

'And then we'd have to walk the rest of the way,' Sheff muttered, grinning at Nyembo.

'You're all heart,' Gonzo told him.

I was running possible scenarios through my head. 'OK,' I said. 'Paul, grab an M72 and come with me. We'll take a quick look at who's doing what by the bridge. You three stay here. If by some miracle the lads on the roadblock have gone home I'll call you through. If someone comes up your backside and you have to risk a CLB we'll RV half a kilometre down the Poma road. Otherwise we'll talk it over when we find out who's where. Clear?'

'As the road we're standing on,' Sheff murmured, shifting his feet to make a slurping sound.

Paul and I reached down for some mud, streaked it across our hands, necks and faces, and set off towards the nearby bend in the road. Like Nyembo had said, it curved downhill, and after a few minutes walking down the verge we could hear the distant sound of rushing water above the dripping jungle. Rapids, I guessed, or even falls.

The cutting of the road had let the sunlight in, encouraging secondary growth along both verges, and by the time we'd forced our way through the tangles and into the open ground behind we were as wet as those who'd not had the good fortune to be sitting in the cab. The usual gloom surrounded us, rendered even more murky than usual by the dark skies outside. 'Look out for snakes,' I muttered, steering clear of a trailing liana the size of a healthy python. I'd always enjoyed London Zoo's Reptile House as a kid, but at the time I hadn't quite appreciated how much that enjoyment relied on the intervening sheet of glass.

We walked steadily downhill for about ten minutes, keeping the faint light of the road about a hundred metres to our left, until our progress was slowed by a steady thickening of the vegetation on the forest floor. Holes were visible in the canopy now, lessening the gloom, and the sound of rushing water seemed much closer. We were clearly approaching the edge of the jungle.

And suddenly, through a gap in the foliage, there was the river and the town on its far bank. We moved more slowly now, down what could almost have been a path, looking for a vantage point which overlooked the still-invisible road junction at this end of the bridge, and found one almost immediately. Just above the point where the slope suddenly steepened, plunging down to the road which ran alongside the river, a tall tree had fallen, creating a hole for the sun to do its work. Through a gap in the tangle of new growth which surrounded the grounded trunk we could suddenly see the rebel position on the junction below.

A lorry was drawn up on the road directly opposite the turn-off to Poma, and three uniformed men were sitting in the back, smoking cigarettes and drinking beer, their legs dangling over the tailboard. Another two men were standing facing them, sharing the conversation and indulging in the same vices. These two had AK47s slung across their shoulders, and I guessed the guns of the other three would be behind them on the floor of the lorry. There was no gate, no hut – as roadblocks went, this was obviously more makeshift than most – and there didn't seem any reason why the men sitting in the lorry would abandon their seats now that the rain had stopped.

Unless, of course, a pick-up full of European soldiers trundled out of the jungle.

I transferred my attention to the view beyond. The

Lowa at this point was about three hundred metres wide, and a study in riverine violence. Rocks littered the uneven bed, channelling enough foaming rushes of white water to make the members of our Boat Troop back home wet themselves with excitement. A whirling cloud of spray hung over the whole river, occasionally partly obscuring the long girder bridge which had been slung across the churning waters by some colonial administration in the distant past.

I was just focusing my eyes on the town beyond the river when gunshots sounded from that direction. There were two single shots, a long burst, a short burst, then silence. The men standing beside the lorry below took a few steps to their left to look back along the bridge, but they could obviously see no more than we could, because they shrugged at each other, and then at their three seated companions. It was clear that the shots didn't worry them, which probably meant that they were being fired by fellow-rebels, either in celebration of victory or in punishment of the recently vanquished.

I took my eyes off the group, fearing that someone's sixth sense might get a hint of our presence before we chose to advertise it. Which, sooner or later, we were going to have to do – if we wanted to drive to Poma, that was. There was obviously no way of getting the Dodge past the lorry unseen, and I couldn't think of any clever diversion which would entice the group below back across the bridge. Once more I considered abandoning the pick-up and taking to our feet, and once more I rejected the idea. If and when we rescued the clinic staff from the Serbs, we would probably need all the speed we could muster to make our getaway.

The conclusion was regrettable but also inescapable. If we couldn't get past the men below we were going to have to go through them. I didn't have much doubt that we could do so – these didn't look like men with much experience of real combat – but I couldn't help regretting the necessity. We were in someone else's country, and we were probably about to kill several men who'd merely had the bad luck to position themselves between us and another bunch of heavily armed Europeans. Men, moreover, who'd taken up arms against the bastard Mobutu, which had to say something good about them.

But like I said, it didn't seem as if we had any choice in the matter. Paul and I discussed the tactical situation in whispers, and then brought in the others on the comm link. Rather to my surprise, Knox-Brown agreed to do the driving, leaving Gonzo and Sheff to provide the broadsides from the back. Nyembo, given the choice of curling up on the floor or being left behind – it wasn't his fight, after all, and taking part in an attack on rebel troops might prove a bad long-term career move – decided on the floor. He said he didn't like the idea of the long walk back to Punia, but I think that by this time he'd become infected with our sense of humour.

I went through the intended sequence of events

one more time, just to make sure we were all on the same page.

We were. 'See you in a few minutes,' Gonzo said, as if he was just coming round to take us for a drink.

'Right,' I said, but at that moment Paul tapped me on the arm and gestured with his head in the direction of the town. A lorry had appeared on the other side of the river, and as it turned on to the long bridge two accompanying jeeps became visible. 'Stay where you are,' I told Gonzo. 'The odds have just taken a turn for the worse.'

Whichever way you looked at it this was bad news. If this mini-convoy turned right on to the Poma road it would be putting itself between us and Serbs; if it was bound for Punia it would run smack into our jeep; and if it was simply bringing reinforcements for the roadblock below us our chances of breaking through looked decidedly bleak. The second possibility was the most worrying, and I was still trying to make up my mind whether to order Gonzo back up the road towards Punia or off it and into the jungle when the approaching lorry came to a merciful halt in the middle of the bridge.

Merciful for us, that was, but not for its occupants. Paul and I watched as about twenty men were brought out of the lorry, where they huddled in a tight group under the watchful eyes of armed soldiers. The captives' hands were bound behind their backs, and as the first man was manhandled towards the parapet it became apparent that their ankles were hobbled as well.

The man struggled briefly, squirming in his captors' grip as they levered him up and over the railing, and then he tumbled like a stone into the rushing channel beneath. He surfaced one or twice in the next fifty metres, his red shirt flashing in the white water, but then he was gone.

The next man was on his way over by then, but he didn't land in the channel. He'd put up more of a fight than the first, and in the struggle to get him over, the guards had lost their place, dropping him on to a group of rocks below, where he lay unmoving for several minutes until a stronger than usual surge of the current carried him away. By this time three more men had been thrown from the bridge.

Paul and I watched all this, and the stunned look on his face pretty well reflected what was going on behind mine. These men might all have been guilty of heinous crimes against humanity – they might well have been raping and murdering their way across country in Mobutu's name – but it seemed much more likely that they were prisoners whom no one could be bothered to look after. Such killings took place all the time in Third World wars. Hell, if you believed the newspapers, my countrymen had disposed of a few inconvenient Argentinian prisoners in the Falklands – but that didn't make it any easier to watch. I felt a sense of helplessness spreading through me, and the temptation to interrupt the executions with a burst over the bastards' heads from my MP5 was surprisingly hard to resist.

On the road below us the five men we knew about

had been joined by another pair from the cab, and all seven had their eyes glued to the events taking place on the bridge. One turned to say something to the man beside him, who laughed, and in that moment I lost any compunction I'd had about taking out him and his companions.

But was this the moment? If we moved against the roadblock now we'd have the men on the bridge to deal with too, but if we waited until the latter had disposed of all their prisoners there seemed a better than even chance they'd go back where they came from. On the other hand, they might just keep coming, making things a lot more difficult for us. I told myself that this possibility alone justified immediate action, but in my heart of hearts I knew that my real reason for wanting to set our attack in motion was that I didn't fancy the idea of watching another fifteen men being casually tossed to their deaths.

I was probably lucky that the decision was taken away from me, but it didn't feel like it at the time. The noise of the river had obviously drowned out the approach of the local civilians on the path behind us, because the first thing I heard was someone shouting in a strange language, and the second was someone crashing away through the foliage. I trained my MP5 in the general direction, saw a running head jump in and out of view, and just about managed to keep my finger off the trigger as I realized the head belonged to a child.

The shouting went on though, and clearly something

was being communicated because three of the seven men below were now spraying the slope in front of them with automatic fire and the other four were grabbing their guns with the intention of following suit. A hundred and fifty metres behind them, in the middle of the bridge, the soldiers had paused in mid-execution, holding on to their next victim while all eyes were turned towards the river's southern bank.

On the comm link Gonzo was asking what the hell was happening.

'The faeces hit the fan,' I told him. 'Move!'

'On our way,' he said cheerfully.

It would take them about a minute, I reckoned. The fire from below was shredding leaves on a fifty-metre front and there didn't seem much point in advertising our position by firing back until the pick-up was about almost here. Two children had now appeared on the road below, and for a few horrible moments they hesitated, clearly torn between the town they'd been aiming for and the possibility of getting shot, before turning away down the Poma road.

'I can see the river,' Gonzo said in my ear. 'I can see the lorry,' he added a couple of seconds later.

'OK,' I told Paul, and we both opened up with the MP5s on the men below, most of whom had stopped firing and were simply staring at the slope above. Three went down immediately, and the other four scrambled for what they wrongly believed would be the cover of the lorry.

Wrongly, because at that moment the free-wheeling

pick-up rolled into view almost behind them, giving Sheff and Gonzo the easiest of chances to take them all out with one broadside.

I was charging down the slope before the last one had hit the ground, one eye on the pick-up, one on the men in the middle of the bridge. Two of these had climbed into the lorry's cab, and presumably more were piling into the back, because there was a definite delay before the vehicle started moving forward.

Paul and I had reached the road by this time, some twenty metres behind where our pick-up had stopped. 'How good are you with that?' I asked, gesturing at the M72 in his arms. The lorry was about a hundred and twenty metres away, well within range for what was effectively a stationary target, even though it was now gathering speed towards us.

'Piece of cake,' he said, dropping to one knee and aiming the stubby barrel down the bridge. The whoosh of its firing was short-lived, drowned by the crash of the rocket's impact on the front of the lorry. There was a sudden flare as the petrol exploded, and pieces of metal, canvas and flesh erupted above the bridge, showering down across the river and what was left of the burning vehicle. Through the smoke I could see the remaining guards and their prisoners, most of whom were just standing there staring in disbelief.

I swung myself into the cab, where Nyembo was busy uncoiling himself from his foetal position on the floor. 'Go,' I told Knox-Brown, as the Congolese and I disentangled ourselves. The pick-up gathered speed and I took one last look back at the bridge, wondering if and when the jeeps would be giving chase, finding myself half hoping that they would. At least then the poor devils waiting their turn by the parapet would be granted a stay of execution or a quicker death.

5

There was no sign of pursuit as yet, and I allowed myself a few moments of satisfaction with the way things had gone. We were past the roadblock, heading down the road of our choice, and all without sustaining any damage to ourselves or our trusty Dodge. Admittedly we now had enemies both behind and ahead of us, but those of us who had joined the SAS hadn't done so for a peaceful life.

For about a kilometre we followed the turbulent river, and twice I thought I saw a body bobbing in the current, but then the road took a sudden turn away, climbing back into the jungle. The roar of the water slowly faded, until only the screech of monkeys and our passage through the puddles broke the re-established silence of the trees.

The sun had not reappeared after the last downpour, and now it began to rain again, lightly at first and then with increasing vehemence. Much of the time the road was protected by overarching foliage, but in those stretches where the sky was visible the surface soon became lake-like, and our speed was reduced to little more than a crawl. In the open back a wet Sheff, Gonzo and Paul were keeping their eyes glued to the road behind, but I wasn't expecting to see any signs of pursuit for some time yet. It would take them a while to get the burnt-out lorry out of the jeeps' way, and if the officer in charge had been killed his men would probably still be arguing among themselves about what to do next. They would have their prisoners to think about, their superiors to inform, their own survival instinct to consult. They wouldn't want to end up like the men at the roadblock.

Against this, there was always the possibility that Yumbi was host to a thousand troops, and that an energetic rebel officer had organized a significant number of them into a Congolese posse that was already hot on our trail. If so, the only good news was that they would have more vehicles to drag through the mud than we did.

We were travelling at no more than fifteen kilometres an hour when we slid into the first hole, rather in the manner of a giant ship easing down a slipway and into the sea. Knox-Brown had been driving well, staring through the rainswept windscreen with touching determination on his boyish features, but neither he nor I saw the danger until it was too late. There was a sort of giant sucking sound, and the pick-up settled gently into the glutinous muck like a very happy hippo.

We all scrambled out on to relatively dry land and stared at the stricken vehicle. For some reason I found myself wishing I could share the moment with all those friends who never stopped moaning about how impossible it was to get around London these days. It was a while since I'd seen an Escort axle-deep in shit halfway down the Mile End Road.

The thought passed. It was raining more heavily now, splattering us with drops large enough to keep goldfish in, and at that moment a rising roar-cum-scream reverberated out of the jungle away to our right. It didn't sound like a monkey.

'Anyone see *Jurassic Park*?' Sheff asked.

Paul sighed. 'This is turning into a really bad day,' he said slowly, which cracked both Sheff and Gonzo up. Knox-Brown gave them both an uncomprehending scowl; Nyembo offered an equally uncomprehending grin.

I looked back down the road, now expecting the pursuit to appear at any second, but there was only the dripping channel between the trees, the ribbon of dark clouds overhead. There was no bend in sight behind us, so I just told Paul to look for a suitable spot some fifty metres or so back up the road. Two men would have been better, not to mention another couple of lookouts a similar distance up ahead, but we needed all the other muscle we had for dragging the pick-up out of the mud.

'Let's get on with it,' I said wearily, and after the inevitable chorus of groans we got down to the task. Half an hour of straining and struggling later we took our first break, all leaning against the rear to stop the pick-up sliding back down again. Sheff managed to smoke a cigarette between gasps for breath and I half wished I hadn't given up myself – a fag might have calmed me down. The day's various tensions had finally got to me, and at that moment I was feeling like exploding with anger at anyone and anything. At myself for joining the Regiment, at the bastards in the Government who'd sent me to this place in the middle of nowhere, at Mobutu, who'd ruled the country for thirty years and left it with roads like this one. Not forgetting the fucking rain which wouldn't stop and the fucking jungle which surrounded us.

The darkness above was more than just clouds, I realized – it would soon be nightfall. And unless this road suddenly mutated into a concrete superhighway we were still at least six daylight-driving hours from our destination. There was no way we could risk travelling in the dark, which meant that we would need to find a camping place off the road for the night. Preferably after we'd put a few more mud holes between us and the rebels.

The faces around me weren't exactly overflowing with joy at the prospect. In fact, all of them looked like they'd been standing under a shower for several hours.

'Christ, I hope we catch up with the clinic people before long,' Sheff muttered. 'They'll be able to help us dig,' he added, just in case anyone had mistaken the reason for his concern.

He actually had a point, I thought. There was

probably some sort of Law of the Congolese Road, whereby speed could be calculated according to the proportion of shovellers per ton of vehicle weight. Or something like that. A jeep with four shovellers would probably travel at twice the speed of one with only two, and so on. I tried to share this theory with my comrades, but they all looked at me as if I'd finally cracked under the strain of leadership.

We almost had the pick-up out now, and were girding our exhausted loins for one final push when the sound of approaching vehicles seeped out of the rain. I almost laughed at the appallingness of the timing. Just when we needed every gun we had, all but two of our hands were fully engaged in preventing the pick-up from sliding back into that ooze from which we'd spent the better part of an hour removing it.

'Get it out,' I told the others, abandoning both them and the Dodge, grabbing my MP5 and splashing back down the road towards Paul. The rain seemed to be letting up, but dusk was taking over from the dark clouds and visibility was as bad as ever. All I could see of the approaching vehicles was two pairs of blurred headlights, which for some reason looked like giant frog's eyes.

They were advancing at a cautious pace, and I found myself wondering why such a small force was advancing at all. Hadn't they noticed what had happened to the lorry on the bridge or were they counting on us only having one of the throwaway M72s? Perhaps the rest of the rebel army, including all the officers, was following these two sacrificial lambs at a respectable distance, but it didn't seem likely, and even if that was the case, our reaction would have had to be the same. We were waiting on a straight and narrow jungle track, and the obvious vehicle to fire on was the one in front.

It was about a hundred metres away, its occupants just about visible behind the twin yellow orbs, when I gave Paul the nod. He squeezed on the trigger and the front of the lead jeep exploded in a burst of orange flame, sending shadowy shapes cartwheeling into the rain-filled air. There was a sound of heavy weights crashing into foliage, and what remained of the jeep seemed to subside with a sigh, as desultory flames flickered all around it.

On the road behind, the remaining two frog's eyes were receding at speed, the jeep's driver having gone into reverse with enviable alacrity. But his steering left something to be desired – the two lights suddenly arced to the left, there was the sound of foliage being torn and then a loud thunk as the rear of the vehicle made decisive contact with a tree trunk. A few seconds later we heard the sound of feet running down the water-logged track, and after a while was silence.

We walked down to the wreckage of the jeep, and with some difficulty managed to find the remains of its occupants. I told myself I was relieved that all four men were dead – we were, after all, in no position to nurse enemy wounded – but a death is never less than a death, no matter how necessary or convenient it might be, and these torn bodies had all meant something to someone.

Back at the mud hole the others were leaning against the side of the rescued pick-up, getting their breath back and generally acting as if Paul and I had just been for a stroll down the road.

Paul suddenly realized he was still carrying the used M72, looked around, and hurled it into the surrounding jungle.

'At this rate we'll have used all four by this time tomorrow,' Sheff said.

And we'll still be a long way from home, I thought but didn't say. At least we were still alive, unlike the men down the road, the men back at the roadblock, the men who'd been thrown into the river.

I suddenly realized that the rain had stopped, and, looking up at the narrow band of visible sky, I could even see a little lightening, as if the sun was struggling to be seen before it made its exit for the night. 'We'll have to camp in the jungle tonight,' I said. 'Let's keep going for another fifteen minutes – mud holes permitting – and then get ourselves off the road.'

We climbed back aboard and sloshed our way down the track for the allotted time, encountering no major mud hole, hardly daring to believe our luck. We must have gone about four kilometres when the beginnings of an opening appeared in the wall of jungle to our left, and after about ten minutes of hacking with our machetes we had a space wide enough to drive the pick-up through. After spending a similar amount of time trying to erase the evidence of our passage, we headed the Dodge deeper into the jungle, a task which proved much easier than might be expected. The ground, though often spongy, was significantly drier than the roads we'd been used to, and in most cases the trees stood sufficiently far apart to allow the pick-up through. On two or three occasions a denser cluster of trees forced a retreat and a rethink of our route, but generally it was like driving through a huge hall of pillars, albeit pillars with protruding roots which occasionally threatened the vehicle's suspension. We had to drive with headlights on full beam, but I couldn't believe the rebels would be sending any more men after us – at least not until the next morning – and as far as I knew no one else was looking.

I was more worried about getting lost than being spotted – the jungle is notoriously easy to lose your way in, and this particular stretch, being essentially flat, seemed easier than most. I relied on my compass to keep the vehicle pointing in a basically southerly direction, and hoped that by reversing this in the morning we should have no trouble re-finding the road.

We'd been driving for about ten minutes, and were probably about a kilometre from the road, when we found ourselves skirting the edge of a clearing. The sun had obviously just about set in the outside world, but I was able to make out several tall stands of bamboo, which would provide ideal for making A-frame bashas.

'Another fifty metres,' I told Paul, who finally

pulled the Dodge to a halt in a natural amphitheatre surrounded by towering tree trunks and lianas thick as cables.

In the canopy above we could hear the monkeys discussing our arrival, and lumps of what looked distinctly like shit started bouncing off the cab roof, but we refused to be deterred. Paul and Sheff were dispatched to cut the requisite lengths of bamboo while Gonzo attended to the urgent business of a brew-up – it had not been a day to remember when it came to meals and drinks. Nyembo was just standing there, with a look on his face that seemed to say, 'How the hell did I get into this?', but when I smiled at him he couldn't help smiling back.

Knox-Brown looked even more worried. Still, he'd acquitted himself better than I'd expected at the bridge, and I was almost ready to count him among the ten per cent of MI6 employees I'd met in a professional capacity who weren't complete wankers.

'I think I should talk to Kinshasa,' he said, seeing me looking at him.

'That was next on the agenda,' I said, and went for the radio, which had spent most of the day between my legs, resting on the floor of the cab. As I pulled it out there was an ominous squelching sound, and I realized for the first time that it had been standing in a couple of centimetres of water. I sighed and cursed myself a little, but not with any great feeling – it had been the sort of day when you noticed if something was dry, not if it was wet.

And it might still work, I thought, as we carried it towards the clearing and a sky at which to aim the antennae. The clouds had disappeared with the light, leaving a star-filled hole in the canopy, and if it hadn't been for the insects buzzing round my face I might even have enjoyed the moment.

The radio was dead as a dodo, of course, a fact which Knox-Brown found much harder to accept than I did. I explained about the Clansman's notorious vulnerability to moisture, but he was more impressed by the fact that we were stuck in the middle of the Congolese rain forest with less chance of phoning home than E.T.

I could see his point. 'When we need to, we'll drop in on one of the missions,' I said, a lot more cheerfully than I felt. 'You heard Father Laurent – they've all got radios.'

He gave me a very unTintin-ish look and strode off in the direction of our camp, leaving me to wonder whether it was worth lugging a dud radio the rest of the way across Africa. Probably not, I thought, propping the offending equipment up against a tree and using it as a seat. My stomach was growling with hunger but I still felt reluctant to leave the patch of starry sky for the dank embrace of the jungle. And if I stayed where I was maybe one of the others would make me a basha, one of those tasks I'd never quite mastered the knack of.

The only problem with calling in an exfil chopper on a mission radio, I thought, was finding the mission to call from. And since the need wouldn't arise until we had the clinic people in tow, one or all of whom should know where the various missions in the area were, that wasn't really a problem at all. I didn't think we had much to fear from the rebel forces behind us, or not for a while in any case, so even without a radio our only real problem was the Serbs. Feeling somewhat cheered by this line of reasoning, I grabbed hold of the radio and walked back to join the others.

They were all too busy slapping on mozzie rep to have put up a basha for their beloved PC, so I spent the next twenty minutes struggling to create the usual masterpiece with bamboo and twine. Insects buzzed, whirred and zoomed all around us, but Nyembo was apparently immune to their attacks, the Hereford Four had their mozzie nets, and Knox-Brown was happy with the de luxe accommodation offered by the Dodge's front seat, or at least he was until he discovered that the windows wouldn't shut properly. Realizing that he was doomed to play the role of tonight's *plat du jour*, Our Man from Kinshasa plastered himself with enough mozzie rep to melt a spacesuit, let alone human skin, and I found myself fearing for his youthful complexion when morning arrived.

Gonzo declared that supper was ready, and we all sat in a circle like boy scouts to consume our freeze-dried fare. It actually tasted good, which only showed how hungry we were, and the mugs of hot, sweet tea we downed almost kept pace with the gallons of liquid we were losing in sweat. It was now about seven-thirty p.m., and the gripping humidity seemed even worse than I remembered it.

As I swatted listlessly at some of the several hundred mosquitoes which had gone into orbit around my head it suddenly occurred to me that we'd actually been on Zairean soil for little over twenty-four hours. And they say time flies when you're having fun.

The meal over, the four of us dutifully cleaned our weapons – a daily necessity in the jungle – and then changed into our equally essential dry sets of clothing. Knox-Brown and Nyembo had borrowed theirs from the clinic, and from the way the two sets respectively hung and clung I gathered that Barry Moir and Andy Waterson were of extremely dissimilar bulk.

Everyone but me then clambered into their snug little hidey-hole a decent distance off the jungle floor, and after swapping a few jokes, insults and hopes for the next day, lapsed into their private silences. I had decided to take the first watch myself, and after a cursory walk around an imaginary perimeter I sat myself on the roof of the Dodge's cab, feet dangling over the sodden floor of the rear. I thought the chances of any night visitors were remote, but the probable consequences of my being wrong were dire enough to justify the loss of two hours' sleep apiece.

Soon several different snores had been added to the collection of clicks, buzzes, whoops and cries which the usual jungle night-life was providing, and for the first time I found myself almost seduced by the sheer otherness of the place. I imagined an older Louise sitting here with me, finding a childlike wonder in it all, and my gnawing claustrophobia seemed to fade a little.

Gonzo had told us earlier that the Pygmies still lived in the eastern Zairean jungle, though not, he thought, in this particular area. They had never discovered how to make fire, he said, but they had no need for modern aids like the match or the lighter, because each band had been transporting its own flame around the forest for hundreds of years, lighting each fire from the embers of the one before.

Gonzo, who took the last watch, woke the rest of us just before dawn with a cup of tea in bed. After that the day sharply deteriorated. There's few things worse than changing into wet clothes, but one of them is watching an ominously mottled snake slide between your legs when you're in the middle of a morning crap. It disappeared as quickly as it had come, and I found out later that it was one of nature's more harmless reptiles, but I swear the fucking thing took several months off my life in that one split second. For what seemed ages, but was probably less than a minute, I just squatted there listening to my heart going boom-boom like a kettledrum, and wondering if the shock had constipated me for life.

By the time I got back to the others I'd just about recovered, and when I casually remarked in passing that I'd seen a two-metre snake – only a slight exaggeration – they were too busy scoffing breakfast to take much notice. Knox-Brown was busy scratching a healthy crop of new bites but I was glad to see that the mozzie rep hadn't dissolved his face into one of those bubbling moonscapes beloved of low-budget science-fiction films.

Light was now filtering down through the canopy, and the monkeys had apparently woken up because every now and then a new shower of shit landed somewhere nearby. We all sat round covering our mugs of tea with our hands, speculating on the delights of the day to come. Nyembo reckoned we were probably about fifteen kilometres from Ongoka, where he said there was a ferry across the Lowa.

'A car ferry?' I asked.

He nodded. 'Two cars or one lorry,' he said.

'What if it's not running?' Knox-Brown asked. Like me he was probably used to London, where cancellations were as much the rule as the exception.

'Then we build our own,' I answered him confidently. I might not be the world's greatest basha-builder, but I knew how to lash enough logs together to carry six men and a pick-up across the average river.

'What's the river like at Ongoka?' Sheff asked, remembering, as I hadn't, the waters at Yumbi.

'Peaceful,' Nyembo said quickly. 'Not like Yumbi.'

Gonzo had another potential problem in mind. 'If the ferry's not working then the Serbs may still be on this side,' he pointed out.

'We're not even sure they came this way,' Sheff added pessimistically.

'They must have done,' I insisted.

'They must have done,' Nyembo echoed helpfully.

'And we won't just go charging in,' I added.

'OK,' Gonzo agreed. 'So, assuming the ferry is working, and they're not there and they haven't destroyed it behind them . . .'

'That would have been stupid,' I said. 'If they can't get across the Congo they'll have to come back this way.'

Gonzo shrugged. 'If they're thinking that far ahead. But say they left it for us, then it's what – thirty kilometres to Poma? Mud holes permitting, we could be there by noon . . .'

'What sort of place is it?' I asked Nyembo.

He shrugged. 'A small town. A big village.'

'Bigger than Punia?' I asked, using the only reference point we had in common.

'No, no. Punia is two times . . . maybe three times bigger than Poma.'

The ground between us was moist enough for drawing on. I broke off a piece of dead branch and handed it over to him. 'Draw us a map.'

He looked doubtful, but started anyway. 'This is the river,' he began, drawing a long line.

'How wide is it?' Sheff asked.

'It is wide. Maybe two kilometres.' He drew another curving line. 'This is the road – it bends round beneath this hill' – he drew a wide semicircle which almost abutted the river – 'and becomes the main street of the town, between the old Belgian buildings and the dock. The rest of the town is on the hill behind the main street.'

We all looked at the diagram, trying to imagine the reality.

'If you were Mejahic, and you couldn't get across the river, what would you be doing?' I asked.

'I'd be buildings rafts as fast as I could,' Gonzo said. 'And I'd have taken over one of the old colonial buildings as my headquarters.'

'Sounds reasonable,' I agreed. 'And once you were across the river – just keep heading west?'

'There wouldn't be much point in staying put. It's either head home to Big Mama in Kinshasa or head for a border, and the way the war seems to be going I reckon I'd be seriously thinking about cutting my losses and looking for a flight out. There must be airstrips around, maybe a transport plane I could hijack.'

'If they find one it'll be bad news for the hostages,' I thought out loud. Their use as bargaining chips would be spent, and Mejahic didn't sound like the sort who'd leave witnesses behind.

'Well, let's hope the ferrymen are all on strike,' Sheff said, getting to his feet. 'Let us depart,' he suddenly added with mock urgency. 'Our sleek chariot awaits,' he declaimed with an outflung arm in the direction of the mud-coated pick-up. 'The road stretches out before our eager eyes!'

Ten minutes later we were inching our way back across the jungle floor towards the hole we'd made in the secondary growth that bordered the road. With the sun now climbing into the sky there was enough light filtering through the canopy for us to follow the tracks the Dodge had made the previous night, and after cautiously checking for signs of other traffic we pulled out on to the track and headed slowly west. Even for junglephobes it was a beautiful morning: the roof of foliage above us could have been a vast stained-glass window painted in a thousand shades of green, and the coils of mist which rose towards it seemed completely other-worldly, like something out of a sword and sorcery novel.

On a more practical level we encountered no more mud holes of epic proportion. Three or four times in the first ten kilometres we had to get out and give the Dodge a friendly helping shoulder, but there was none of the previous day's 'now you see the wheels, now you don't'.

We passed through several roadside villages. The first two of these looked deserted, but there was still smoke hanging in the air above one clearing, and Nyembo reckoned the inhabitants had simply gone to ground. Either the men of the third village were made of sterner stuff or their warning system had let them down, because a group of them were happily chatting on a roadside pile of tyres when we drove in. They looked less than pleased to see us, but warmed up a bit when Nyembo told them we were English, and I half expected to hear Gazza mentioned. He wasn't, but Nyembo did gather two important pieces of intelligence: the Serb convoy had apparently passed through the village the previous afternoon, and the ferry across the Lowa at Ongoka had been running, at least until yesterday.

'So they're across,' I muttered.

'Looks like it,' Gonzo agreed.

We took the last five kilometres very slowly, because Nyembo wasn't at all sure he'd recognize the last lap when he saw it and we didn't want to announce our arrival until we'd sussed out the place. As usual, we met no traffic coming in the opposite direction – it seemed to all intents and purposes as though the roads of Zaire had all been reserved for our personal use during the last day and a half. Of course, what this really meant was that we were the only people in the country dumb enough to be out driving in that shifting no man's land which lay between the advancing rebels and the retreating Government troops. Anyone else with wheels was keeping them off the road, partly to avoid their vehicle's instant sequestration, partly to save the driver from any possibility of contact with the soldiers of either army.

Still, it was a beautiful day, and our first view of the river at Ongoka, seen down a long tunnel of trees which disgorged the track practically into the water, brought back memories of the Tarzan comics Uncle Stanley used to read to me when I was little. It all looked so peaceful: the glistening forest, the sun-dappled road, the wide river and the trails of smoke rising above the village on the far bank. I couldn't see any hippos wallowing in the shallows, or crocodiles in pre-slither mode on the muddy banks, but I was certain they were there. This was the Africa of my boyhood, in all its exotic glory. *Tarzan and the Serbs*, I thought – a film whose time had come.

Back in the real world, the English contingent all got out of the Dodge, leaving Nyembo to drive the last hundred metres to the river's edge, where he blew a couple of hefty toots on the horn. We followed on foot, keeping to the shadows of the jungle verge, hoping that the Serbs weren't burning their ferries behind them, and that one would appear in answer to Nyembo's summons.

It did. The river was about three hundred metres wide at this point, and it took the three men on board the wooden ferry some five minutes to pull it across the gently swirling red-brown water. The ferrymen's smiles disappeared when they saw more European soldiers emerging from the shadows, but Nyembo quickly explained that we weren't Serbs, Frenchmen or Belgians or any other group against whom they could conceivably bear a grudge, and this argument – along with the guns we were carrying – persuaded the Congolese to give us the benefit of the doubt. The pick-up was driven aboard and we started across, Sheff and Paul helping with the chain, Gonzo and I scouring the approaching bank for an unlikely ambush.

It had taken four trips to get the Serbs across the river, Nyembo learnt, and yes, there had been women in one of the vehicles – one white woman, one African and one from Asia. For a moment I was afraid the two nurses had already been killed, but then realized that I had no reason to believe they were white. My experience of British hospitals over the past few years should have led me to the opposite conclusion, and the fact that it hadn't could have cost us dear. We could have spent hours looking out for white prisoners who didn't even exist, and looking right through black ones who did.

I felt stupid, and not a little worried – there are few people more inclined to racism than the Slavs, and my expectation of how the Serbs would be treating their prisoners had just taken a turn for the worse.

We paid the chief ferryman – his helpers were his grown-up sons – with money I'd found lying on the clinic floor, climbed back aboard our trusty pick-up, and, with yours truly at the wheel for the first time, started out on what we hoped was the last lap of our journey west. The village seemed empty, and Nyembo knew why. 'The Serbs shot a woman here yesterday,' he said. 'The man on the boat told me.'

'Why did they shoot her?' I asked, but I could have guessed the answer.

'There was no reason,' Nyembo said. 'They were just firing their guns.'

I thought about the run-in we'd had with some German hunters in the mountains of Kirghizstan the year before. They'd only been murdering endangered species, which seemed kind of tame when compared with using people for target practice. I was beginning to warm to the idea of meeting Colonel Mejahic, if only to borrow his copy of the Geneva Convention.

We left the silent village behind and burrowed once more into the jungle. Only a few minutes had elapsed since the sun's disappearance, but dark clouds were already filling all the sky we could see, and before you could say Radovan Karadzic the rain was coming down in sheets and the Dodge was aquaplaning again. This time, though, it stopped as suddenly as it had started, the clouds rolled away like a sliding roof to reveal the purest of blue skies, and much to my dismay Gonzo and Sheff broke into a rendition of 'Dancing Queen' in the back. Nyembo's face was a study in culture shock, Knox-Brown was probably wishing he'd stayed at home, and I could just imagination Mejahic's face when his lookout reported incoming Abba-impersonators. It was everyone's good luck that they only knew the words to one verse.

Another half-hour and Nyembo announced that we were almost there. 'Just two kilometres,' he said, as we passed a small roadside clearing with three huts, and that seemed close enough to me. The jungle's not what you'd call quiet, but mechanical noises have a timbre all their own, and if Mejahic and his men were still on this side of the river I wanted to make sure they didn't hear us coming. I went into neutral and free-wheeled down the slight incline, looking for a suitable place of concealment. An even muddier track suddenly appeared on the right, and after thinking about it for a few seconds I decided it was a better bet than the road we were on. I pulled the Dodge round and together we began to descend, alternately sliding and sloshing our way through the mud, brushing aside successive veils of overhanging branches. About two hundred metres in, a gap suddenly appeared in the trees to the left, and I swerved into an overgrown clearing, almost burying the pick-up in ferns and young saplings. A red corrugated roof was visible above the foliage, but the rest of the building had been conquered by the vegetation.

It wasn't the best car park I'd ever seen, but it looked cheap.

We gathered in the back of the pick-up for a conference. Nyembo reckoned that the track we'd just abandoned probably curled round the back of the slight riverside hill to which Poma owed its existence. If he followed it, he said, he could enter the village from the rear and ask the locals whether the Serbs were still here. If they were . . .

I stopped him at this point. 'If they are, I want you to come straight back here,' I told him. 'Someone might recognize you from the clinic, which probably wouldn't do much for your health or ours.'

'No one would recognize *me*,' Paul offered, which saved me making the same suggestion. There was a faint look of amusement in his eyes, as if he'd already intuited my reluctance to make use of his natural camouflage. 'There's the dry clothes we brought from the clinic,' he added.

'Just so long as you don't burst into "God Save the Queen",' Sheff murmured.

'No chance – I'm a republican.'

'Well, I'm glad we got that sorted out,' I said, looking at my watch. It was almost three o'clock, which gave the two of them just over three hours of daylight for their exploration. 'We need an OP,' I told Paul, 'and preferably not one that's right in the middle of the village.'

'OK,' he said, rummaging through the suitcase we'd crammed with clothes before leaving the research clinic. 'These should do,' he murmured, and a few minutes later he was modelling a pair of light-blue slacks, a short-sleeved white shirt and a pair of flip-flops for us.

'A male Naomi Campbell,' Sheff murmured.

Paul grinned and moved the Browning's holster into the small of his back, where it would hidden by the hanging shirt-tail. 'OK,' he said.

Now that the moment had come, Nyembo looked less eager than he had, but he managed one more gap-toothed grin before the two of them disappeared into the sea of foliage which surrounded the Dodge. The sky above was still blue, which was fine for the moment – I was still hedging my bets on what sort of weather I'd like later that evening. If there really were twenty-five assorted mercenaries on the other side of the hill, we'd be needing all the help from the elements that we could get. The trouble was knowing what would be helpful. A moon makes movement easier for friend and foe alike, rain the opposite. The only meteorological aid I'd have unequivocally welcomed was a lightning bolt between Mejahic's eyes, but that was probably too much to ask for.

Waiting is not something I do very well, and the next couple of hours didn't pass very quickly. We hadn't really spent much time in the sun since our arrival, but there wasn't room in the cab for four of us, which meant we took turns either baking under a tarp in the back or risking a close encounter with the local wildlife in the shade between the wheels. No one seemed in the mood for chatting, so the threesome in the front just sat there picking their noses, staring through the windscreen at leaves and thinking. I thought about adopting another life in the not too distant future, one that didn't involve snakes, killing people or two rivers of sweat running down my sides.

Paul reported in every half-hour as ordered, and once on his own initiative. The regular check-ins were that and only that – he obviously didn't want to risk giving us a running commentary from Poma High Street in case he got mistaken for Kate Adie. The unscheduled one followed a single burst of gunfire from down near the river – he just wanted us not to worry.

It was about half-past five, and the sun had long since disappeared behind the hill in front of us, when he and Nyembo arrived back, both looking pleased with themselves. We all clambered back into the Dodge's conference room, passed round newly brewed mugs of tea and the mozzie rep, and fought for the right to sit next to Sheff, reckoning it was better to die of passive smoking than get eaten alive by the insect life.

'OK, give,' I told Paul once we were all sitting comfortably.

He gave, drawing a map on a piece of paper as he talked, and pointing out the places as he came to them.

About fifty metres along the track they'd found and taken a path which led up the hill, emerging from the jungle to climb across a stretch of cultivated slope. Soon they could see the Lowa away to the left, flowing into the much wider Congo. Immediately above them a church sat atop the flattened hill, and down to their left, astride the main road out of Poma, two men were sitting in a stationary jeep. Paul grinned and said he'd almost dropped to the ground when he spotted them, but had remembered just in time that he would look a lot less suspicious just walking across the field. And as far as he could tell, the Serbs, if that was what the two men were, had hardly given them a second glance.

He and Nyembo had reached the back of the church, walked round it and found themselves at the top of a street which descended into a straight line to the dock area beside the river. This street, though not metalled, was lined with fairly solid-looking, one-storey buildings, but the quality of accommodation dropped sharply along the side-tracks. Here the houses were basically shacks, their mud and wood walls topped off with rusting corrugated roofs.

'We'd just taken all that in when the priest appears

from inside the church,' Paul said. 'He was obviously a bit nervous, but I think his curiosity got the better of him, so he came out and asked us who we were.' Paul looked straight at me. 'I took a risk,' he said. 'The town seemed dead, like everyone was hiding indoors, and I reckoned the Serbs had to be pretty unwelcome visitors. So I told the priest Nyembo and I were with the rebels . . .'

'Advance scouts,' Nyembo said with a grin.

'Yeah. And I asked him to tell us what was going on.' Paul smiled. 'He was only too willing. He took us inside and told us how the Serbs arrived yesterday evening, and that they'd gone ballistic when they found the ferry was on the other side of the river . . .'

'Did he say why it had been taken across?' I asked.

'They were warned that the Serbs were coming, and they guessed that once they'd carried them across the Serbs would burn the ferry to slow up any pursuit. It's standard practice round here apparently, and the ferrymen didn't want to lose their livelihood. Anyway, the Serbs burnt a couple of buildings, more out of frustration than anything else, and the priest says that several of the local women have been taken away somewhere. There's no way of communicating with the other side of the river, so they can't actually threaten the ferrymen with reprisals, which must piss them off no end.'

He turned back to the map. 'The priest gave us a run-down on the rest of the geography. The only luxury digs are here,' he said, drawing a couple of neat rectangles which faced the river across the incoming road from Ongoka, just to the left of where it met the street running down from the church. 'They're European villas with verandas, like the ones we saw in Punia. On the other side of the junction there are several old warehouses fronting the docks, and they've been empty since the local rubber plantation went bust.

'The other thing the priest said was that he'd heard a lot of banging that morning, as if the soldiers were building something . . .'

'A raft,' I said.

'He didn't know,' Paul went on, 'and he admitted he didn't fancy walking down the street to find out.' He smiled wryly. 'He was in the middle of telling us that when we heard the gunfire coming from down by the river, so I decided we'd have to be a bit on the careful side ourselves. So we walked down through these fields' – he indicated them on the map – 'to the path which goes round the bottom of the hill and followed it down to the river, here. I left Nyembo there to cover our backs and worked my way down past the warehouses, looking for a decent view of the dock area. The first thing I saw was a body floating in the water – probably the gunfire we'd heard – but then I found a pretty good spot among some piles of rotting netting on one of the old jetties . . .'

'Explains the smell,' Sheff murmured.

'. . . and from there I had a pretty good view. I

counted thirteen white men.' Paul smiled to himself at the description. 'Four of them were chatting in the road outside the villas, two more sitting outside the door of one villa, like they were on guard, and the rest gathered round the raft they'd been building.' He looked at me. 'But it's more like a cross between a raft and boat – it's not that big and it's motorized. They've found a couple of outboard motors from somewhere, and fixed them to one end.'

'Big enough to carry a jeep?' Gonzo asked.

'Nope.'

'But big enough to carry a squad across the river,' I suggested. 'Where they won't have much trouble persuading the ferrymen to change their minds and give the whole convoy a ride.' I turned to Paul. 'Where are their vehicles, by the way?'

'Here,' he said, indicating the stretch of road between the villas and the river. 'They're parked in a line, facing north.'

'I don't get it,' Sheff said. 'Once the ferrymen hear the outboards they'll just disappear into the jungle.'

'The Serbs'll still get the ferry,' Gonzo said.

'And they may not be planning to use the outboards,' I said. 'Maybe they're planning to row across, and just use the outboards in an emergency. They probably have no idea how strong the current is.'

'And at this moment they're just waiting for dark,' Gonzo added.

'Looks like it,' I agreed, suddenly feeling much more

optimistic about the night ahead. 'And while they're in midstream . . .'

Sheff nudged Gonzo in the ribs with an elbow. 'This is where we hear the master plan,' he said knowingly.

6

I led the way up the muddy track, trying not to think about how ill-equipped we were for the job we had to do. The pungent smell of the mud plastered across my face was a constant reminder that we lacked cam cream, but that was just a minor inconvenience. Our shortage of weapons – particularly our lack of explosives – might prove much more serious, depending on how alert and well armed the Serbs were. And our failure to bring a reliable radio could yet prove fatal, both for us and the people we were on our way to rescue.

It had been dark about half an hour, but the sky was still clear, and the stars offered a degree of illumination that was just about perfect for our purposes. In this we'd been lucky – a lightless sky would have hampered movement, while a moon might well have betrayed us.

Knox-Brown was walking behind me, having insisted on taking part. I hadn't been hard to convince – another gun was another gun, and he was probably earning better money. Twenty-four hours ago I would have worried more about his ability to keep cool in a drama, but I had to admit to being impressed by his performance at the bridge. I was also pleasantly surprised by how little he'd tried to interfere with the way I was running things.

Paul was last in line, and he was definitely in my good books. The fact that he'd twice done the business with the M72 didn't count for so much as his conduct of the CTR that afternoon, which I thought had demonstrated an almost perfect balance of daring and caution. He might have been able to find out more – the exact whereabouts of the hostages, for example – but not without putting the whole op in jeopardy. 'Who dares wins' is a great motto for some occasions, but look what it did for the Light Brigade.

Nyembo had wanted to come too, but he had no experience of guns and was more likely to get in the way than be any real help. I'd persuaded him we needed someone to wait with the Dodge, taught him how to use one of our Motorolas and left him there waiting for the call. If Sheff and Gonzo failed in their attempt to steal a jeep, we'd be relying on him to come and pick us up.

We'd spent some time wondering whether we needed another vehicle, and eventually decided that the greater flexibility, as well as the greater amount of room, more than made up for having to shoulder another set of wheels out of the mud holes as we headed back east in search of a radio. If the worst came to the worst we could always abandon a second vehicle, preferably in a mud hole for the pursuit to deal with.

Whether or not the Serbs would bother with a pursuit was another matter. With any luck they'd just adopt an easy come easy go attitude to our recovery of their hostages, and push on westwards, particularly since chasing us would take them back towards the advancing rebel armies. But who knew what a bunch of enraged Serbs would do? I remembered being told by a journalist in Bosnia how many Serbs it took to change a light-bulb. The answer was three – one to take the old bulb out, two to plug in the Muslim.

We'd been walking for about ten minutes now, and the jungle had given way on both sides of the track to rather ragged-looking fields. On top of its hill the small church was silhouetted against the stars, and I hoped the anxious priest was still hiding inside. The silence all around was almost total – we had left the strange squawks and howls of the jungle behind, the birds had gone to bed, and the vast river which we knew was just beyond the slope ahead offered up no more than a deep murmur. No screams or bursts of gunfire had punctuated the night so far, and an optimist might have been forgiven for thinking that the mercenaries were too busy for rape and murder.

We walked on, hoping we were as invisible as we felt against the backdrop of the dark fields, until the church was back over our left shoulders and the huge expanse of water lay dead ahead. To our right the jungle reached out over the river; to our left, about fifty metres away, stood the first of the abandoned warehouses.

The river itself had to be at least two kilometres wide, and the few pinpricks of light which glimmered on the far bank only seemed to emphasize its enormity. Some places in the world – cities, rivers, mountains – have names which are bywords for exoticism, but up close they often seem disappointing, like shadows of their reputations. But, standing there looking at the Congo – a name which for me had always conjured up hearts of darkness, vast jungles, forbidden continents – I felt truly satisfied. This was the 'mighty Congo' all right. This was majestic. A mother of a river.

I was only glad Gonzo wasn't there to spoil the moment with one of his statistics, like how many Olympic swimming pools this river could fill per second. Which reminded me – it was time to talk to the Thompson Twins.

The jeep was still there, Sheff told me over the comm link. The lights were off, but both its African occupants were awake, chatting away and smoking what smelt like local cigarettes. He and Gonzo had found a good OP some fifty metres upwind of the enemy, about halfway between the Lowa and the road.

I told him I'd call again when we had an OP of our own, cut the contact and gave my two companions an update. Paul looked like he was enjoying himself, Knox-Brown like he was just eager to get it all over with, which pretty well mirrored my own feelings. Now that there was more than a track to follow, I told Paul to take the lead, put myself in second place and left the MI6 man to play what I hoped would be a no-show game of Tail-end Charlie.

We reached the first warehouse, edged along the side facing the river and slipped across a wide area of concrete which the jungle was still in the process of reclaiming for its own. A vague yellow glow was now visible further up the riverbank, and after creeping along the wall of the second warehouse we could see what was obviously one of several kerosene lamps hanging from the wooden rail of a jetty about a hundred metres in front of us.

Paul now took a turn to the right, heading along behind a derelict shack and on to the upright arm of a T-shaped jetty which jutted some twenty metres out into the river. It obviously wasn't used for its original purpose any more, because piles of rotting fishing nets were sharing the boards with an assortment of rusting oil barrels. The planking creaked beneath our feet as we advanced to the far end, which offered a satisfyingly concealed view of the dock area and the houses behind it.

The first thing we noticed was that the motorized raft was almost ready to leave. About fifteen men were milling around beside the ramp where the ferry usually docked, all of them wearing variations on camouflage fatigues, many of them sporting Uzis or AK47s. One tall man with crew-cut blond hair and a butcher's face was just standing there, gazing out across the river like Cortéz confronting the approaching Mexican coast. I couldn't see his eyes, but I'd have bet on their being blue and empty. He had to be our deranged quarry, the phoney colonel with the taste for sadism and torture.

I felt a pang of pity for the ferrymen on the other side of the river, and hoped to God they saw him coming in time.

Apparently satisfied, Mejahic strode down the ramp and on to the raft. This looked like it had been efficiently put together, neatly cut logs having been lashed together into a rectangle some five metres by four, the whole craft given added buoyancy by a dozen empty oil barrels. Paddles had been fashioned from planks and two outboard motors fixed in tandem at one end, as Paul had explained. Looking at it, I decided that if anyone ever asked me to recommend a construction company for psychos this bunch would get the nod.

Ten of them were now on board the bobbing raft, which, not surprisingly, was more than I'd feared and less than I'd hoped. They were given a push-start by two of the men who were staying behind, and once the raft was a few metres from shore one of those on board engaged the outboards. This was bad news – I'd been hoping they'd be relying on paddles and stealth for the outward journey, which would have increased the time we had for doing our business. At the speed it was now going – about ten kilometres an hour, I reckoned – they could make the crossing in ten minutes, and even allowing for another ten minutes to beat the shit out of the ferrymen, that gave them only half an hour for the round trip.

Which didn't leave us with much leisure time. I took one long look at the scene in front of me, just to make sure there were no major surprises in the picture, and called up Sheff and Gonzo on the comm link. 'Phase One,' I told them.

'On our way,' Sheff said.

We hadn't discussed how they would take out the two men in the jeep, but everyone knew how important it was that it be done in silence. A burst of gunfire at this stage would probably not only alert the soldiers hanging round the buildings in front of me, but might well persuade Mejahic to turn his raft round. I could almost see the Serbs and their allies grabbing for their guns, all their faces turned towards the darkness down the road, wondering what had happened.

I forced myself to concentrate on what was actually there in front of my eyes. The nearest of the three villas had a wraparound veranda facing both the river and the street up to the church, and there were five soldiers sitting on it, their feet up on the rail in front of them, bottles of beer in their hands. Two of these were black and three white, and as I watched, another white man put his head through one of the windows. He was apparently naked, and it crossed my mind that the villa had probably been turned into an involuntary brothel. In Bosnia the Serbs had specialized in the staffing of such places with kidnapped Muslim and Croat women.

Another three soldiers were standing outside the second villa, two on the veranda and one in the street.

They were all black, and I hoped it wasn't just wishful thinking when I decided that they looked like guards. Across the road from them, lined up under a row of tall palms which flanked the river, were the vehicles of the Serbs' convoy – two jeeps and two open lorries.

I did some mental arithmetic. There had been eight Serbs on the boat and two Africans, which, together with the men in front of me and the two Africans in the jeep, left three Serbs and one African unaccounted for. Most or all of whom were probably taking their pleasure inside the first villa.

The thought was barely out before the door of the house in question suddenly burst open and a naked girl came hurtling out. She raced past the startled men on the veranda, half tumbled down the steps, then went sprawling in the dust as she tried to turn. A man was right behind her, a young man with longish, blond hair wearing only a heavily stained T-shirt, and as she tried to scramble back to her feet he kicked her legs back out from under her and threw himself astride her, trying to turn her face up and pinion her arms up above her head. She squirmed violently, and apparently her knee made contact with something tender because the man suddenly lashed out with his fist, punching first her face and then her breasts in a frenzy of anger.

She was just lying still now, and he seemed to have lost interest, because he climbed back to his feet and walked across to the veranda, where he took a swig from one of the other men's beer bottles. Then he made a gesture to one of them, who passed something over the rail.

He walked back towards to the girl, and I saw it was a gun.

Shit, I thought, but he'd already raised it and fired. Once, twice, three times, as if he was trying to make the corpse dance.

Twenty metres away a man had just come into view. He was carrying a tray of steaming food, and even at this distance I could see it was visibly shaking in his arms. I could almost hear the thoughts running through his head – the sorrow, the rage, the realization that he could precipitate his own death with nothing more than the wrong expression.

Maybe it was his daughter, or maybe a friend's, and maybe he had others to live for, a wife, children. With what must have been an enormous effort, he resumed his forward progress, climbed the veranda steps and put the tray down on a table for the soldiers who were seated there. He waited a few seconds, presumably to make sure he was no longer needed, then retraced his steps, allowing himself only one quick, heartbroken glance at the dead girl in the dirt.

Her killer meanwhile had stepped back on to the veranda and was helping himself to the newly arrived food.

I closed my eyes for a moment and tried to let the anger drain away. It wouldn't help.

A few seconds later Sheff's voice sounded in my ear.

'Phase One was a walk-on,' he said. 'They were both half asleep.'

'Phase Two, then,' I said.

'At your service.'

The next wait felt longer than it was. For a few minutes the men on the veranda seemed slightly sobered by what they'd just witnessed and the body sprawled in front of them, but gradually the volume of their conversation crept back up, the laughs became more frequent and the dead girl just became part of the scenery. The killer finished his meal and disappeared back inside the villa, probably in search of another victim.

By this time Mejahic and his party should have arrived on the far shore, but so far there had been no noises to confirm this. Maybe the current was a lot stronger than it looked, and outboards notwithstanding, they'd been swept downstream. Some serious rapids would get the job done, but I couldn't help hoping that the crocodiles got them.

At last Sheff's voice sounded in my ear again. He was in position close to the river, just beyond the last vehicle in the line, and quite a lot closer than we were to the villa which we hoped held the clinic staff.

'I can't see anything inside,' he told me. 'But there is a light on.'

I thought about it for a minute, and decided we had to work on the assumption that that was where they were. They obviously weren't in the vehicles, and it didn't seem likely that they'd be in the makeshift brothel. So where else could they be?

'Phase Three,' I told Sheff, who wished us luck.

I led the way off the jetty, through a gap between empty warehouses and up the hill behind. Either the shacks on the lower slopes were also empty or their occupants were sitting quietly in the dark waiting for the nightmare to end – a pretty understandable reaction in the circumstances. I heard nothing as we threaded our way between several dwellings and finally reached one of the dirt tracks which followed the hill's contours.

The main street leading down from the church was about seventy-five metres away, and as we started towards it the sound of guns firing drifted across the enormous river. Mejahic was having his revenge.

We walked on, pausing at the main street before slipping across. Down to the right the street glowed yellow from the villa's windows, but where we were the only light was supplied by the stars, and once on the other side we had some difficulty in finding a route down the hill which would bring us out behind the second villa. Eventually we realized there was nothing for it but to clamber through the empty chicken coop which someone had used to block our path.

This done, we found ourselves in what had once been a European-style garden, but which was now almost chest-deep in tropical greenery. Half this space was dimly illuminated by lamps inside the first villa, but the other half, behind the second villa, was wreathed in dark shadows. As we crouched there for a few seconds, taking the time to be certain we'd seen all there was to see, a naked man appeared at one of the windows in the first villa, took a last drag on a cigarette, before flicking it out into the bushes and disappearing.

There was no sign of light in the windows of the second villa, which didn't seem like a good sign. I was just gesturing to the others to follow me when Sheff's voice sounded in my ear: 'One man entering villa two, carrying a handgun. One of the three men outside has walked off towards villa one.'

Shit, I thought, and crouched down again. If we were lucky he'd be in and out; if not . . . If not, I didn't know what we were going to do. Mejahic and the rest of his Serbs could be back in ten minutes, doubling the odds against us if it came to a fire-fight. And the longer we waited the more chance there was of something going wrong . . .

There was a sudden wail of alarm from inside the second villa, followed by the sound of upraised voices. Pleading voices.

The image of the terrified girl running out of the brothel imprinted itself once more on my retina, burning away any reserves of sensible caution I still had left. And as if to prove me right, at that moment music started playing somewhere in the first villa, loud African music, all drums and bass. I sent a silent vote of thanks to the music lover and whispered, 'Let's go.'

We pushed through the foliage to the back of the villa, where a few iron steps led up to a decrepit-looking door. It was locked, but the wood was so rotten that the whole thing almost fell off in my hands.

I edged into what must have been the kitchen, and through an open doorway into a short corridor. There were no sounds of struggle to be heard, only a rasping noise towards the front of the house, as if someone was fighting for breath. I started forward, only to be stopped in my tracks by the sudden sound of a woman starting to cry behind the next door.

I tried the door, expecting it to be locked, but it wasn't. There was almost a squeak of alarm, and someone scuttled away from me in the darkness.

'Shhh,' I said stupidly. 'SAS,' I added, feeling like someone in a very bad film.

'Come to take you home,' Paul whispered beside me.

'He took Nell,' the woman said.

'Take care of her,' I told Paul, and accelerated round the bend in the corridor, not worrying too much about being heard. A male voice suddenly shouted, 'What's happening, Nell?' from behind another door, but I ignored it in my headlong rush to prevent the abductor getting away.

I reached the dimly lit expanse of the wide living room just in time to see the front door closing behind them, and for a second I hesitated, not knowing what to do. Sheff was just starting to tell me that the man had come out again, dragging a woman with him, when she started to shout at the top of her voice, in English, repeating the words 'you bastard' over and over in an hysterical litany. There was a loud slapping noise, a male laugh that was instantly followed by a curse, and the woman suddenly burst back through the door, falling as she did so.

A figure appeared in the doorway, gun in hand. It was the same man who'd killed the African girl, and he hardly had time to register my presence before I sent a triple tap through his chest, throwing him out on to the veranda. The two men on guard duty outside reacted no quicker – they still seemed to be trying to convince themselves that Pretty Boy was dead when I raked the front windows and doorway, letting my anger out with a burst of fire that killed them both instantly in a satisfyingly bloody shower of glass.

'Sheff,' I said, 'if anyone starts down the road, open up.' I whirled to find a group of stunned-looking doctors and nurses huddled in the doorway with Knox-Brown. Paul was helping the black nurse to her feet.

The elder of the two rescued men started to say something but I ignored him. 'Get them out the back,' I told Paul and Knox-Brown. 'You get them to Gonzo,' I told the MI6 man. 'Paul, you take the back.'

They both nodded, and started herding their charges towards the rear.

'Gonzo,' I said into the mike, 'get ready for passengers. And tell Nyembo to get the Dodge out on to the road.'

'Right.'

I looked at my watch, and then put an eye round the edge of the open door. I couldn't see any Serbs advancing in my direction. 'What are they doing?' I asked Sheff.

'Running around trying to get their trousers on, probably . . . no, here come a couple . . .'

I heard his MP5 in stereo, through both the earpiece and the door.

'One's a little wiser, and his friend won't get any older,' Sheff said smugly.

I looked at my watch again. Forty seconds had gone by, and I was reckoning on giving them a two-minute start. 'Everything OK, Paul?' I asked.

'Not a whisper.'

More seconds went past, and still the Serbs seemed unwilling to come after us. With the two minutes about to run out I started systematically shredding the right-side tyres of the two jeeps and two lorries with the MP5. That done, I called Paul through from the back. We waited for Sheff to give us covering fire, edged out of the door and along the veranda, then accelerated up the edge of road, which almost immediately bent to the left, taking us out of any line of fire from the river frontage.

Two minutes of running and we were joining our own convoy. We had no idea where we were going, but that didn't matter for the time being, because there was only one road to take. Gonzo and I took the jeep; Sheff, Knox-Brown and the woman doctor shared the cab of the Dodge; Paul, Nyembo and the rest of our rescuees clambered into the pick-up's rear. As we pulled off into the jungle night I was feeling pretty pleased with the way things had gone. I didn't know I'd just killed Stojan Mejahic's only son.

7

The ribbon of sky above the jungle track was still clear as we set out on the first lap of the night's journey, and occasionally the landscape would open briefly to reveal the most fragile of moons riding just above the trees. It was a sight for peaceful contemplation, but not surprisingly my mind was racing considerably faster than our vehicles, trying to conjure away all the obstacles which lay between us and a slap-up supper in Brazzaville the following evening.

The road was an obstacle in itself, but there hadn't been any five-star mud holes between Poma and Ongoka that morning, and I was hoping none had appeared in the meantime. It had hardly rained all day, but then I didn't have the faintest idea how these mud holes were formed. For all I knew, they were a cataclysmic response to a slow cumulative process, one minute solid ground, the next a Venus fly-trap for pick-ups and jeeps. The lack of light was keeping us down to about fifteen kilometres an hour, which was probably just as well.

The enemy behind us could hardly be in our way,

literally speaking, but Mejahic and his merry men could turn themselves into an obstacle to our progress if they so chose. I'd only been able to take out the tyres on one side of their vehicles, which meant that, with the spares, they probably had enough left to outfit their two remaining jeeps. Give them half an hour to do the work, another fifteen minutes to get themselves organized, and they'd be less than an hour behind us, which wasn't much on these roads. In my ignorance of Mejahic junior's fate I was banking on them not bothering. They presumably had their ferry by this time, so why not cut their losses and head on west? Surely, I thought, that would seem a much better bet than chasing after a few hostages they hardly needed, particularly when such a move was likely to involve them in a head-on collision with the advancing rebels.

I wasn't too eager to meet the latter again myself – our first two run-ins hadn't exactly set the stage for a beautiful friendship. But while I couldn't think of any reason for them to have abandoned their position at Yumbi, I could think of quite a few why they might be advancing towards us. Not at night, I hoped – not on roads like this. We probably had a few hours' grace, but that was all.

So what should we do? The thought occurred to me that we could just take ourselves off the road and into the jungle, and let the rebels bypass us on their triumphant march into the west. If Mejahic and Co really were following us, our two enemies would run straight into one another. They'd actually have to use their guns on people who could fire back, which would be a bit of a change for both sets of thugs.

This was an appealing notion, but not, I decided, a very practical one. There was no way of knowing how long it would be before the rebels resumed their march westwards, and we didn't have the supplies to set up a semi-permanent jungle camp for eleven. Nor did I really like the idea of hanging around in Zaire for a minute longer than I needed to. Better to find a radio, call up an American taxi, and get the hell out, before we ran into any more men with guns. Once we'd reached Ongoka and put the Lowa between us and the Serbs, I'd have a talk with our grateful rescuees, maybe sign a few autographs and rack their brains about the local radio situation.

It was about nine-thirty when we found ourselves rolling down towards the river, earlier than expected but apparently not early enough to catch the locals still up. We parked the two vehicles by the berthed ferry, and after promising Moir and Knox-Brown a conference as soon as we were across the river, I sent Sheff and Paul back up the hill to cover the road and took Nyembo along with me to find the ferrymen. Three shacks and two wary helpers later, we were waking the family, all six of whom shared the one room. The ferryman seemed more resigned than pissed off, but he'd probably had a lot of practice lately at concealing his anger. The youngest son actually seemed pleased to see me again, but then he was only about five – he hadn't yet learnt that men with guns nearly always mean trouble.

The father and his two older sons walked down to the river with us, yawning infectiously, and the pick-up was slowly driven on to the ferry. I checked with Sheff on the comm link that there was no sign of a Serb pursuit, and was told that there was no sign of anything but bloody mosquitoes. There didn't seem much chance of the jeep being stolen where it was, so Gonzo and I went across with the pick-up and the clinic staff, just in case the rebels picked this moment to arrive on the far bank. Once we got there I dispatched Gonzo a hundred metres up the road to give us warning of unwelcome visitors, sent Nyembo back with the ferrymen as some sort of insurance that they wouldn't just disappear round a bend in the river, and told Sheff and Paul to make their way down to the water.

What with our hurried escape, my place in the jeep, and the need to help pull the ferry across the river, this was my first chance to look over the people we'd been sent to collect. They were all sitting on an old mud wall that someone had thoughtfully provided by the landing ramp, looking remarkably like what hostages would be expected to look like after thirty-six hours in the company of fifteen Serb mercenaries and their deranged leader. They looked drained, exhausted, stunned, hardly able to believe their sudden luck in being rescued.

The married doctors were both in their late thirties.

Barry Moir was about five foot nine, and from the way his clothes hung I guessed he'd lost a little weight since leaving England. He had crinkly brown hair which was just beginning to grey and recede at the temples, and one of those faces which would look handsome when its owner felt in charge of things. The dark bruises on one cheek were proof that lately he'd been anything but.

He wore black-rimmed glasses, which at that moment he was cleaning with a front tail of his shirt. My immediate feeling about him – one that was to be borne out over the next few days – was that here was a man who had not taken to Africa, and who had been obliged to fight the continent to an exhausting draw merely in order to continue working here.

His working-class background was no more apparent than his wife's middle-class background at first sight, but other differences certainly were. Rachel Moir was a big-boned, blue-eyed blonde with an attractive Nordic face and a devastating smile. She was as tall as her husband, and looked in rather better condition. Unlike him, she had obviously thrived in the jungle, and if Nyembo's devotion to her was any indication, not at the expense of the locals.

Over the next few days, as with so many couples in the past, I would find myself wondering what on earth this pair had once had in common. The only answer I ever came up with was what they still shared – a fierce commitment to medicine. And they even seemed to see this from different ends of the stethoscope.

The two nurses were both attractive young women in their twenties. Nell Campbell was a tall, long-legged, wide-hipped and big-breasted West Indian with short hair, big eyes and skin almost dark enough for a Congolese. She was the one whom the Serb had been dragging, with some difficulty, from the villa, but on the surface she didn't seem that fazed by the experience. The Asian beside her, whose name was Rubina Patel, seemed much more troubled. The worst might be over, but her eyes were still brimming with fear, and alongside the much bigger Nell she seemed like a small and very vulnerable child.

The arm round her neck belonged to Andy Waterson, who looked like he wasn't long out of school. He was very tall, with tousled, blond hair, a fashionable goatee and beach-bum good looks. I later learnt he was a second cousin of Rachel's, seeing the world before starting the grind of medical school, but at that moment all I knew about him was that the joy of having Rubina's head on his shoulder had completely driven out any residual feelings of anxiety over his own recent kidnapping and possible murder. Oh, to be young again, I thought.

A mental picture of Louise slurping back a mini-tin of peaches and custard flashed across my mind. Oh, to be home again.

I introduced myself, which seemed almost Monty Pythonesque in the situation, and checked that Paul,

Sheff and Knox-Brown had filled them in on why we were there and what we were hoping would happen next.

They'd been filled in all right, and they had their own ideas on where we went from here.

'We have to get back to Kima,' Barry Moir said straight away.

'Why?' I asked.

'The doctor hid the computer discs before they were all taken away,' Knox-Brown explained on Moir's behalf.

'What's on them?'

'Our research findings, of course,' Moir said testily.

'A cure for AIDS?'

'Not exactly,' Moir replied.

'Exactly enough to risk all our lives?' I asked. What with the rebel roadblock at Yumbi and the Government forces at Punia, not to mention enough mud to keep a thousand wallowing hippos happy from here to Christmas, I could think of journeys I'd rather take. 'Do you know what we can expect to meet between here and Kima?' I asked.

'They know,' Knox-Brown said, and for the first time I felt completely clear about his role in this particular venture. He was the coach who'd been sent to make sure we kept our eyes on the ball – or, in this case, computer disc – for fear that, left to our own devices, we might be diverted by other trivial considerations, like our own survival.

'There's one mission just north of Yumbi and

another south of Isambe,' Rachel Moir volunteered. 'And from what we've been told it looks as though those would be harder to reach than our own one near Kima.' She smiled. 'So it looks as though we don't have much choice.'

'There's a manned roadblock outside Yumbi, and after what happened yesterday I think we'll need more than charm to get us through,' I said.

'At least they won't be expecting us,' Sheff put in, coming up behind me. He gestured back over his shoulder, to where Paul was still standing on the ferry. Though his gun wasn't pointed at one, it was clearly deterring the ferry's departure. 'What do we do with this lot?' Sheff asked. 'We could sink the ferry, but who knows when we might need it again?'

I sighed. The thought of spending a life racing to and fro between Poma and Yumbi was not pleasant to contemplate, and neither was sinking this family's means of livelihood. I'd seen their home, and I didn't want the memory of having made them even poorer; but just leaving the ferry for Mejahic hardly seemed sensible.

I glanced across the river, just to make sure the Serbs hadn't crept down to the far bank on tiptoe.

'You can't just destroy the ferry,' Rachel said abruptly, as if she'd just realized what we were thinking about.

Resisting the temptation to ask her why not, I turned and signalled to Paul to bring the three Congolese ashore. 'Tell them they're coming with us,' I told Nyembo. 'Tell them we're sorry, and we'll pay them for their trouble, but they'll have to walk back from . . . don't know, Yumbi, I suppose.' I looked across at Rachel, who didn't seem sure whether I was behaving like a brute or a genius. Nyembo had begun explaining my Pilate-like ruling to the Congolese, who seemed relieved by it. They'd probably been expecting worse.

None of which helped much in the wider scheme of things. I found it hard to believe that the closest available radio was the one near Kima, but if it was . . .

A best-case scenario would have the rebels too busy burying their comrades and victims to mount a nocturnal roadblock, the Government troops gone from Punia, and Congolese road crews busy filling all the mud holes with concrete. Arriving back at Kima before dawn, we'd find a new Little Chef waiting to serve us breakfast.

The worst-case scenario would have us running into an overwhelming force of advancing rebels before we reached the junction outside Yumbi. We'd then have the choice of retreating into the arms of the Serbs or going to ground in the fucking jungle and sending up smoke signals in Morse for the American satellite boys to wonder over. We might not starve to death, but then neither would the local parasites with us to feed on. If we were really lucky we might end up having a lethal virus named after us.

But I didn't think we'd run into advancing forces

in the middle of the night. So look at the middle-case scenario, I told myself. A little hassle here, a little hassle there. We'd done it one way in about sixteen hours, admittedly in daylight, but our acquired knowledge of the road should provide some compensation for the difficulties of driving by night. And maybe there would be no manned roadblocks between dusk and dawn – after all, the roads weren't exactly crammed with vehicles to check. If we could get through Punia before dawn then we should be safe, and I could see no problem with bringing a Super-Stallion down at either the mission or Kima itself.

I looked at the others. 'Any suggestions?' I asked Sheff and Paul.

Sheff shrugged. 'We don't seem to have many options, boss,' he observed.

'Keep heading east until someone stops us,' Paul said.

'OK,' I agreed, turning back to the others. 'If we can get past Yumbi and through Punia, fine. But we'll need to be east of Punia before it gets light, and there's a lot of mud between here and Yumbi. Everyone'll have to dig or we won't make it.' I gave them a questioning look to make sure they were listening, and a couple of them nodded back. 'And when it comes to the bridge outside Yumbi,' I went on, 'we'll have a good long look from a distance before we make any decisions. If there's a big force in the way then we'll have to take to our feet.'

'And then what?' Knox-Brown asked.

'And then walk to Kima.'

'It's about seventy-five kilometres!'

'A long walk,' I admitted, and in this sort of climate it was. 'But no longer than the walk all those women prisoners of the Japanese did in *A Town Like Alice*.'

'Very inspirational,' Sheff murmured in my ear a few minutes later. 'You do know that *A Town Like Alice* was a novel?'

We shuffled the seating arrangements and set off. Sheff was now driving the jeep, with Gonzo beside him, Barry and Andy behind. I was at the wheel of the pick-up, sharing the cab with Rachel and Rubina, leaving Knox-Brown, Paul, Nell, Nyembo and our three guests from Ongoka to fill the back. As we climbed away from the Lowa and back into the clammy embrace of the jungle I flirted with the idea of myself as a tropical Josey Wales, spewing tobacco juice through the pick-up's open window and leading a disparate group of misfits to the eventual safety of a mission radio.

It was going to be a long night. We were no sooner trapped in the tunnel of trees than the first of the minor mud holes glistened hopefully in the moonlight before us, and the all-too-familiar chore of pulling, digging and shoving the vehicles back on to solid ground began once more. We had more willing arms to help us this time, not to mention the ferryman and his sons, and even with the need to post sentries both fore and aft, the extra labour more than made up for the extra vehicle. There were three of these holes in less than a kilometre, but then, unless memory was playing me false or more had spontaneously appeared in the last twelve hours, we had more than twenty kilometres of dig-free road.

It took us about two hours to get through this stretch, and for much of the last half-hour I was half expecting to hear the Serb vehicles coming up the road behind us. I knew this wasn't logical – unless they'd borrowed the *Enterprise* transporter beam there was no easy way across the river at Ongoka – but I felt it just the same. If it had only been the four of us I would have had no worries – we could either fight or retreat into the jungle if need be – but with six civilians and an MI6 man in tow I felt trapped on the road.

So it was with some relief that I started off on the easy stretch. All I had to do was keep the pick-up on the road, not ram the jeep from behind, and hope to hell that no oncoming head-lights suddenly pierced the darkness behind or in front of us.

'How long have you been in Africa?' Rachel suddenly asked me.

I did a quick mental calculation, and could hardly believe the answer. 'About ninety-six hours,' I said. 'We arrived in Brazzaville on Tuesday morning, and were told we'd probably be hanging around for a while. You know what happened next.'

'Colonel Mejahic came to Kima,' she said simply, as if she was reading from a children's book.

'How did they arrive?' I asked. 'Did you have any warning?'

'Not much. We heard the lorries coming, and we knew it must be soldiers, though of course we didn't know whose.' She laughed, but not with amusement. 'I must admit that when I saw they were white mercenaries I felt a twinge of relief. Shameful really. Our Africans – the people on our staff – they seemed to know straight away that these soldiers were really bad news, and most of them had the sense to just run off into the jungle. I don't know how many . . . I should have asked Nyembo but . . . I don't know how many were killed.'

'We saw three bodies,' I told her. 'Two men and one woman. I think Father Laurent said the woman's name was Cécile.'

'Oh Christ,' she said, and I could tell she was genuinely distressed.

'What happened next?' I asked.

'Oh, they just rounded us up like animals. Barry tried playing the outraged Englishman, and Mejahic just hit him in the face with his pistol. Then we were all bundled into the back of a lorry, and kept there until we reached Poma. Andy and Barry were taken out to help with the digging when the lorry got stuck, but Nell and Rubina and I weren't even allowed to use the jungle for a toilet – we were just given a plastic bucket to empty on to the road. It was better when we got to Poma – we were given some food and water at least, and Mejahic made a point of telling us women that we were safe from his men. The Western media and the UN liberals wouldn't bat an eyelid at their raping a thousand Congolese, he said, but three white women were another matter. He didn't seem to have noticed that Rubina and Nell weren't white, and it didn't seem a good time to tell him.'

'So it was a case of when the cat's away?' I asked. 'The attack on Nell, I mean.'

She grimaced. 'From the little I saw of the son I doubt it was that calculated,' she said. 'He . . .'

'That was Mejahic's son?' I asked with a sinking feeling in the stomach.

'That's what Nell said.'

'It was him,' Rubina said almost inaudibly. 'I saw him when he came to the room to take her.'

'We saw him shoot a Congolese girl in the street,' I told them. 'There was nothing we could do to stop it,' I added, which, though true enough, didn't make me feel much better. I wondered how devoted a father Mejahic was, and whether his particular set of psychic disorders would include a penchant for the blood feud. It seemed rather likely.

I took a look in the wing mirror, but there was only the jungle dark behind us. This stretch of the road looked familiar, and I realized we were passing the spot where we'd headed off into the trees for our night's rest two evenings ago. The idea of doing so again was truly tempting – I felt twice as tired after eighteen hours on the go as I would have felt in a temperate setting – and I was forced to retrieve the down side from my memory banks: the blizzard of biting insects, my friend the snake, the shit-throwing monkeys. If, as I half hoped, there was a regiment of rebels camped out on the site of the old roadblock, we could still return to sample the jungle's hospitality.

We were only about fifteen kilometres away now, with one more major mud hole to traverse. The fact that the weather was holding up was becoming less of a blessing and more of a curse – I rather fancied approaching the roadblock in either a major downpour or a dense fog – but at least there had been no further deepening of the hole in question. According to Rachel these holes had been known to swallow a lorry to its roof, so we'd been a lot luckier to date than I thought we had.

It still took the better part of an hour and a half to get the two vehicles through this one, and at the end of the experience I was feeling much more like a shower and a good meal than another encounter with the local gunmen. We compromised with a brew-up and some half-melted Mars bars which Sheff magically produced from his bergen, and the look on the face of the ferryman's younger son as he took his first chew of this British nectar would be one of my abiding memories of the whole business. The boy's face seemed to light up, his eyes widening with wonder at this assault on his taste buds.

After the feast this seemed like a good time to cut our captives loose. Sheff and I managed to cobble together thirty-two dollars for a parting gift. It didn't seem like much compensation for what we'd already put them through, not to mention the long walk home, but the ferryman seemed really excited by this sudden wealth, which made me feel a bit better. The nearest *bureau de change* was probably in Kisangani, four hundred kilometres downstream from Poma, but that didn't seem to worry him too much, and he insisted on shaking us all by the hand before leading his two sons off into the dark.

The rest of us climbed reluctantly back aboard our vehicles and set off in the direction of Yumbi. Ten minutes later we were pulling to a halt again, about a hundred metres short of the spot where the road joined the river for the last two-kilometre stretch to the bridge. It was only one-thirty in the morning, which left us plenty of time to do a CTR of the junction up ahead and reach Punia before first light, provided there was nothing substantial in our way.

Sheff and I carried on up the road to find out, walking quickly, not wasting our breath on speech. To our right the jungle was a black wall; to our left the river churned happily away, white waters glinting in the light of the slender moon. The bridge up ahead slowly took shape against the far bank beyond, but we could see no lights in the distant town.

The same could not be said of the junction ahead, where the bright orange glow of a small fire was beginning to imprint itself on my retina. We abandoned the open road for the concealing jungle, worked our way with some difficulty to a position near the one Paul and I had used on our previous visit, and examined the view below.

My heart sank. A large force would have been deterrent enough; no force at all and we'd have just sailed through. But here were three jeeps and a dozen men, most of them apparently awake. Five men were sitting round the fire smoking, another three playing some sort of game by the light of a kerosene lamp. Two more were standing and talking by the edge of the river; the last pair sat in separate jeeps, probably dozing. None of them was that far from his gun, and though there were a few discarded beer bottles in the grass no one seemed to be actually drinking.

'Shit,' I murmured.

'Looks like we have to jump into this frying pan before we can jump into a fire,' Sheff said.

I tried to look on the bright side. There was certainly no tank and I couldn't see any sign of anti-tank weapons. Nothing was physically blocking the road. They didn't look like they were expecting us. And with all the noise the river was making they wouldn't hear us until we were almost on top of them. I strained my eyes to the left, trying to visualize the background that would frame their view of our approaching vehicles, but we were too high up.

But still, it looked possible. In the Second World War the Regiment's units in France had often attacked in similar circumstances, barrelling out of the dark in their jeeps – free-wheeling silently downhill wherever they could – and overrunning stronger positions through sheer speed and surprise. Of course, they'd had Vickers and Browning machine-guns mounted front and rear on the jeeps, but a man with an MP5 was a pretty good substitute.

The only alternative I could come up with was the seventy-five-kilometre walk which had so horrified Knox-Brown, and which I fancied even less than taking on the men below. Our maps weren't good enough, we had civilians in already weakened condition and our supplies were inadequate. Neither option was exactly mouth-watering, but my blunt reckoning was that we'd lose more people taking to the jungle than taking on the rebels. And as I discovered on our walk back to the others, Sheff had come to the same conclusion.

Rachel wasn't so convinced. When I told them all the plan – Sheff, Knox-Brown, Gonzo and me taking the vehicles, Paul leading everyone else through the jungle to an RV point on the Punia road – she suggested the exact opposite. 'The rebels have got no reason to stop us,' she explained, meaning herself and the other clinic people, 'so why don't we take the vehicles and pick you five up?' That way there'll be no bloodshed.'

Knox-Brown obviously liked this idea even less than he'd liked the long walk, and I could see his point.

'They'll recognize the pick-up,' I reminded Rachel.

'And there's a very strong chance you'll all be arrested and taken into Yumbi,' Knox-Brown added. 'Our chance of getting you out of the country will be gone.' He didn't add that the rest of us would be left with a long walk home, which I suppose was to his credit.

'We need the discs,' Barry said tiredly, as if he couldn't believe how we could have forgotten their importance.

'I think I could talk us through,' Rachel insisted.

'You always do,' her husband said nastily.

I didn't like being on his side, but I had the feeling that in this instance he was right. 'When we were there yesterday,' I told her, 'they were throwing bound prisoners off the bridge and into the river. And I don't think their run-in with us will have made them feel any more kindly towards their fellow human beings, particularly the white ones.'

She gave me a stony look.

'I don't like it any more than you do,' I said, 'but that's the way it looks to me.'

There were no more protests. Paul was obviously disappointed to be the odd man out, but I had more faith in him than any of the others when it came to jungle navigation, and I quietly told him so. 'You'll have to carry all the food and water,' I added, 'because if we don't make it you'll be on foot for at least a couple of days.'

'Then you'd better make it,' he said with a grin.

Ten minutes later he and Nyembo were leading the British clinic contingent off down the road. All but Rachel were clearly still half in shock from their ordeal, and I felt a little guilty using their passivity to get my own way. But only a little – after all, they were going for a walk in the jungle, whereas we were going to get shot at.

'So how are we organizing this raiding party?' Gonzo asked me.

'The jeep first,' I thought out loud. 'The people in the pick-up'll be less vulnerable to fire from the rear,' I explained. 'Sheff, you drive the jeep and I'll ride shotgun. Knox-Brown, you drive the pick-up with Gonzo in the back.'

We spent the next few minutes 'armouring' the latter vehicle, stuffing the space behind the tailgate and the area behind the driver's head with anything we could lay our hands on that would absorb or slow bullets. Then we just sat and waited, following the progress of the jungle-walkers in our minds, hoping that they weren't having a time-consuming close encounter with a hungry leopard. Because if one thing was certain, it was that we didn't want to hang around by the kerb waiting for them with half the rebel army charging after us.

Half an hour had gone by, and I was beginning to think they really had got lost, when Paul finally came through on the comm link to say they'd reached the Yumbi–Punia road. 'Party time,' I told the others in my best Stephen Seagal voice.

The road to the bridge was in pretty good condition, and I was hoping we could make enough speed to keep our engine noise down. About sixty kilometres an hour seemed a good target to aim at, and provided we didn't aquaplane ourselves into the river the men at the junction would be in for a bit of a shock. A siren would have helped turn shock into panic over the last hundred metres, but we didn't have one. I remembered the tank crews in *Kelly's Heroes* playing loud country music as they went into battle, considered an Abba singalong in four parts, but decided it was probably against the Geneva Convention. And in any case we didn't have time to teach Benny's part to Knox-Brown.

We took our places and began to trundle down the slope towards the river, picking up speed as we hit level ground. Clouds were beginning to mass in the west but the moon still sat in a depressingly open patch of sky. My heart was thumping, my veins pumping adrenalin like there was no tomorrow, and the thought flashed through my head that at least the Light Brigade had a buzz before they died.

The whole business seemed unreal, absurd. Here we were rattling down a muddy track in the middle of nowhere, about to do our Roadrunner routine one more time for the soldiers at the rebel roadblock, and risking our lives – our only lives – in the process. In a couple of minutes Ellen could be a widow, though God only knew how long it would be before she found out. This is the sort of thing single men should be doing, I told myself – not happily married fathers.

I glanced across at Sheff; a slight smile was puckering the corner of his mouth as his eyes and hands concentrated on keeping the jeep on the road. He was probably thinking about the nurses, I thought. The lucky bastard was still too young to have felt mortality's clammy hand on his shoulder.

We were almost there now, the bridge separating itself from its background, the sudden spark of the fire ahead. I looked back to make sure that the pick-up hadn't fallen too far behind, and found it only about fifteen metres behind us – Knox-Brown was driving like Damon Hill. There were about four hundred metres to go and it was hard to hear our own engine above the tumult of the river, let alone an Abba singalong.

Two hundred metres, and I could see the figures of individual soldiers up ahead. We had to be travelling at about sixty kilometres an hour, which meant we were covering each hundred metres in a little over five seconds, but it seemed a lot longer. At about a hundred metres I heard the first shout rise up above the noise of river and engine, and suddenly the darkness in front of me was full of movement. I opened up with my MP5, emptying the thirty-round magazine in a couple of second-long bursts. Firing from a moving jeep over the rim of an armoured windscreen, I didn't bother trying to aim, only to fill the air with enough danger of imminent death to get the rebels diving for cover.

We were probably about thirty metres from the junction when I exchanged my MP5 for Sheff's and tried, probably ineffectually, to target the tyres of the rebels' jeeps. We were still not receiving any return fire, and for a second or so I had the luxury of worrying whether Sheff was going to overturn our jeep as he hurtled into the right-hand turn. But either luck or judgement was with him, and we were back on four wheels when the first rebel bullets pinged against the back of our vehicle. Squirming round in my seat I managed one last burst before the pick-up slewed around the corner behind us, cutting off my line of fire.

Judging from the noise – like hailstones on a tin roof – it was taking a lot of hits, but I could still hear Gonzo's MP5 rattling away, and if Knox-Brown wasn't alive and well then he was doing a great El Cid impersonation in the driving seat.

And then we were sweeping uphill into the shelter of the trees and I was feeling that almost hysterical sense of relief that floods through you when the jaws of death slam shut a little too late to catch you. 'We're through,' I told Paul on the comm link.

'I see you,' he said. 'I'm two hundred metres ahead of you. The rest of them are another hundred metres back.'

A couple of seconds later we could see him emerging from the jungle verge, the stubby M72 cradled in his arms. We drove on to where the clinic people were standing by the side of the road like a group of hapless hitchhikers, pale smiles of relief on their faces. I jumped out and walked back to the pick-up, only to find a blood-soaked Knox-Brown climbing somewhat unsteadily down from the cab. 'It's not serious,' he said, and he was right. A bullet had cut a quarter-inch groove through the flesh of his upper chest, causing a lot of bleeding but no significant damage. He'd been lucky.

I left Rachel to look after it, told Gonzo to get everyone aboard, and jogged down the road to join Paul, half expecting rebel headlights to appear round the bend before I reached him. But they didn't, and after a couple of minutes there was still neither sight nor sound of pursuit. Maybe Gonzo and I had put their jeeps out of commission, but I thought it more likely that they were still recovering from the shock of another drive-by. Maybe trying to convince themselves that they'd imagined this second visitation.

'Ready to move,' Gonzo told me on the comm link.

'Let's go,' I said to Paul, and we jogged back to the waiting vehicles, ears straining for sounds of movement on the road behind us. One last look back and we were in our seats, ready to roll.

8

We didn't run into any more rebels on the road to Punia, but it wasn't what you'd call an uneventful drive. My hysterical sense of relief wore off almost immediately, giving way to what was probably an equally hysterical sense of foreboding. Knox-Brown wasn't the only one who'd been lucky – we seemed to be just blundering round in the dark, and sooner or later . . . I suddenly thought of the perfect metaphor for our trip to date – we'd turned part of the Zairean jungle into our personal pinball machine, and we were the ball, hurtling to and fro along the channels, just flippering ourselves back into play each time we looked booked for oblivion. But sooner or later the ball was bound to find the gap, because that was the only way the game could end. We had to get ourselves off the fucking table, and quickly.

I was still congratulating myself on the metaphor when we passed the first of the refugees camped out by the side of the road, and for most of the next half-hour a catalogue of despair flickered in the dim peripheral glow of our headlight beams. Most of the refugees seemed asleep, but more than a few of those lying still and open-eyed were probably dead. A few were standing by the road, arms outstretched towards us as we passed, their faces gaunt, their bellies distended. No shouts followed us, no yells of recrimination – only the occasional sound of a baby crying.

We all knew we couldn't stop, that we would have had nothing to offer but useless sympathy if we had, but the logic of the situation had no power to alter the way it felt, which was bad. People say that wear on the soul is every bit as exhausting as wear on the body, and we'd had our share of both that day. By the time we reached the outskirts of Punia I was ready for about twelve hours' sleep, not another confrontation with the local gun club.

But that, of course, is what we got. It was about three-thirty in the morning, and I'd been hoping for a downpour to clear the streets, but the rainy season seemed in temporary abeyance, and the gathering clouds had so far refused to coalesce and drop their load. The moon was gone, but the gun club had thoughtfully hung out enough lamps to illuminate the barrier it had strewn across the end of the main street. There were about ten men wearing rebel uniforms, and they'd arranged themselves in line, rather as if they were expecting a re run of the Gunfight at the OK Corral. The local Wyatt Earp was standing a few metres ahead of Doc and the brothers, clutching an Uzi and trying not to look scared.

The whole thing felt ridiculous.

Sheff had pulled to a halt about seventy metres short of the barrier. I climbed down from the cab of the pick-up and walked towards the jeep.

'If we just keep going I think they'll break,' Sheff suggested.

He might have been right, but I didn't fancy the consequences if he was wrong. They might be too panicked to break, and we'd all end up killing each other because there didn't seem any other option.

Fuck that for a game of soldiers, I thought. 'I'm going to talk to Wyatt Earp down there,' I said. 'Tell him we're harmless.'

I started walking slowly towards the Congolese, keeping my eyes open for itchy-looking trigger fingers. The man in front didn't come forward to meet me, but he did lift the barrel of his Uzi slightly in my direction.

I stopped about ten metres from him. He was obviously not far out of his teens, which didn't bode well for my lecture on unnecessary deaths, but at least he didn't have that blank look on his face which meant I might as well be talking in Urdu. '*Bonne nuit, Colonel*,' I said cheerfully, giving him what was probably at least a couple of promotions for good measure.

He didn't smile back, and for a moment I wondered whether news of our contretemps with the other road-block had got through to Punia. But if it had, I found it hard to believe that we'd be facing only ten men.

'Who are you?' he asked. 'Who do you have in your vehicles? Where are you going?'

On impulse I told him the truth, or as much of it as he needed to know. We were just looking after our own nationals, I told him. We were no threat to the rebel war effort – we were, in fact, anxious to get out of their way, and we wished them a speedy victory over Mobutu.

He wanted to be convinced, but he was finding it hard. Even if he believed my story – we might be English, we might be Serbs – he couldn't quite contemplate the notion of letting a bunch of armed Europeans loose in recently conquered rebel territory. I could see his point of view, and I wasn't surprised by his decision – we would have to remain in Punia until higher authorities arrived to decide our fate.

I moved to Argument Two, which was simpler.

'We cannot remain here,' I said flatly, 'but we will remain at Kima, and if the authorities wish to question us, then they can come there.' I brushed aside his interruption with a colonial sweep of the hand. 'Colonel, you have guns, we have guns. We can fight it out and maybe both die here, but for what? You have real enemies to fight, and we just want to get back to our own country.'

Josey Wales had just scowled at Ten Bears, but I gave my adversary what I hoped was an appealing look.

He looked at the ground, then at me, a smile playing at the corners of his mouth. 'OK,' he said, 'you may travel on to Kima.'

I felt like embracing him, but I just turned and walked back to our vehicles, listening to the pleasant sound of the barrier behind me being shifted. A minute later we were driving through the gap, turning left down the main street and rumbling downhill towards the now-welcome embrace of the jungle. Dawn was still a couple of hours away and we were off the main road. The optimist in my head was dancing on the moon, the pessimist reduced to the odd murmur of dissent.

We kept going, only stopping when we reached the first of six familiar mud holes. There we arranged a brew-up on the back of the pick-up before starting work, and shared a few of our remaining freeze-dried specials when we'd manhandled both vehicles through to the other side. By this time the first hints of light were appearing in the sky, and in the surrounding jungle the day shift was gearing up to relieve the night shift. Almost immediately it began to feel hotter, and the sweat started pouring off us in buckets.

When it was completely light I called a brief halt to investigate the road for any signs of recent traffic, and rather to my surprise we found a wealth of tyre prints, none of which matched those of our pick-up. The consensus was that the recent traffic had been heading west – it might even have been Wyatt Earp and Co – but when we finally approached Kima at around ten that morning, I sent Sheff and Gonzo in ahead to check the place out. They reported back that it was as empty as the day we'd left it, though rather the worse for wear.

There'd been visitors all right, and they seemed to have gone through the place with a bailiff's eye, removing anything which could later be exchanged for money. In the research lab everything which hadn't been broken by the Serbs had now been taken, as had all the personal clothing which we'd left behind. Barry and Knox-Brown hardly noticed any of this, of course – they were too busy worrying about the precious discs. The doctor headed straight through the research lab and out into the jungle, the MI6 man close behind him. A couple of minutes later they returned with exultant faces, the doctor clutching a plastic-wrapped bundle of discs.

Maybe it was a cure for AIDS, maybe not – although I tended to put more faith in Rachel's scepticism than her husband's obvious ambition. Still, I hoped he was right and she was wrong – it didn't seem like a nice way for anyone to die.

Paul and Gonzo, meanwhile, had been investigating the muddy tracks outside, and found more evidence to support our earlier conclusion that the most recent vehicles on this track had been heading west. Which suited me, since with any luck they'd run straight into any Serbs heading east.

The other clinic people reappeared one by one, having collected anything that was left of their possessions. Nell was carrying just a dog-eared photograph. 'My family,' she explained, as she showed it to me. There were only males in the picture: a man in his fifties and two boys in their late teens. 'My mother died when I was ten,' she added.

Rachel was the next to emerge, and her hands were

empty. 'I'm surprised our people didn't come back,' she said thoughtfully, looking across the road at the abandoned huts.

'Maybe the latest visitors scared them off,' I suggested. 'They're probably at the mission.'

'I hope so. I wouldn't like to just fly out of here without saying goodbye.'

Andy and Rubina finally came out, he carrying a canvas bag, she empty-handed. He was talking animatedly, and she suddenly smiled, which completely transformed her face. The two of them were halfway to the vehicles when they both turned and stood for a second, taking a last long look at the buildings in which they'd lived and worked for several intense months. Personally, I didn't think it was the kind of place they'd be able to forget, even if they wanted to.

We drove up the Mangombe road and turned left on to the track which led to the mission. The sun was out again, sending shafts of light through the canopy which reached across the track, and the words 'last lap' kept running through my brain as if I couldn't quite believe it. While I'd been waiting on the veranda at Kima I'd suddenly pictured myself as a kid on the beach at Clacton or Walton-on-the-Naze, standing proudly inside the sand fort I'd built with Uncle Stanley, as the tide swept past us.

I smiled wryly to myself. It didn't seem like a coincidence that my mind had pulled that memory to the surface.

The light at the end of the tunnel grew steadily larger,

and we sloshed our way through the last stretch of puddles and into the clearing. The first thing I noticed was the clear sky – there were no cooking fires. The second thing was the absence of movement, the third that the mission gate was hanging open.

Sheff pulled the jeep to a halt, I followed suit with the pick-up, and we all stared at the sun-dappled clearing. It looked so peaceful, so still. So dead.

But there were no bodies lying on the grass, no smouldering buildings. Maybe those who lived here had just been taken somewhere, or had fled into the jungle.

Gonzo was examining the tracks in the mud. 'Same vehicles,' he said after a while. 'They must have come here before they came to Kima. The outgoing tracks are on top of the incoming.'

We left him on sentry duty and drove slowly across the clearing, stopping outside the mission gates. I ordered the clinic people inside, where the walls would at least offer them some protection against a surprise attack, and told Sheff and Paul to take a careful look around the clearing. I followed Knox-Brown, who was already making a beeline for Father Laurent's radio.

It was smashed, of course; smashed so comprehensively that you could probably have started a DIY radio shop with the bits.

'Fuck!' Knox-Brown said, with rather more feeling than I'd have thought him capable of. I think he was beginning to realize that he was stuck in the same sand fort as me and Uncle Stanley, only this time round it seemed to be a sea of death that was lapping at the walls.

I tore my eyes away from the pieces of our salvation littering the floor, and noticed a dark stain on the rug just in front of Father Laurent's record player. The blood was still sticky, but then so was everything else in the fucking jungle. I let my eyes focus on the record which was still sitting on the turntable and found out I'd been right – it was Edith Piaf.

There was a chorus of female lamentation from outside, and I walked out to find Paul holding a small limp, blood-coated body in his arms. It was the boy, Gérard, and his head had been nearly severed from his body, most likely with a machete. Paul looked up at me and I could see tears in the corners of his eyes. 'He was in the shed where we worked on the pick-up,' he said.

'There's a lot of blood on the floor inside,' I said, as if we were holding a competition to discover the most victims.

'Oh my God,' one of the women said, just as Sheff appeared in the gateway. 'Boss, I think you'd better see this,' he said, and from the tone of his voice I knew whatever it was, it wasn't going to be pretty. He led the way round the compound wall, heading for the back of a clearing, where a path delved into the jungle. I followed him, and found that everyone else was following me.

'There were a lot of footprints,' Sheff explained over his shoulder as we headed into the trees. I could see another clearing some fifty metres in, and guessed that was where we were headed. It was.

Just inside the clearing an area of beaten-down grass the size of a large room was thick with blood. It hung in clotted drips from the grass, it sat in crusty pools, it glistened in the sunlight that was streaming through the hole in the canopy. Beyond this red-brown swamp a larger area of turned red earth marked the mass grave, and it didn't take more than a few seconds to notice that in several places limbs were protruding through the surface.

We all just stood there in silence for a minute or more. Tears were coursing down Nyembo's cheeks and I realized I didn't even know whether he'd had family here.

'Father Laurent was a good man,' he said to me, as if he'd felt my eyes on him.

'I'm sorry,' I said, and I was, but my attention was already turning back to the business of saving the living. 'There's nothing we can do here,' I told the stunned faces, 'so let's get back to the compound. We've got some decisions to make.'

'We could bury them properly,' Rachel said, but there was no force behind the words, and she allowed herself to be led away by Nell.

'I'd like to bury the kid,' Paul said, appearing at my shoulder.

'OK,' I agreed, and turned to Sheff. 'Give him a hand, and then I want both of you to go through the whole place, see what you can turn up which might be useful.

Food, water containers, fuel, whatever.' I stopped at the gate and told the clinic people to wait for me on Father Laurent's veranda. Rubina's smile was certainly gone again, and she was biting her lower lip with anxiety. Even Rachel looked overwhelmed for once.

I jogged across the clearing, feeling the sweat running down my sides, and told Gonzo what we'd found. Neither the destruction of the radio nor the massacre of the refugees seemed to worry him much, but Gérard's killing got through. 'Paul really liked that kid,' he said sadly. 'That first day after we left this place he kept on and on about how much he reminded him of his youngest brother.'

I stared down the tunnel of jungle, wondering how long we had before someone caught up with us. At least a few more hours, I decided. 'We need to sort out a plan,' I said, looking at my watch. 'All of us. So give it fifteen more minutes and then come on in. If the Serbs turn up while we're in conference, we'll have to ask 'em to wait.'

Gonzo grinned. 'It looks like a good time to say, "Beam me up, Scottie."'

'Right. Except the *Enterprise* is a zillion light-years away and we forgot to pack our intergalactic pagers.'

I walked back across the clearing. Off to the left, beneath a huge splash of yellow hibiscus, Paul and Sheff were lowering the boy's body into the grave they'd dug. He must have been about eight, I thought. He wouldn't be getting any older. I'd never been able to understand how anyone could kill a defenceless child, but I knew who I wanted to string up right then – the vain bastard who'd ruled this country for thirty years, stolen all the money donated for its development and thereby ensured that its people stayed where the Belgians had left them – in the Dark Ages. It looked like Mobutu was going to lose this civil war, but I'd have laid odds he'd escape with his life and his loot. And as long as people like him got away with it, the longer others would follow in their scumbag footsteps.

I took a deep breath, allowed the anger to subside a little, then walked back in through the gates of the mission, wondering how Father Laurent had felt as the machetes had rained down, ending his tenure among the people he'd come to teach Christian values to.

The cross on the little church poked into the sky, reminding me of the dead limbs sticking out of the mud.

'What are we going to do now, Sergeant?' Barry asked as I came up the veranda steps. I don't think he much liked the idea of taking orders from a mere NCO, but he was trying to convince himself an SAS sergeant was anyone else's officer.

'I don't know yet,' I told him curtly. I paused at the door to Father Laurent's house. 'But we'll be talking over the options in a few minutes, and whoever wants to stick an oar in will be welcome to do so. OK?'

Without waiting for an answer. I pushed on into the house, closed the door behind me to discourage interruptions, and started going through what was left of the priest's possessions. Most of what was portable had been taken, but the shelves of books had hardly been touched, and it was among these that I found what I was most looking for – a set of decent government maps covering the eastern third of the country. Separated from these by a quartet of bird recognition books were even more detailed maps of the Virunga and Kahuzi–Biega National Parks.

I went round the room one more time, found nothing else of use, and took the maps out on to the veranda, just as Sheff and Paul returned with their inventory. For reasons best known to himself, Father Laurent had accumulated enough fuel to get both of our vehicles halfway to Europe, but when it came to food the story was very different. Pooling our own supplies, the stuff we'd taken from Kima the first time round, and the little Paul and Sheff had just found, we probably had enough to feed the whole party, at subsistence level, for four or five days.

When Gonzo joined us all on the veranda a couple of minutes later I told them this at once, hoping it would serve to concentrate minds. I didn't want to scare people, but on the other hand I didn't want them to think we were just experiencing a temporary glitch. We were in real trouble, and the sooner everyone realized it the better. We might have the cure for AIDS in our duffle bags, but getting it anywhere useful was going to take some doing.

Just to make it crystal clear that we were up shit

creek without the makings of a paddle I pointed out that we'd managed to severely piss off elements on both sides of the civil war which was raging all around us. 'The people in Punia and Yumbi will have talked to each other by now,' I said. 'Which means the Yumbi people now know where we are. And if I were Mejahic I'd have bet on us coming back this way. All of which means we can't stay here.'

With this thought hanging in the air, I hung our large-scale map of eastern Zaire across the balustrade, and pretended I was in the Kremlin at Stirling Lines.

'So where can we go?' Rachel asked.

'The way I see it we've got three options,' I said. 'All of which start with driving east to Mangombe and then on to Kasese. Option one: we just head in that general direction – which will hopefully take us away from the war – and hope to find a mission with a radio where we can wait for an exfil – a helicopter pick-up. Two: we can try heading south from Kasese towards the Copper Belt and Zambia. Three: we can keep heading east towards the border with Rwanda.'

'If all roads go through Kasese, why make any decisions until we get there?' Knox-Brown asked intelligently.

'No particular reason,' I said. 'I'm just trying to make everyone aware of what they're in for.'

'You don't think we'll find a radio?'

'I think the rebels are destroying them as they head west, and they've already passed through this area.'

'That makes sense,' the MI6 man admitted.

'So it's east or south,' Rachel said impatiently. 'It's a much longer journey to the south.'

'But the rebel HQ is still in Goma,' I said, jabbing a finger in the direction of the eastern provincial capital. 'And a lot of their soldiers are either Zairean Tutsis from this region or Rwandan Tutsis. We'd be heading into their heartland.'

'Kabila's from the south,' Gonzo pointed out. 'And the last report we got in Brazzaville suggested the rebels were closing in on Kabalo.' He searched for and found a river port on the upper Congo. 'Going south would certainly mean a much longer journey, but I wouldn't like to bet on it being any safer.'

'How far are we from the nearest border?' Sheff asked.

'The Rwandan border . . .'

'Just our luck.'

'. . . is a hundred and seventy-five kilometres. As the parrot flies, that is.'

'And as the jeep skids?'

'More than twice that if we take the metalled road from Musenge to Bukavu.'

'Which will be full of military traffic.'

'Probably,' I admitted. 'By the Goma road it's more like four hundred and fifty.'

'OK,' Sheff said. 'So if we keep to our current average of about ten kilometres an hour, we're talking about a forty-five-hour drive.'

I nodded, then looked at the clinic people. As I did

so, I couldn't quite suppress the inner voice telling me how much easier it would have been for the four of us without them. 'Four nights, dawn to dusk,' I went on. 'We'll sleep by day in the jungle.' I looked around the faces again, and saw less than total enthusiasm. But then maybe discovering a mass grave had taken away their appetite for debating the options. 'If anyone's got a better idea, now's the time to share it,' I said.

No one had.

9

The sky had begun to darken as we talked, and by the time we set off once more the rain was beginning to fall. We reached the tunnel of jungle just in time to miss the full bucket-of-water-over-your-head effect, and immediately needed the headlights to see more than a few metres in front of our faces. Lightning suddenly crackled overhead, and thunder rolled out in an almost instant response. 'Not a good day for golf,' Sheff shouted at me.

We reached the Mangombe–Punia road, which looked more like a stagnant river, and splashed our way left. It was not long past noon, but even if we hadn't all been in dire need of some rest I wouldn't have wanted to risk Mangombe in daylight. We were almost certainly the subject of a several alert by this time, and I needed some sleep before I tried bluffing our way through any more roadblocks.

The blue-black clouds seemed to be almost brushing the tops of the trees, and I could practically see the water level rising in the almost continuous puddle which constituted the road.

'Look for an opening,' I yelled at Sheff, just as another fork of lightning ripped at the canopy above our heads. This time the thunder seemed instantaneous, and almost loud enough to deafen.

The words were hardly out of my mouth when I noticed a gap in the jungle wall. Sheff backed up, the jeep's rear wheels churning water like a Mississippi riverboat, and we got out to investigate. There was about three metres of stuff to clear before we hit the relatively open ground behind, which was about right – anything less would have been hard to replace convincingly.

Everyone set to work willingly enough, but the looks on their faces weren't exactly cheerful. We were tired, soaked through, and the subject of at least two manhunts – none of which was calculated to lift the spirits. I realized after a few minutes that I hadn't even sent a lookout down the road. It was almost as if I couldn't believe our luck would get that much worse.

Once the gap had been made and the vehicles moved through we set to work erasing the evidence of our passage. The waterlogged road only needed work at the edges but the artful restoration of the forest wall took quite a time, and the way Gonzo gazed at the completed work I was tempted to ask him to sign it. Back inside the jungle the two vehicles had been moved a hundred metres or so from the road, and then camouflaged with ferns and other floor foliage. They were hard to spot across even fifty metres of open jungle floor, and there was no chance they could be seen from the road.

At least it was relatively dry under the canopy, even if we weren't. A brew-up on the hexamine stoves was quickly underway but a fire was out of the question, so there was no chance of drying the clothes we were wearing. We could change into our dry set, but come dark we'd be putting the wet stuff back on, which wasn't a very enticing prospect.

While the tea was brewing the four of us went into business mass-producing basha frames for people to sleep in. We'd managed to find several mosquito nets in the mission, and after an hour's work we'd put up a pretty impressive imitation of a jungle camp. Lunch was served in celebration, though neither the quality nor quantity of the food was cause for much enthusiasm, and gathered there in the semi-darkness of the ever-dripping trees we looked a pretty sombre group. There wasn't much in the way of conversation, and I got the feeling that with time to think the realities of the horror behind us and the dangers ahead were finally sinking in.

'We'll leave at ten,' I said, working on the assumption that we didn't want to reach Mangombe before midnight. 'So get as much sleep as you can between now and then,' I told them, feeling like a scoutmaster addressing his pack. We were bound to hear any approaching traffic on the road, so there didn't seem much point in sacrificing anyone's much-needed rest for a sentry duty.

But once settled in the creaking basha, alone behind the veil of the mosquito net, I found my mind was still too hyper to let my body sleep. The jungle noises didn't help much either, particularly the squawking birds, who, now that the sky outside was clearing, seemed intent on practising Red Arrow manoeuvres just beneath the canopy roof. Lying there with my eyes open, watching the sunbeams brighten and fade as the sky broke up, I found myself remembering those summer evenings as a kid when bedtime came, against all reason or common sense, before nightfall.

A long time ago. A few more years and Louise would be protesting about the same absurdity. I thought about her and Ellen back in Hereford, and how worried my wife would be about our sudden disappearance from the world of the reachable. Would the fact that she'd been through this before make it easier or more difficult? Would last time's happy ending encourage her to expect the same, or would she worry that I'd used up in Afghanistan all the luck I had coming to me? I sometimes worried about that myself.

I thought about the people around me: the mismatched doctors and their possible cure, the two nurses who'd come to do good and ended up in a nightmare, the young student seeing more of the world than he'd expected, the intelligence man who seemed as much a stranger now as he had on the tarmac at Brazzaville. He'd nearly been killed by the bridge and Nell had nearly been raped in Poma, but so far our little party of Brits seemed to be leading a charmed life, sidestepping potential tragedies while all around us the locals were dropping like flies.

And now here we were in the middle of the jungle. A charmed life, I told myself again, and on that cheerful note I fell asleep.

It was dark when the vibrator alarm woke me – dark as an underground cave and twice as damp. I lay there for a minute, getting my eyes used to the lack of light and half-heartedly cursing myself for not having persuaded the Yanks to lend us some night-vision goggles. After willing myself back into the soggy set of clothing, I just stood there for a few moments, staring blankly at the pale band of light which represented the distant road, then groped my way across to the hexy stoves. Having set a brew-up in motion, I started waking the others. Only Nell managed a smile, but that was one more than I'd expected.

Though I'd shortened this night's driving to give us some extra rest, I was still hoping to cover roughly a quarter of our four-hundred-and-fifty-kilometre journey to the border. A hundred and ten, I reckoned, would take us through Mangombe, all the way to Kasese, and a few kilometres farther up the long road to Musenge. The following night we should be able to get within striking distance of Musenge itself, which lay on the metalled road between Kisangani and Bukavu on the Rwandan border. That road might be too busy for us to use, but we'd still have two days' worth of supplies in which to find ourselves some less frequented route out of Zaire.

That was the plan, at least for the moment, and as the light slowly improved over the next half-hour it seemed like fate was intent on giving us a helping hand. By the time we'd packed up camp, stripped and loaded the vehicles, then moved them up to the camouflaged hole in the jungle wall, the puddles in the track beyond were just rippling in the breeze and clouds were scudding across an opening sky. The moon appeared a little later, a little fatter than the night before, hanging over the track which ran back towards Kima.

The drive soon turned into a variation on a familiar theme. Three times in the thirty-kilometre drive to Mangombe we had to dig and shove ourselves out of sizeable mud holes, and – a new twist this – we had a particularly hairy time fording one bloated and surprisingly fast-flowing river. But we encountered no traffic – Zairean roads at night were still apparently cleared for the sole use of SAS rescue missions.

It was nearly one when we approached Mangombe, easing the two vehicles halfway down an unusually precipitous hill which could see service as a toboggan run if Zaire ever gets to host the Winter Olympics. Nyembo had drawn us a rough map of the overgrown village below, which sat on the west bank of one of the Lowa's larger tributaries. It was a crossroads of sorts – while our road crossed the river on a smaller version of the bridge at Yumbi, another track ran north along the western bank to eventually link up with the metalled road to Kisangani.

Leaving Gonzo and Paul watching the road behind us, Sheff and I walked down the rest of the hill and into the village. There were no artificial lights visible, just a sea of roofs glimmering softly in the moonlight, with the steady murmur of the river beyond. A couple of dogs barked as we slipped quietly down towards the bridge, but if any humans were aware of our presence they didn't let on. The bridge itself, and the track which ran north alongside the hundred-metre-wide river, were both empty of movement.

'All clear,' I told Gonzo on the comm link, and a couple of minutes later two dim shapes rattled into view, free-wheeling down between the silent houses. 'Doesn't look like there's much to do of an evening,' Sheff observed, as if he'd just noticed the sleeping village for the first time. The two of us climbed back aboard, and the jeep led the way across the low girder bridge. The river beneath us would have been considered a major waterway in England, but here it was probably thought of as not much more than an overgrown stream.

It was about sixty kilometres from Mangombe to Kasese, most of which seemed uphill. The slow, winding climb to higher ground seemed to help in terms of the mud – we only had two minor stretches of glop to deal with – but it didn't seem to agree with the pick-up, whose engine was beginning to complain noisily. It certainly wasn't our speed which was taking the toll – held down for the first couple of hours by a lightless, cloud-covered sky, this was then reduced still further by a rainstorm of depressingly typical ferocity. The two stops we made to stretch our legs and brew up were pretty sombre affairs, though I did notice that Sheff and Nell were obviously beginning to enjoy each other's company. The rest of the clinic team seemed to be wondering glumly whether they'd been right to put their faith in yours truly, and I was beginning to have nightmares about the pick-up. Paul tinkered away beneath the bonnet, but the tone of his mutterings sounded distinctly pessimistic to me, and packing eleven people into the jeep was more likely to get us into the *Guinness Book of Records* than out of the country.

Still, the pick-up hadn't given up the ghost, or not yet at least. The rain stopped when we were about four kilometres short of Kasese, and by the time we reached the outskirts the pre-dawn sky was almost clear. The town had looked bigger than Mangombe on the map, but in the dark it was hard to get a real fix on its size. Set in a valley among jungle-covered hills, it offered the same panorama of roofs and the same street winding down to the centre, which in this case really did straddle an overgrown stream. There were more shops than in Mangombe, and what looked like the site of a market on the floor of the valley. A garage and petrol station stood nearby, but there was no sign of any stealable replacement for our ailing pick-up. We saw only one of the town's inhabitants, a man curled in a doorway who'd apparently been woken from his sleep, and who gave us one bored look before slumping back into the foetal position.

At the bottom of the opposite hill there were several old colonial-style buildings, and we climbed up the road between them, the pick-up now making enough noise to wake the town, before disappearing with loud sighs of relief into the anonymity of the jungle. It was just gone five o'clock by this time, so we started looking for a suitable place to stop for the day.

We found this about four kilometres from the town, and were soon at work widening an existing gap in the jungle wall. 'One night's journey, three more to go,' I was telling myself as Sheff and Paul began to bring the vehicles through. The jeep's engine fired, the pick-up's didn't. Paul took another look under the bonnet, fiddled a bit, then tried again. Same result.

The first hint of light was showing in what little we could see of the sky. 'Let's just push it through,' I suggested.

'I was just wondering how to work up a sweat,' Sheff muttered.

Everyone applied a shoulder or a pair of arms, and the pick-up reluctantly allowed itself to be ushered through the screen of hanging foliage and across the jungle floor to the camp-site chosen for Day Five of our Adventure Holiday. Four go mad in Zaire, I thought. And why not? When in Rome . . .

Breakfast, needless to say, was not a particularly happy occasion. It didn't take a genius to work out

189

the possible implications of a dead pick-up. We'd either have to replace it, with all the attendant risks which that would imply, or do a lot more walking. Either way we'd be adding at least a day to our journey, a day moreover for which we had no easy source of food.

For the moment all we could do was get some sleep and hope Paul could work his magic. Having the last watch, I went straight to my basha, hoping to shut out all the 'what ifs' in blissful unconsciousness. It didn't work, of course, and when Gonzo finally woke me at three I felt as if I'd been asleep only a few minutes. I drank a cup of the last brew-up – to say it was stewed would have been a gross understatement – and glanced through the day's log. Eleven vehicles had passed on the nearby road, seven going east and four west. Three had been private cars, eight lorries of some sort or other. None, so far as could be seen, had been in military use. Perhaps we'd finally ducked out from under the war, I thought hopefully.

I walked across to where Paul still had his head under the pick-up's bonnet. He said he'd had a few hours' kip, but the tiredness on his face told a different story. 'I'll take some more now,' he said, 'because the bad news is I can't fix it, or not without a vice-grip.

'And where can we find one of those?' I wondered out loud.

'Any garage. That one in Kasese should have one.'

I nodded. 'But will they take American Express?' I murmured.

Paul laughed. 'They said you were nuts.'

'Get some sleep,' I told him, and with one last lingering look he managed to tear himself away from the engine.

Both pick-up and jeep were only camouflaged on the sides facing the distant road, so I was able to use the jeep's front seat as an OP. Not that there was anything much to observe – invisible parakeets were squawking, invisible monkeys were howling and invisible snakes were probably slithering, but the visible jungle was just a selection of buttress trunks, hanging lianas and a dappled canopy overhead. I remembered rain dripping on my basha roof sometime that morning or afternoon, but the sun was out now, turning water to mist and reducing SAS men to pools of sweat. I sat there asking myself what would be a good time to visit the local garage, and as usual failed to come up with a clear answer. Not too early to draw the crowds, not too late to use up good travelling time. About seven-thirty, I thought. It was a Monday, so everyone would be watching *Coronation Street*.

I was still smiling at my own little joke when a flash of red caught the corner of my eye. A macaw, I hoped; or a colour-blind chameleon. An animal anyway. But as my eyes scoured the jungle depths for confirmation I heard the first of two voices, both of which sounded high and shrill.

'Children,' a deeper voice said behind me, and I turned to find Rachel staring into the distance.

'Maybe,' I said, and walked swiftly over to where my three colleagues were still happily wandering the

Land of Nod. 'Visitors,' I told each in turn as I shook them awake. 'Probably civilians,' I added, once they were *compos mentis*.

We waited in silence, MP5s at the ready, but Rachel had been right. The first of the visitors ran happily into our camp, only stopping abruptly when he suddenly realized that there were soldiers all around him. He was about to bolt back the way he'd come when a panting woman came chasing after him, only to do the same double-take when she saw us. Her face suddenly filled with fear, and she seemed rooted to the spot for a second, before she suddenly caught sight of Rachel.

'You needn't be afraid,' the doctor said immediately in French. 'We are friends.'

The woman looked at her, fear and hope mingling in her expression, and after a few seconds the latter won out. If she wasn't convinced of our friendliness she was too tired and hungry to care.

As we eventually found out, she had good reason for both the fear and the exhaustion. There were five children with her, ranging in age from around seven to around fourteen; the boys, in ascending order, were Patrice, Jean-Pierre and Camille, the girls Console and Sylvie. The woman's name was Imaculée Kabakira, and she was a thirty-year-old teacher from the Rwandan capital, Kigali, who'd been wandering eastern Zaire in search of sanctuary ever since the rebel uprising cleared the Hutu refugee camps near the border with her homeland. Only Sylvie was really hers; the other four children, their parents either dead or lost, had been adopted piecemeal over the months. They all looked malnourished and exhausted, and Camille had what looked like a seriously infected machete cut on his left forearm.

Rachel immediately wanted to treat it, but the boy backed away, suspicion in his eyes, and it took a lot of urging from his adoptive mother before he would submit the arm for examination.

She was just beginning the process when Patrice, who'd been staring at me for a while, suddenly pointed back the way they'd come and blurted out: 'More soldiers over there!'

'Where?' I asked him.

'Over there!' he repeated, shaking his arm for emphasis.

'There's a camp on the road,' the woman explained. 'About two kilometres in that direction, at the bottom of the hill.'

'Rebels?' I asked.

'Tutsi,' she agreed.

'And they're not moving?' I asked just to make sure.

'No, they have set up camp where the roads meet.'

Oh great, I thought. 'How many soldiers?' I asked.

She shrugged. 'Twenty, thirty . . .'

We'd have to take a look, and we'd see more if we did so before dark. Sheff and Nell were busy cooking food for our guests, Paul had sneaked his head back under the bonnet, so I decided to take Gonzo. We smeared some sodden earth on our arms, necks and faces, grabbed our MP5s and set off, walking parallel to the road. We covered the first couple of kilometres pretty quickly, but then holes in the canopy above grew more frequent and the jungle floor more choked with secondary growth. After another ten minutes of fighting our way through tangled foliage with no camp in sight, I was beginning to wonder if they'd made up the whole story.

A ploy to split us up, my paranoia suggested, but at that moment another rent in the canopy revealed a thin plume of smoke in the late-afternoon sky.

We advanced cautiously down the slope, looking for sentries but not really expecting to find any, and stumbled upon an ideal OP overlooking the soldiers' camp. On the floor of the valley below, an area the size of two football pitches had been cleared on either side of a small river. Our intended road to the east continued along the near side of the watercourse, but another road headed south across a flimsy-looking wooden bridge and past a hamlet's worth of circular huts. Several soldiers could be seen outside them, talking with those I presumed to be the local inhabitants, but their camp was on this side of the river. I counted twenty-nine men in all, and there were doubtless a few more inside the parked lorries and tents. The fact that they'd bothered to erect the latter seemed proof of an intention to sit astride this junction for at least one night, and maybe more, which wasn't good news. One way or another we had to get ourselves on to one of the two roads below, but short of rendering ourselves invisible it was hard to imagine how.

One problem at a time, I told myself – by the time we got the pick-up running this lot might well be in Kinshasa.

Satisfied that we'd seen all there was to be seen, Gonzo and I made our way back towards our own camp. The sky was beginning its swift descent into darkness as we drew near, but there was no sign of the thunderclouds which often provided us with an evening downpour, and with any luck we'd be visiting romantic Kasese and its garage by moonlight. Not that there was a shortage of storms in the area, as soon became apparent. During our ninety-minute absence a humdinger of a row had broken out among the happy campers, with the Moirs cast in the role of chief antagonists. The main point at issue, as I should have had the sense to anticipate, was how we intended to deal with the refugees.

When Gonzo and I appeared, both parties immediately started pleading their respective case, as if I was the circuit judge and he was my humble scribe. There could have been a hundred Serbs down the road for all they cared at that moment – this was a matter of principle.

'Sergeant,' Rachel began heatedly, 'we cannot possibly leave these people here to fend for themselves. The children won't last another week without regular food and . . .'

'We hardly have a surfeit of food ourselves,' I said gently, more in the interests of accuracy than argument.

'Exactly,' her husband said triumphantly. 'We don't even know if we can save ourselves, Rachel, and you're still trying to save the world. There's hundreds of thousands of people in the same situation as these. I know it's tragic, but we just don't have the means to help them all . . .'

'We can help these,' she said coldly. 'And I intend to.'

'There are other lives at stake,' Knox-Brown said reasonably, looking first at me and then at her. 'Think of all the people who will die needlessly in the future if your vaccine doesn't get back to civilization.'

And all the profits that'll go by the board, I thought. 'That's your priority, not mine,' I told him.

He didn't like that. 'Yours should be to get these people to safety,' he said. 'The people you were sent in to bring out. Not to take sides in a civil war.'

Rachel laughed out loud at that, and she had a point. Unfortunately, so did Knox-Brown, much as I disliked hearing it. We'd been sent in to do a particular job, and sorting out Africa wasn't it.

'Anyone else?' I asked.

'I think we should take them with us,' Nell said immediately.

Rubina shook her head but didn't say anything, and Andy just looked down.

I looked at the refugees – the dignified woman, the

sullen adolescent, the hopeful children – and wondered if they knew what we were talking about. Probably, I thought – people usually do when their own survival is at stake. I decided to temporize. 'If we can't get the pick-up repaired,' I told them all, 'then we're in a totally different situation, so let's see how that goes before we take any big decisions.' I looked round at the faces, hoping I could please all of the people at least some of the time.

Two hours and a decidedly inadequate meal later, Paul, Nyembo and I were on our way into Kasese in search of a vice-grip. I'd left Sheff watching the road, and if there was any movement in our rear he'd be letting us know, always assuming we weren't beyond the often erratic range of the pagers. Any movement up ahead, and we'd be seeing it ourselves.

I had to admit it was a beautiful night. The moon wasn't up yet but there was a wall-to-wall carpet of stars, and the Milky Way seemed to be flowing in our direction like a glinting veil caught up in a breeze. Every now and then there'd be enough space on one side of the road for a tall tree to silhouette itself against the sky like a rain forest exhibition poster, and during our frequent listening stops – we wanted to be absolutely sure we heard an approaching vehicle before it heard us – the jungle was rolling out a magical soundtrack which would have had your average New Age freaks wetting themselves with stress relief.

'Do you think we should take them with us?' I asked Paul during one of these stops.

He looked surprised to be asked, but answered readily enough. 'Yeah, why not,' he said. 'I think we're going to need more food anyway, so let's share what we've got. And you never know,' he added, 'we might run into a situation where we can use some protective colouring.'

'Uh-huh,' I said. I think I'd already decided that we would if we could. Josey Wales would have done as much, and he hadn't had Rachel Moir to deal with.

We started forward again down the dark tunnel of living matter, and I glanced across at Paul. He had a serious expression on his face, and I found myself wondering whether he – and Sheff and Gonzo – were old enough yet to appreciate the life they were living. OK, he was sweating like a pig, scratching his bites, feeling hungry. He hadn't seen a TV or a flush toilet for days, and he certainly had more chance of being dead this time tomorrow than your average disc jockey. But a night like this, a situation like this – how many people in England ever got to see it, feel it, to put themselves on the line and find things inside themselves they didn't know were there? Things like coolness and clarity of thought under intense pressure, things like the wonder of a jungle night.

I didn't want to do it any more, but only because I knew that sort of life was completely incompatible with the one I wanted with Ellen and Louise. I knew I'd miss this one, would miss nights like this. And if that was because, like most men, I wanted the chance to keep playing boy's games, then that was

OK. It's the men who can't do anything else that have a problem.

'Getting close,' Paul said, and right on cue a yellow glow suddenly appeared up ahead. It was the window of a house on the other side of the valley, and as we breasted the rise above the town a sparse sprinkling of lights opened up below us.

Paul looked at me as if he was expecting new instructions. 'Just keep going,' I told him. 'And keep praying the troops are somewhere else.'

The jeep rolled down the hill towards the centre of town. During our previous visit some fourteen hours ago Kasese had been sleeping the sleep of the dead, but this time round many of its citizens were definitely awake. There were groups sitting on rotting verandas, groups lolling on circles of tyres, individuals leaning in doorways, and their heads all slowly turned to watch us pass. No one smiled or shouted a welcome, and I began to wonder whether the Serbs had passed through in the last few weeks.

We drove past the few modern buildings at the bottom of the hill, crossed the river and drew up in front of a dark and obviously closed garage. Two men sitting on the concrete steps of a shuttered business just across the street were staring at us, and Nyembo walked across to ask them where we could find the garage owner. After only a moment's hesitation – any reluctance was probably overcome by the sight of our MP5s – they pointed him in the direction of a tumbledown house just up the hill.

Paul and Nyembo went off to tell the owner he had business, leaving me as the focal point of the locals' attention. '*Français?*' one of them asked, and while I was still wondering what to answer the other chipped in with '*Belge?*'

'*Non, anglais,*' I admitted. '*Norvégien*' would probably have been a better bet – no one hates the Norwegians.

It was only a couple of minutes before Paul and Nyembo returned with the garage owner, a man of about thirty in light-blue shorts and a Batman T-shirt. He didn't look too happy at being dragged away from whatever he did in the evenings, but maybe it was just the guns making him nervous.

He says he doesn't have one,' Paul told me, 'but maybe he's got something else which'll do the job.'

I nodded. 'Take a look.'

As the two of them disappeared into the workshop, I turned to Nyembo. 'How about asking our friends over there if there's any food to be bought in this town?'

He walked across the street for a second conversation, this one rather more animated than the last, and returned a couple of minutes later looking glum. 'They say the shops are empty and the market has had nothing for several weeks. Mobutu's men took everything they could carry when they fled to the west, and the rebels have commandeered the rest. They say everyone here is hungry.' Nyembo glanced back at the two men. 'They may be lying, and people will have their own supplies hidden away, but . . .'

'Yeah,' I agreed. I didn't fancy going round stealing people's last Weetabix at the point of a gun.

Inside the garage I could hear Paul and the owner talking in French, and a few moments later Paul emerged, an unidentifiable tool in his hand. 'This should do it,' he said. 'If it doesn't . . .' He shrugged. 'I can't find anything else.'

I peeled a few dollars off our rapidly shrinking wad and handed them to the owner, who at first looked surprised to be paid, but then made a great recovery to demand twice as much. I grinned at him. 'A for effort,' I told him, 'but we're not American tourists.'

He grinned back, but our fraternal farewell was interrupted by the last sound I wanted to hear – wheels rumbling down the road above us, the road from the west. There was no engine noise – whoever they were, they were free-wheeling.

'Get in,' I told the others. Paul, who'd been standing on the driver's side, ended up behind the wheel, and as the garage owner scuttled off in the direction of the nearest shadows, he started the engine and lurched forward into a tight turn through the semicircle of ruts which constituted the forecourt. As we straightened out and headed for the bridge I squirmed around in my seat, just in time to see two jeeps emerging into a lighter stretch of street about a hundred metres above and behind us. They were showing no lights themselves, which enabled me to catch a glimpse of pale faces and pale caps in the lead vehicle.

Serbs, I thought instinctively, wondering how the

hell they could have got this far this fast across a rebel-controlled region which had just been given several great lessons in maintaining vigilance by the cream of Hereford.

The answer came almost as quickly. Somehow the bastards had got hold of some pale-blue UN berets. They'd bluffed their way eastward. They were disguised as humans.

For a moment I toyed with the possibility that it really was a UN convoy behind us, but the first burst of automatic fire over our heads put paid to that idea. As Nyembo, with what sounded like a low groan, squeezed himself down into the gap between front and rear seats, Paul accelerated the bucking jeep up the rutted road and I let off a short burst in the Serbs' general direction, just so they didn't start getting overconfident. But that was all. The gap between us and their lead jeep had widened slightly, the state of the road made aiming next to impossible, and it seemed wiser to conserve ammo.

By this time the whole town was probably wondering what was happening, and if it hadn't been for the gunfire they might have just thought the Trans-Africa Rally had been re-routed. Either way, they must have been more than happy to hear the sound of three jeep engines fading away as we passed the last houses, then the sloping fields, and delved once more into the wretched jungle.

Tunnels of trees alternated with sky-ribboned channels, darkness with ghostly light, solid mud with glistening sheets of water. In these conditions even one medium-speed chase was exhilarating enough for me. Both we and the Serbs now had our headlights on, but we had the advantage of having travelled the road twice before, and gradually we were extending our lead.

Which sounded great until you took in the fact that in less than ten minutes we'd be racing into the rebel camp, much in the manner of shit hitting a fan. Even if by some miracle we emerged unscathed on the other side, both they and the 'UN' Serbs would be right behind us. When would we get the chance to double-back and get the others?

A mad plan, certainly. Trouble was, the only alternative – diving off into the jungle somewhere between here and there – was just as impractical. Even if we could manage it without being seen – a feat which would require a considerably larger lead than the one we now had – the Serbs would soon learn from the rebels that no one had passed the junction. They'd tell the rebels that we were American mercenaries in the pay of Mobutu, war criminals on the run from the UN's international justice, something along those lines. And once their combined forces came back up the road looking for us we'd be dead ducks.

Another clearing flashed by, another tunnel, and for some ludicrous reason I got a mental picture of Bruce Forsyth standing beside a big clock ticking out the time.

What the fuck were we going to do? Tell the

others, I told myself, and reached for the comm link.

'So what's the plan?' Sheff wanted to know.

'I'm still working on it,' I told him.

'Remember to wave as you go by,' he said, and for want of anything better to do, I laughed.

I fought back the panic which seemed to be seeping round my skull, tried to forget that the distance between Serbs and rebels was shrinking at about a hundred and twenty kilometres an hour with us caught in between, and tried to get my fucking brain to work. It was already too late to stop and take on the Serbs – the gunfire would bring the rebels running. Somehow we had to get them fighting each other . . .

'I've got it,' Paul said, jerking me back to reality. 'You and Nyembo – you'll have to jump for it once we get a bend between them and us. I'll just keep going until I reach the rebel camp.'

'And then?' I asked. Had he finally lost it?

'Then I'll tell them there's a bunch of Mobutu's Serb mercenaries wearing UN berets right behind me,' he half shouted over the roar of the engine as the jeep barrelled up a long slope.

'Why should they believe you?'

'Because they'll see them coming and they'll have already heard this.' He tapped the MP5 in his lap. 'It'll make sense.'

'And who the fuck do they think you are?'

'God only knows. They won't have time to ask

me, will they? The Serbs are only about fifteen seconds back.'

He had a point there. 'And what about afterwards?' I asked.

'I'll play it by ear.'

'No, I don't . . .'

'Any better ideas, boss?'

'No, but . . .'

'Then get ready to jump. You too, Nyembo.'

We slid round another bend and on to a suddenly familiar stretch of road. 'I can hear you,' Sheff said over the comm link.

'Nyembo, get ready,' I said. He didn't look too happy at the prospect, but I think he realized a close encounter with the verge was a better bet than staying aboard.

'Fifty metres,' Sheff told me.

'Go,' I told the Congolese, who disappeared into the darkness without a sound.

'And you,' Paul said. He was beginning to sound downright pushy, not to mention insubordinate.

'I'm coming with you,' I said, without really knowing why. It just didn't seem right to let him take all the risk alone.

Paul wasn't having any of it. 'No way, boss. They see a white man and a black man, they'll be suspicious right off. But if they see a black man being chased by white men I've already got them half believing me. Understand?'

I understood.

'They've just gone by,' Sheff's voice said in my ear.

'OK,' I told Paul, 'but I'm getting off further down the hill. I need to know what happens.' I reached for the comm link again. 'Sheff, leave Gonzo with the others and jog on down to meet me,' I said.

More trees rushed by, the headlights behind disappeared and appeared again. We had to be nearly there, I thought, and the road took a winding dive downhill to prove me right.

'We'll wait till midnight in the camp,' I told Sheff. 'And we'll make the ERV a couple of kilometres past Ibondo, midnight tomorrow. Got it?'

'Got it.'

A light suddenly glimmered through the trees below, then another. 'Next bend,' I said.

'You'll be needing this,' Paul said, handing over the vice-grip substitute as he slowed to take the bend. I grabbed it, shouted 'good luck' and launched myself out on to the verge, rolling into the foliage with the sort of elegance which deserved an action replay, then forced my way through the dense undergrowth and out of the headlight beams as fast as I could manage. I'd just reached the hollow inside of some giant, fern-like plant when the pursuing jeeps swept into view, painting a moving swathe of illumination across the jungle above me.

First one jeep swept past, then another, and as I clambered back through the foliage to the road I heard Paul fire the promised burst on the MP5. And then, for half a minute, there was total silence.

10

The seconds ticked by, and still there was nothing. Had I misjudged the distance to the camp? Had Paul and the Serbs just driven straight through it, leaving a line of gobsmacked rebels in their wake? If so, why hadn't he told me so on the comm link? I looked at my watch and then up the road, thinking that Sheff should be with me in less than five minutes.

My vision was improving, but it wasn't just acclimatization – the pale light suffusing the trees and sky must have its source in a risen moon. I looked down the hill, just in time to see the first flashes of light, and a split second later the crackle of automatic weapons began. A loud, grinding sound followed, like metal scraping on metal, and then the crash of a heavy impact, before the guns once more came to the fore.

The cats were obviously among the pigeons, and vice versa. Paul's plan had worked, but I was still not feeling too happy about giving him the go-ahead to play the hero. He was down there somewhere with about eight Serbs and thirty rebels, and the temptation to rush down and grab my share of the excitement was almost overwhelming. I felt like one of those moronic footballers who say they can't watch the team when they're not playing themselves.

It seemed like for ever, but eventually the gunfire lost its seamless quality, breaking down into increasingly desultory bursts. It was almost over, I told myself. Paul was either OK or he was dead, and my charging down the hill wouldn't help anybody. I had my travelling commune of multicultural misfits to worry about, and Sheff would be with me in a couple of minutes. Until then I had nothing to do but scratch my bites and wait.

Or so I thought. Having reduced the jungle to silence, the gunfire now stopped, and suddenly the slightest sounds were audible. I heard a bird utter a peevish squawk, then there was what sounded like a car door slamming in the distance. More to the point, I heard feet on the road below, moving at more than a walking pace. For a second I thought it might be Paul, but there were more than two feet jogging my way, and more than one angular shape materializing out of the shadowy mosaic beneath me. One of them was wearing a pale beret.

I instinctively knew that they wouldn't see me unless I moved, but Sheff was unlikely to be so lucky, so I couldn't just let them go by. The sensible thing would have been to let them come within ten metres and just cut them down, and five years earlier I think that's just what I'd have done, but this time around I couldn't do it. I'm not sure why – and since this was a failing which could well have killed me, I've thought about it quite a lot since – but I just couldn't. I do remember thinking at that precise moment that the Mary Whitehouses of this world had got it completely wrong, and that it was my being raised on righteous TV violence – and the code which says killing people is only OK in self-defence – which actually stopped me from squeezing the trigger.

My teenage TV heroes usually had the script on their side; I just had luck. 'Throw down your guns,' I shouted, or something like that – I can't even remember what language I used. It might have been English, might have been French, but it certainly wasn't Serbo-Croat, and the only result of this ludicrous warning was that the figure on the left had his sub-machine-gun in the firing position at the exact same moment as me. His aim was no worse either, and we both pressed down on our triggers at the same moment.

The difference was that his magazine was empty, whereas mine was full. The body jerked backwards, all flailing arms, and my finger loosened on the trigger. As the other man's head jerked round, exposing his face to the thin light from above, I saw it was Mejahic. He had no SMG, and his fingers were still struggling with the holster on his belt, but I couldn't see any fear in the face, only what looked like the beginnings of a snarl.

I squeezed down on the trigger again – just a short burst – and his gun fell to the ground, sending up a spray of silver droplets as it landed in a water-filled furrow. One hand seemed to sweep outwards, as if it was conducting traffic, and then the mercenary leader just slumped forward, landing face down in thick mud with a dull squelching sound. He'd come a long way from Srebrenica, but he didn't seem to have learnt very much from his journey.

I was starting across to make sure they were both dead when I thought I heard more footsteps, this time on the road above. 'Sheff?' I said into the mike.

'I think I'm just above you. What was . . . ?'

'It's all clear. Come on down.'

He joined me a few seconds later.

'Grab a pair of feet,' I told him. 'Whoever's in charge down there may send someone up to see what the hell's going on.'

We pulled the two bodies through the thicket lining the road and dumped them in the ferns. I expected their mothers had loved them once, but from what we'd seen at Poma I couldn't believe they'd inspired much affection since, and I had no trouble believing that humanity as a whole was a bit better off for their sudden demise.

Once inside the jungle I tried in vain to raise Paul on the comm link and then successfully filled Gonzo in on the current state of play. That done, Sheff and I started off downhill. The thick crescent moon was occasionally visible through the canopy to our right, and the filtered moonlight made the going easy enough, but making sure of our direction was something else. Every now and then I thought I recognized the huge buttressed trunks of particular trees from our previous recce a few hours earlier, and then I'd notice one which I was sure I'd never seen before.

Our other big worry was running into other Serbs, but that, as we found out when we finally reached the afternoon's OP, was not going to happen. There were a lot of bodies strewn around the rebel camp below, and six of them seemed to be white. Four had been dropped in a pile near the spot where their jeep had suffered a head-on collision with a lorry, and the other two were sprawled farther up the road, as if they'd been running for it. Their overturned jeep was just being righted by a group of rebels.

The latter had also suffered casualties – at least four that I could see – but I could spot no trace of either Paul or our jeep. Had they just let him drive on through? It seemed ludicrous, but where else could he be?

As we crouched there watching, a couple of the rebels began dumping the Serb bodies into the back of one of their own jeeps, stacking them like logs or sardines across the back seat. Their own dead were being buried by another party, in graves that looked none too deep on the edge of the clearing. The whole unit was moving out, I realized, which could only be good news for us, particularly if it continued westward.

Twenty minutes later, it did. Sheff and I exchanged grins and thumbs up, and narrowly resisted the temptation to stand up and cheer. The luck had been with us that evening. If Paul really was OK, we were in clover.

We waited till the sound of their vehicles had faded into the jungle soundtrack and then worked our way west across the slope to rejoin the road. Another twenty minutes later we were re-entering our camp, where the last couple of hours had added a few anxious lines to most of the faces. They'd heard a lot of gunfire, heard jeeps go by in one direction, lorries in another, and despite Gonzo's best efforts to explain – or perhaps because of them – still seemed none too sure what their SAS minders had been up to. We still had over two hours to wait for Paul, so while Sheff went to work on the pick-up I gave them a detailed run-down on what had happened, from our first sighting of the Serbs in Kasese through Paul's brainwave to my meeting with the good colonel. The expressions on their faces said they could hardly believe what they were hearing, but that was understandable – I was telling the story, and even I found it hard to credit.

I'd just about wrapped up my description of the camp below when the pick-up's engine suddenly burst into life a few metres away, reducing the jungle to shocked silence for several lovely moments.

'Have you decided what we're going to do with these people?' Rachel asked abruptly. 'Because I have to tell you . . .'

'If they want to come with us, they can,' I interrupted, before she could deliver whatever ultimatum it was she had ready for me. 'Though if we've lost the jeep,' I added, 'they may end up wishing they'd shared a vehicle with more innocent company than four white soldiers.'

I waited for protests from the opposing camp, but, to my surprise, none were forthcoming.

A voice sounded in my ear instead. It was Paul. He reckoned he was about three kilometres east of our position, and would be with us in less than an hour. I heaved a huge inner sigh of relief, saved my questions for when he arrived, and told everyone else the good news. The lad had obviously made himself popular, because the smiles on the faces almost lit up the jungle for a couple of seconds.

When he did walk back into camp about forty minutes later he himself was grinning from ear to ear.

'About fucking time,' Sheff said. 'We've been working while you've been joyriding and forging nature trails.'

'I love you too,' Paul said, giving him a big kiss on the forehead.

'So tell,' I said. 'How the hell did you get away from them?'

Paul laughed. 'It was fucking amazing. I just screeched to a halt, shouting, "Serb mercenaries", and pointing back up the road, feeling like a crap actor in a crap movie, and they were all staring at me with their mouths open, and then they heard the Serbs' jeeps, and everyone was grabbing for their guns. I hadn't turned off the engine, and I just eased the jeep forward, as if I was going to park it in the rear or something, and just kept going. I don't think anyone noticed, and if they did they were all too busy worrying about who was heading their way to worry about someone disappearing. I was about seventy metres up the road when the first guns opened up, and then there was this huge crash. I don't know what it was, but one of the Serb drivers probably got hit and his jeep just ploughed into one of the lorries.'

'That's what it looked like,' I told him.

'So who won?' he asked.

I gave him the score. 'And the jeep?' I asked at the end.

'It's OK. I just drove on for a couple of kilometres, made sure no one was after me, then found somewhere off the road to hide it. We can pick it up on our way.'

I grinned at him. 'Great job,' I said.

'Fucking right,' Sheff agreed. 'We'll be using you a lot from now on.'

We left a few minutes later, with Paul edging the pick-up forward across the root-strewn jungle floor, the rest of us following on foot like an army of supplicants. We now had seventeen in our travelling party, which I think beat Josey Wales's group by quite a few, and it was going to be a tight fit once we'd recovered the jeep, let alone before. I dreaded to think what the weight of seventeen bodies was going to do to the just-repaired vehicle, but at least the first few kilometres were all downhill.

Once the pick-up was on the road two of the kids joined me and Paul in the cab, while the rest of the party put up with standing room only in the back.

As Nell later told me, this was easier said than done – the road was uneven, the sides of the pick-up not high enough to lean on, and they all had to join in a sort of standing scrum to keep everyone aboard.

While they were all having fun in the back I was reflecting on another night, another throw of the dice. Sooner or later we'd meet an enemy we couldn't sidestep, and then, I thought, remembering my pinball metaphor, the flippers would be batting only air and the ball would be gone. We needed a new edge, something . . .

And then the idea occurred to me. I didn't much like it – in fact I felt slightly ashamed of having thought of it – and I told myself we hadn't really got the time to spare, but then again . . .

We rumbled out of the jungle and into the clearing where the rebels had camped. The huts on the other side of the river were dark – the local civilians were either sleeping or gone, and if it was the former I didn't think they'd be rushing out to see if we were an ice-cream van. 'Stop once we're back in the jungle,' I told Paul, and explained to him what I intended to do.

He didn't say anything, but just smiled faintly as if he found the idea amusing and did as I asked. I jumped down, pulled the mission spade out from behind the seat and summoned a reluctant Sheff from his place beside Nell in the scrum in the back. 'Ten minutes,' I told everyone, but didn't offer any explanation. It didn't seem like the right time or place for an argument.

I explained to Sheff as we walked back into the clearing, and he seemed as put out as I'd expected.

'Who were that famous pair of grave-robbers?' he asked. 'Burke and Hare? Something like that.'

I didn't say anything.

'It's nice to know we've got tradition on our side,' he muttered.

We reached the spot and started to remove the six inches of earth which covered the dead rebels. Once they were exposed, we held our breath and peeled off the uniforms, which in both cases were still sticky with blood. Lying there almost naked, the two dead soldiers looked more helpless than they had, more pathetic.

'Cover them up again,' I told Sheff, before carrying the tunics and pairs of trousers across the clearing to the river. There I scrubbed them as clean as I could on a convenient rock, thinking as I did so that of all the strange things I'd done in strange places, doing dead men's laundry in a rain forest by the light of a silvery moon had to be near the top of the list.

But who knew? These plain, dark-olive uniforms most of the rebels seemed to wear looked very different from our camouflage fatigues, and on the right shoulders – Paul's and Nyembo's – they might well give us a few seconds more than we could have otherwise counted on. The owners wouldn't miss them, and they might mean the difference between life and death for one of us.

I rejoined Sheff on the road and we walked together back to the pick-up. Five minutes later Paul was pulling the Dodge to a halt beside the spot where he'd driven the jeep off the road, and ten minutes after that we were ready to set out in tandem once more. Sheff drove the jeep with me riding shotgun and Nyembo and Knox-Brown behind us. Paul drove the pick-up, sharing the cab with Rubina and the two weakest children, which left the two doctors, Nell, Andy, Gonzo, Imaculée and her other three charges to fill the back. We might not have the food for a big picnic, but we certainly had the people.

That night's drive turned out a lot like the others: long, hot, bumpy and eventually drenching. It started out better than it ended, with the moon riding behind us and a rather better road surface than we were used to for the first thirty kilometres or so. Then, in short order, we encountered two recently broken bridges across small rivers. Fording them proved distinctly risky, but, once across, I at least felt they were a change from the usual digging, shoving and cursing our way through mud holes, although there were a few of these too.

The changes as we headed east weren't dramatic, but they were apparent. I knew we'd been slowly climbing ever since we left the Congo, from an altitude of around four hundred metres at Poma to something over a thousand now, and the mountains still ahead of us, which bordered the western edge of the Great Rift Valley, would be more than twice as high again. Both the temperature and the flora were gradually changing with the altitude; though still very humid it was noticeably cooler than it had been in Poma, and the jungle canopy was lower and more patchy. This had the disadvantage of increasing the floor growth and making movement inside the trees more difficult, but it also created a markedly lighter, less claustrophobic world. Now we were driving between walls of foliage, not down dark and dripping tunnels.

We needed all the light we could get when the rain started again at around two in the morning. The other two young children swapped places with Rubina in the pick-up's cab, leaving seven adults and an adolescent to struggle with the heavy tarp in the back, while the four of us in the jeep, for all the protection our convertible roof offered, might just as well have been driving along the bottom of the English Channel.

Still, we weren't likely to die from a soaking, which was more than could be said for the children, who'd already been weakened by their nomadic life of the last few months. Rachel was naturally worried for all of them, and particularly the younger girl, Sylvie. She made what use she could of the medicines we had – those from our emergency kits and those we'd picked off the floor of the ransacked mission – but what they really needed was food and rest, which we couldn't give them. In the lighted cab of the following pick-up I could see Paul joking with them, and wondered whether running a kindergarten should be made part of Continuation Training. This was the third country in as many years that I knew about – first Bosnia, then Liberia and now Zaire – where an SAS team had ended up escorting a bunch of kids out of a war zone.

We struggled on, our pace markedly reduced, down roads which looked more like canals. Not surprisingly, we encountered no other traffic, and the occasional villages by the side of the road passed by like rainswept ghost towns. As we passed through one of the larger settlements I suddenly had a mental picture of people jerked awake by the noise of our passage, lying there with eyes open and ears straining, breathing sighs of relief as the noise faded back into the rain beating on their grass roofs.

I felt a little more relieved myself with each village we passed. When we reached the bank of the River Luka I reckoned we weren't much more than a hundred kilometres from the Rwandan border, and for a few seconds I let myself bask in that thought, before admitting to myself that I was talking at least two hundred kilometres by road, and the most difficult two hundred of the whole journey at that. Twenty kilometres up the Luka was Ibondo, and thirty kilometres beyond that, in the adjoining valley, lay Musenge, a small town straddling the paved road between Bukavu and Kisangani. This road would be full of traffic, probably both day and night, and about a hundred and fifty kilometres south-east of Musenge it emerged from the concealing shelter of the jungle to wind up across a mountain pass and down to the Rwandan border town of Bukavu. Neither the open road nor the town was likely to be safe for us, but as yet I had no idea how we were going to avoid them.

We drove up the Luka valley, the river on one side,

signs with a gorilla logo on the other – we were skirting the edge of the Kahuzi–Biega National Park. The signs felt comforting somehow, as if conservation was some sort of down payment on civilization. There was more to the world than endless jungle and warring armies, they seemed to say.

Ibondo was about the same size as Kasese, its serried ranks of roofs covering the slopes above a fast-flowing river. We saw no sign of either soldiers or the town's inhabitants as we rumbled through the empty centre and across the bridge, but then not many places are jumping at four in the morning. Musenge was still at least an hour away and I wanted to pitch camp as close to the town as possible, preferably within reach of an OP overlooking the main road which ran through it. There was also the option of sending a party into the town itself in search of food. Barry had pointed out during one of our rest stops that the war had passed through this area some weeks ago, so that the food situation might have had time to get back to normal.

We climbed again, listening to the straining engine of the pick-up behind us and half expecting to hear I breathe its last at any moment. But in half an hour we were over the watershed and coasting down the slopes of the next valley. Here the jungle had been cleared in several places for what looked like tea plantations, and we seemed to be passing through sleeping villages with ever-greater frequency. I began to wonder whether we were going to have trouble finding somewhere to hide out for the day, and decided to take the jeep ahead on its own to look for one.

Luck was with us again. Not far short of Musenge's outskirts we found an overgrown track leading off into the jungle which both offered the necessary concealment and seemed to provide the planned OP. It was hard to be sure in the dark – though the rain had stopped, clouds still filled the sky – but as far as I could tell we were almost exactly above the town, and it shouldn't be hard to find somewhere nearby with a view of the relevant road.

Leaving Sheff to watch the road and the other two to find a camping ground, I went back in the jeep to collect the pick-up. Gonzo and I covered the vehicles' tracks as best we could and followed them into the jungle, passing a ruined house which had all but disappeared beneath the foliage growing in and around it. Another couple of hundred metres and we found ourselves in a clearing surrounded by an almost perfect circle of huge trees. I only hoped it wasn't a favourite picnic spot for the locals, since it wouldn't be possible to do a thorough check for traces of any recent human presence until dawn, and of course by then it would be too late to move.

It felt OK to me, or maybe I was just too tired to care.

As everyone piled in to the familiar routine of setting up camp and starting a meal on the hexy stoves, I idly wondered whether there would actually be a market for this sort of adventure holiday, the sort where you were dropped into a strange country and had to slog your way out, risking starvation and fighting off real soldiers. It was a depressing thought, but there probably would be.

After we'd all consumed another inadequate meal, most of the party wasted little time before turning in. The children were all sleeping in the pick-up, and Rachel looked in on them with Imaculée before following her husband, Knox-Brown and Nyembo to bed. Nell, Rubina and Andy still seemed too wired to sleep, or maybe they just needed some time to stop and think out loud after several days of alternating motion and high tension. Whatever their reasons, as the first light of dawn filtered down through the canopy above us, Sheff and I found ourselves sharing the first real conversation we'd had with any of our rescuees.

It was a strange feeling. We could have been sitting in a pub in Hereford, but we weren't.

I soon found out I'd been right about Nell – she was a carer from way back. Her mother had died when she was still young, leaving her to play surrogate mother to her two younger brothers for more than ten years. Her father had apparently expected her to stay on for ever as his personal housekeeper, but when the boys reached their late teens she had decided she'd done her job and it was time the three men of the house learnt to look after themselves. She had moved north to put some physical distance between herself and her family, trained as a nurse and worked a year in a Manchester hospital before seeing an ad offering work in Africa.

She was obviously politically motivated in the sense of wanting to help her fellow-blacks, but not stridently so, and I had the feeling she was still searching for a real focus for her life. One thing I was certain of – wherever she ended up, her colleagues would be glad to have her.

Rubina was a very different kettle of fish. She was also on the run from home – in her case, restrictive parents and their desire for an arranged marriage – but I didn't get the idea she had any real idea who she was or what she wanted from life. She'd ended up in Africa because it was long way from Bradford, but she couldn't hide here for ever, and the way she kept bringing the conversation back to her parents and her little sisters made me wonder how she would ever manage to keep the family at bay when she eventually returned home.

Andy clearly hoped he'd have a say in this, but somehow I doubted it. He didn't contribute much to the conversation, and I had the feeling he was still trying to work through all the things that had happened over the past few days. He was looking pretty dishevelled, and most of the time his eyes had that far-away look of someone suffering from shock. He might emerge older and wiser from this business, but it hadn't happened yet, and for the moment he seemed to need his self-cast role as Rubina's protector more than she did.

Nell asked about Sheff and me – mostly out of politeness in my case, I think – and seemed surprised when I told her about Ellen and Louise. 'I thought you needed to be single for the sort of work you do,' she said innocently.

'We do,' I said. 'My lives have just overlapped a little, that's all. I've only got another ten months to serve.'

'And you?' she asked Sheff.

'I'm available,' he said with a grin.

'I'll bet you are,' she said with a laugh.

'But now he has work to do,' I added, looking up at the canopy. The dawn was now far enough advanced for us to start looking for an OP.

Sheff looked as pleased at the prospect as I was, but we dragged ourselves to our feet, wished the other three a good sleep, and started exploring the slope to the east of our camp. It didn't take long to find the perfect spot – a tangle of fallen trees just below the crest of a ridge which overlooked the town. A sea of pale-grey roofs stretched away to the broad, dark line of the river, and by the time we'd sufficiently improved on nature's offering and Sheff had dug himself in for the first watch, the road to the north was also visible. A succession of small, unidentifiable sounds began disturbing the silence, offering proof that the town was waking up. Visual confirmation of this was soon available in the form of two thin columns of smoke, which drifted lazily upwards into the fast-lightening sky.

'I'll wake Gonzo at nine, then,' Sheff said.

'Make it ten,' I told him. 'There'll only be three of us taking watch today – I've got other plans for Paul.'

'An afternoon shop?'

'Something like that.'

I made my way back to the camp, where the growing din of birds in the canopy above had not prevented most of my travelling companions from falling asleep. After wasting a few moments worrying about whether we should have another lookout up the track, I changed out of my wet clothes and into the dry, slumped into the protesting basha, set my alarm and closed my eyes. Another day to tell my grandchildren about, I thought, and promised myself never to let Louise have a parrot. If the noisy bastards weren't endangered then they damn well ought to be.

11

They were still rehearsing for the parrot version of *The Dam Busters* when the alarm's vibration woke me. Everyone one else was still asleep, and who could blame them? – five and a half hours just wasn't enough for the sort of nights we were having. I changed back into the wet clothes and set off in search of a place to crap, preferably one without snakes. That mission successfully accomplished, I walked down to the OP, where Gonzo was staring red-eyed at the valley below. He seemed to have more prominent rings round his eyes than his Muppet namesake.

I studied the view, which wasn't that different from what I'd expected. Beyond the roofs stretching down to the gently curving river lay low red cliffs and jungle-covered hills. To our left the road ran in from the north between the river and the farmland which occupied the valley floor.

It was just starting to rain, and a large drop of water splattered across the movement log which Sheff and Gonzo had compiled. The density of daytime traffic on the road by the river, though heavy by our recent standards, was about what you'd expect on a rural B-road in deepest Wales. There had been a few lorries, a few cars, even something that Sheff had taken for a tourist bus, but there hadn't been much in the way of military traffic – just two troop lorries heading north, neither of which had stopped. The view of the town below was only partial, but there had been no sightings of soldiers on foot, and no other indications that the place was playing host to a rebel garrison.

It looked good, as did the fact – apparent now in the daylight – that the road in question was two lanes wide. I pointed this out to Gonzo, who for once was slow on the uptake. 'If we meet a rebel lorry we won't have to stop to get past each other,' I explained. 'So they won't have so much time to wonder who we are, and if they do get suspicious, well, by that time we'll be heading in opposite directions. It's always easier to let something go by if it's already gone.'

Gonzo scratched his curly head. 'How far is it to Bukavu?' he asked.

'About a hundred and sixty kilometres.'

'A long way to hold your breath,' he murmured.

'Yeah,' I agreed. 'And a long way for our trusty pick-up. But if it comes to the worst we'll just have to get out and walk.'

Gonzo grunted, as if he found the thought amusing. 'Are you still planning on sending Paul and Nyembo into town?'

'Yeah. I'd better go and wake them up and tell them the good news. I'll be back when I'm done.'

Gonzo raised a weary hand, blinked and turned his eyes back to the road. I retraced my steps to the camp, where both Paul and Nyembo were already awake. I told them what Sheff and Gonzo had observed, and told them what I wanted them to do. Nyembo wasn't at all happy with the idea of putting on a dead rebel's uniform, but as it turned out they were both too big for him, so we agreed he'd pass himself off, if necessary, as some sort of administrator from the rebel capital, Goma. Paul could be his military escort, one of the rebels' Tanzanian allies who didn't speak the local language.

They drove off in the jeep, and I decided to make myself a cup of tea before going back to relieve Gonzo. As I squatted on my haunches waiting for the water to boil, I overheard Rachel and Imaculée talking about the children. Camille, the Rwandan woman was saying, had not spoken to her for more than two weeks after they first met, and he still didn't say much. But that wasn't unusual. In most of the refugee camps there were many children who had lost the power of speech, and each day a few more would die of sorrow.

I sat there for a moment wishing Louise had a kinder world to inherit, then made my tea and walked back down to the OP. The rain was still falling, though with rather less force than we'd become used to, and if it hadn't been for the heat and the straw roofs I might have imagined I was having a bad day in the Brecon Beacons. The traffic on the road had dwindled to almost nothing over Gonzo's last hour, and it didn't pick up during the rest of the afternoon, which I hoped boded well for the night to come. There was no sudden outburst of gunfire in the town below, but I wasn't really expecting one.

My intuition that Paul and Nyembo would return safely was borne out soon after dark, when they drove back into camp with triumphant grins on their faces and fresh supplies in the back seat. There were two sacks of dried manioc – the staple ingredient in many Zairean meals – and smaller quantities of beans and carrots. There were even eight tins of milk, which Rachel immediately requisitioned for the children. We wouldn't be starving for a while yet.

The news of the town also sounded good.

'No sign of troops,' Paul said. 'It looks just like an ordinary town. We had a couple of beers and Nyembo talked to some of the locals, and they said that there was a rebel unit stationed here until a few days ago. It left for Kasese, so it was probably the one we ran into.' He took a gulp of the tea Nell handed him. 'They were part of the hunt for a group of French mercenaries who attacked a rebel outpost outside Yumbi and a mission near Mangombe. Ring any bells?'

'They're blaming you for what happened at the mission?' Nell asked incredulously.

'Looks like it,' I said.

'Maybe they'll get us mixed up with the Serbs, and think we're dead,' Paul suggested. 'Then they won't be looking any more.'

'Maybe,' I said doubtfully. 'But if anyone puts two

and two together they'll wonder what happened to the pick-up. And a lot of people must have seen two different groups of white men. That bunch of rebels in Punia for one. The locals in Kasese for another. And for all we know, we killed the local rebel leader's son as well as Mejahic's. I think we have to go on assuming someone's looking for us.'

Paul made a face. 'OK, so what's the plan?'

'Go and get the other two,' I told him, reaching into the jeep for our soggy map.

'I'll get breakfast started,' Nell said.

Five minutes later the other three returned, Sheff bitterly lamenting the fact that Paul had neglected to include a crate of beer on his shopping list. We sat around the crumpled map and I traced our prospective ride with a convenient piece of dead root. 'It's more of a gamble than a plan,' I admitted, 'but I reckon we should just tootle down this road as fast as we can go, and get as close to Bukavu as we can before dawn. Then we can use the day to suss out the border for a crossing the next night. The border follows this river between the lakes, but there's no way of telling from this map how wide it is or even whether there's a bridge or a ferry. But it's not the Berlin Wall, is it? If we can get near enough I don't think we'll have any trouble getting across.'

There were no dissenting voices, so I called the rest of the party together to tell them what we proposed for the night ahead. They didn't look too happy about it, but no one had any better ideas.

'I think we've got a good chance of making it all the way,' I said, 'but if we don't . . . well, the further we get down that road the closer we are to Rwanda, and if something happens to stop us then our last hope may be to strike out across country on foot. So before we go I want to make sure everything's portable, and I want everyone to be completely clear which supplies they're responsible for. We don't want to get five kilometres into the jungle and then realize we've left something vital back at the road.'

I could see that broaching this possibility wasn't exactly a morale-raiser, but there didn't seem any point in pretending we were off on a joyride. 'It's the last lap,' I said to cheer them up.

And one way or another it would be.

We broke camp soon after eight o'clock. Given the quality of the road, we might reach Bukavu in four hours, but I reckoned we had to factor in almost as much again for possible repairs to the pick-up, so it didn't seem worth delaying our start until the good people of Musenge were all safely tucked up in bed. Once again Sheff and I rode up front in the jeep, with Paul at the wheel of the pick-up and Gonzo playing Tail-end Charlie in the rear. The overall mood was nervous and subdued, and for once even Sheff seemed at a loss for words. Only Imaculée seemed outwardly cheerful, and that had more to do with the dramatic and apparently milk-induced improvement in Sylvie's condition. The

Rwandan woman had spent the last couple of hours in camp making *chikwanges*, concoctions of manioc batter wrapped in banana leaves which she claimed were ideal provisions for the road.

Several locals watched us drive down through Musenge to the junction by the river, but none of them were wearing uniforms, and none of them seemed in a hurry to rush off and claim the reward for information leading to the capture of desperate French mercenaries. We turned on to the wonderful smoothness of main road, and for a few seconds it felt like we were gliding on air, so accustomed were we to the sudden jolts, skids and bumps of the back roads.

Our speed was pretty impressive too. The road ran more or less steadily uphill as we ascended the valley, but we were touching the dizzying heights of forty kilometres an hour, which is a lot faster than most drivers in London ever get to go these days. There was even a cool breeze in our faces. We were heading into the mountains of the eastern border area, whose distant peaks were now hidden from view by the jungle which rose beyond the river.

The rain had stopped soon after our departure, and an hour into our journey the clouds had cleared away to reveal a moon almost half full. The light made for easier driving and a lovelier night, but a continuing downpour would have been much more useful, cutting visibility and keeping nosy people inside their homes and driving cabs. After all, how many times do you see plods getting out of their cars to stop speeders in the rain?

Still, even with a moon to drive by the road wasn't exactly humming with traffic. We only passed two lorries in the first seventy-five kilometres, and neither driver seemed that surprised to see a jeep full of white men heading towards Bukavu. There was no telephone line accompanying the road, so intelligence of our position could only be passed south by radio.

Another hour and we'd be out of the jungle, five and half long days after we'd dropped into it. I found it hard to believe that only four episodes of *The Archers* had been broadcast since our arrival in Kima the previous Wednesday. West Ham couldn't have lost more than two games. Louise would still be thinking I was doing one of my usual week-long stints in the Beacons, monitoring training exercises.

I could see her face in my mind, and I couldn't imagine anything nicer than just walking up the path to our house and being home again with her and Ellen. Across the border tomorrow night, I told myself. Call up the embassy and get a lift to the capital, then most likely a flight to Nairobi, and then home from there. We could be back in Hereford by Thursday.

'Boss,' Sheff said urgently, breaking the spell. Just ahead of us a lorry stood alongside the road, showing lights and facing south.

We motored past, catching a glimpse of two uniforms in the cab.

'Shit,' I muttered, my eyes glued to the wing mirror. 'Where are we?' I asked Sheff.

'About ten kilometres north of Bunyakiri.'

The stationary lorry was now about a hundred metres behind the pick-up, and I allowed myself a moment's hope.

Then it started to move, slowly accelerating until it was matching the speed of the vehicles in front of it. Perhaps it just liked driving behind other vehicles, I thought. Perhaps there were remnants of Mobutu's army in this part of the jungle, and the locals felt safer in convoy.

But this, of course, didn't explain why they'd been waiting by the side of the road. The lights which I suddenly noticed up ahead, on the other hand . .

The road at this point was bordered by trees to the right and the edge of a steep, five-metre slope to the left. The slope ran down to thirty metres of flat valley floor and a tumbling river. Beyond this lay another jungle-covered hillside, and beyond that, eventually, lay the mountains, Lake Kivu and Rwanda. It wouldn't be an easy trip, but it seemed a better bet than surrender to the local rebels. We'd killed their comrades and we'd seen the mass grave. We weren't going to be sent home with a slapped wrist. We weren't going to be sent home at all.

I suppose the thought process and the decision took me all of three seconds, slow by computer standards but quick enough for Zaire in the middle of the night. 'Stop,' I told Sheff. 'Stopping,' I said to Paul on the comm link. The lights on the road ahead were probably still at least a kilometre away – it was now or never. 'Time to abandon ship,' I told the others, and leapt out on to the still-moving ground before Knox-Brown could put words to the dissent I could see on his face.

I ran back towards the stationary pick-up. Farther down the road the following lorry seemed to be slowing down. 'Everybody out,' I yelled, first in English and then in French. 'Paul, get down here with the 72s.'

The lorry had stopped about a hundred and fifty metres behind the pick-up, and at that moment the driver switched off his headlights. This was a mistake in itself, but he compounded it by allowing the cab light to remain on, and for a few vital seconds he and his partner were as visible as we should have been. Both men were wearing rebel uniforms, and the non-driver was speaking to someone through a walkie-talkie.

'Take it out,' I snapped, and Paul, who was already down on one knee, the butt of the M72 braced against his shoulder, wasted no time squeezing the trigger.

There was the usual whoosh of the rocket, the yellow-white flash as it impacted the front of the lorry, the silhouettes of men dying a horrible death briefly imprinted on the mind's eye.

With the enemy behind us destroyed I wondered whether we should turn and make a run for it. I dismissed the idea partly on grounds of reason – what chance did we have of outrunning a chase in that direction? – but also on grounds of pure gut feeling. There was no way I was heading back into Zaire's heart of darkness, not when every nerve in my body was telling me I wanted out. It was the jungle or surrender.

Behind me our civilian charges were just standing there waiting for instructions, the stronger ones trying to look after the weaker, all the adults clutching their assigned luggage like *Titanic* passengers waiting for a lifeboat. Two of the children were shivering violently and not from the cold. Their faces were full of terror and I could only begin to imagine what memories this was reawakening.

'Sheff, get everyone across the river,' I ordered. 'And once you're across, just head due east for half a kilometre and wait.'

As the first people began scrambling down the bank I turned my eyes up the road, just in time to see the lights beginning to move. There were at least three vehicles up there, and they were all heading our way.

'Paul, stay here and cover the road behind us. Gonzo, you're with me.'

We jogged up the road towards the oncoming lights, which were now not much more than half a kilometre away. They were coming slowly though, and were obviously anxious not to share the fate of their comrades behind us. Thrice bitten, once shy, I told myself – it was a pity we were down to our last M72.

We were about seventy metres from the jeep now, which seemed far enough to run, particularly with a bergen full of manioc. The river curved here, and there was room for a small copse between the road and the bank which led down to it. Gonzo and I took up position inside the trees, just in time to see the advancing headlights stop. Looking back, I could just make out the shadowy figures down by the river, some of them already in the water, their arms linked to protect each other from the force of the current.

Out in front, other shadowy figures were advancing towards us along the road, and I caught sight of a couple disappearing over the bank, presumably in the hope of using the flat ground beside the river to outflank us. They were still out of range, but I fired a short burst anyway, just to keep them cautious. We didn't have the ammo to sustain a fire-fight for any length of time, but I hoped we had enough to cover our own retreat once the civilians were across the river and into the jungle.

Several guns opened up in response, and the trees above our head suffered some damage. Up the road someone was shouting, probably in an attempt to get his troops moving again. I could hardly fault their reluctance to advance down the moonlit road, and the ground by the river wouldn't offer them much more in the way of cover. The jungle on the other side of the road was their best bet for concealment, but it looked comfortingly dense from where we lay.

A couple of minutes went by without much sign of enemy mobility, and I was just beginning to feel more optimistic about our chances when a gun opened up from not much more than a hundred and fifty metres away. The rebel soldiers must have been using the time to creep their way forward through the long grass by the side of the road.

'We're over,' Sheff said in my ear, and from the breathless tone of his voice I could tell that the crossing had taken its toll.

'Just tell Nyembo to take everyone a couple of hundred metres inside the trees,' I said, reversing my previous decision, because I didn't get the feeling this particular enemy was going to pursue us aggressively, and splitting the party in unknown jungle seemed like an invitation to disaster. 'Paul, get across the river. Then the two of you cover our backs. And careful with the ammo.'

I watched Paul half slide, half leap down the bank, sprint across the flat ground and wade out into the rushing, knee-deep water. 'Any time you're ready,' I told Gonzo, just as another burst of fire raked the air and foliage above our heads. He backed out on his stomach and disappeared down the bank behind us like a backward-running film of someone crawling up over a rim. On the way down he'd be out of enemy sight, but the moment he hit the open ground beside the river they'd see him.

Just as he came into view several guns opened up. He slipped, stumbled and fell, and for a second I thought he was hit, but as he scrambled back to his feet I realized the bullets were still shredding our refuge among the trees. I fired another short burst, hoping to take their eyes off the river, and emptied the magazine. I shoved in the last one, checked on Gonzo's progress – he was just entering the water – and made my own inelegant way down the stony bank, finally landing with a painful jolt right on the bum bone.

I raised myself into a crouch, took a deep breath and surveyed the seventy-metre dash in front of me. It looked a long way, and my mind went back to the last time I'd made a run like that. I hadn't reached the finishing tape on that occasion, ending up instead with a creased skull and three months in prison.

But there didn't seem much point in dwelling on past failures. I broke straight into a run, wishing I still had eighteen-year-old legs, wishing I didn't have the bergen like a lead weight across my shoulders, seeing myself in the enemy's eyes as a great lumbering juggernaut of a target, too slow for anyone to miss. Sheff said later that he'd never seen anyone run so fast, but that seventy metres seemed to take about a minute. I was dimly aware of bullets whizzing around my head as I zigzagged wildly, then there was the double-whammy shock of the water – first the unexpected cold, then the strength of the current, which almost swept me off my feet.

I don't think I've ever felt more vulnerable in my life, and once I'd scrambled up the far bank and squirmed into the cover of some vegetation I just lay there for several seconds breathing heavily and thanking all the gods I could think of for the life still pulsing through my ageing veins.

'Boss?' Sheff said on the comm link, sounding almost worried.

'I'll be with you in a minute,' I said. 'And cease

firing,' I added. What bullets we had left were going to have to count.

The rebels were still pumping bullets in our direction, but with diminishing direction and ferocity. I wriggled farther into the cover of the trees, then took a left turn in the direction of the others. Sheff, Gonzo, Paul and Knox-Brown were about twenty metres away, and had either chosen or stumbled on an ideal defensive position. Several tall trees with wide trunks offered protection from all but the most oblique angle, but there was still a wide view of the river and the elevated road beyond. Given time, the rebels could always cross the river farther up or downstream, but for the next few minutes at least we were in a commanding position.

What to do with the time? I wanted to put more distance between the civilians and the rebels, but not at the expense of their losing touch with the five of us. And if we all just upped sticks and headed off into the jungle there was nothing to stop the rebels from sneaking up behind us an hour later. Not unless we gave them something to think about first.

I was still wondering what this might be when all the rebel guns seemed to open up at once, creating a crackling wall of sound. I felt several bullets bury themselves in the tree I was sitting against, and watched the jungle around me turn into a whirling snowstorm of shredded vegetation. The sheer ferocity was impressive in a scary sort of way.

The gunfire died away as abruptly as it had begun, and I could almost feel my opposite number waiting for the response which would tell him we were still there. When none came, what would he do? He'd think we were gone, but he'd still only have one way of finding out for sure, and, First World War generals always excepted, any commander would think twice before sending men forward across open ground and a fast-flowing river defended by SMGs. Even if he didn't care a fig for his men's lives he'd still end up having to defend the losses to his own superiors.

And then there was another relevant question – if he did find us gone was he intending to organize a pursuit? The more I thought about it from his point of view, the less probable I thought that was. It seemed unlikely that his unit would be carrying the sort of supplies they'd need for a long jungle trip, and they probably wouldn't have much inclination either. The pygmies were the only Zaireans who actually lived in the jungle; the rest of the population lived either on its edges, in clearings by rivers and roads, or in the grasslands and hills to the south and east. I was ready to bet that the four of us had spent a lot more hours surviving in the jungle than the men across the road.

Their commander didn't know that, of course, not unless he had one of Andy McNab's books in his back pocket. If at this moment we were heading deep into the jungle, then he probably thought the jungle would do his work for him. And if we were just circling round to rejoin the road somewhere else, we'd be easy prey for the mobile patrols he was mentally organizing.

Almost four minutes had now passed since the

gunfire had stopped and there was no sign of forward movement by the rebels. If they were coming, they were taking it slowly, turning our flanks farther up or downstream. But I didn't think they were even doing that – I thought they were just waiting to see if we popped back out again, like a fox who thinks the dogs have gone.

I gave the others the hand signal to withdraw, and we all began the laborious process of crawling deeper into the jungle, only rising to our feet when we'd covered about fifty metres. We met no snakes, but then our luck seemed to be running pretty well that night. True, we hadn't reached our destination. True, we now had a killer of a route march ahead of us. All the same, I couldn't help feeling relieved. In abandoning the road we'd probably left our human enemies behind, and now we'd be pitting ourselves against the elements – the terrain, the weather, our own limitations. That seemed a winnable battle to me, and, even more to the point, one over which I had considerably more control. I liked the idea that getting home to Ellen and Louise was down to me, and not to some chance meeting on a muddy road with a bunch of trigger-happy rebels.

The jungle was denser on the ground than we'd been used to, and it wasn't hard to follow the swathe cut by the rest of our party. We found them huddled in a small moonlit clearing, as if they were using the glowing lunar half-orb for security, rather like a child's night-light. They were relieved to see us, but there was also anger

in several of the faces, and I could understand why –
they were frightened, they felt powerless, no one was
telling them anything. I understood, but that didn't
mean I had time to do anything about it, and when
Rachel started to say something I just cut her off. 'I
know you're all fed up with being ordered about,' I
said, 'and you've all got questions, but they'll have
to wait for a couple of hours. We need to put some
distance between ourselves and the rebels.'

'Are they following us?' Barry wanted to know. At
that moment I think he'd have swapped the discs in
his pocket, and all the riches which would probably
flow from their contents, for a job stacking shelves in
a supermarket.

I almost said yes to get them moving, but I was
afraid there might be a panic. 'Not yet,' I replied.

'But where are we going?' Rachel wanted to
know.

'Home,' I said succinctly, and no doubt rather
glibly.

'This must be a short cut then,' Nell said, and
somehow the joke broke the tension. I think that
was the moment I realized she and Sheff were made
for each other.

12

The silent column of seventeen adults and children set off deeper into the jungle, with Nyembo and myself leading the way. Occasionally we needed to use our machetes, but the farther we got from the road the clearer the jungle floor seemed to become. In the rear of the column Sheff and Gonzo would stop from time to time to listen for any tell-tale sounds of pursuit.

Rachel had asked where we were going, but the real question was how we intended to get there. Just heading due east was all very well in the short run, but a straight line doesn't always provide the quickest route, particularly when there are numerous river valleys and a major mountain range in the way. Fortunately for us, Father Laurent's map of the Kahuzi–Biega National Park stretched to include that area of countryside, just to the north and west of the park, where we now found ourselves. It wasn't a great map for detail, but it offered a pretty good picture of the general lie of the land and a specific point for us to aim at – a three-thousand-metre-high pass across the mountains. The pass lay slightly to the north of an easterly route, and I was following a rough course on the compass which took this fact into account. Later, when I was less worried about the possibility of pursuit, I was planning to do a little directional fine-tuning.

We spent most of the first hour slowly climbing out of the Luhoho valley, sweating buckets and struggling for breath as the uphill slog and high humidity took their cumulative toll. The mosquitoes were even worse than usual, and my hopes of respite from them at higher altitude were soon dashed when the land fell away once more, leading us down into a long, densely forested valley. The going was more difficult here, the moon was sinking fast behind us, and I'd almost decided to call a halt for the rest of the night when we suddenly stumbled on what had obviously been a path in the not too distant past. Any path offered the threat of an unwelcome contact, but in the middle of the Zairean night I decided it was more than worth the risk. The rules of jungle movement we'd been taught in the Brunei training camp didn't seem so relevant with a bunch of civilians of various ages to look after.

More than fifteen years had passed since I'd some-how got through that last phase of the SAS training programme, but I could still remember those days like they were yesterday. The first shock of the humidity beneath the jungle canopy, the humiliating collapse of my first basha in the middle of the night, the instructor's tales of cocksucking leeches, even the do's and don'ts of life in the wretched place. You were supposed to move directly across country, climbing in and out of the difficult river valleys and ravines, because to follow the obvious paths, the ones which kept to the easier higher ground, was simply to invite ambush. You were never to cut wood, or even push through a cobweb, because any tracker worth his salt would look for such signs above ground level should rain wash away the ground-signs. You were supposed to keep noise to an absolute minimum, wear cam cream or dirt on exposed areas of skin and clean your guns at least once a day.

We were keeping reasonably quiet and carrying clean guns, but we also walking into any number of potential ambushes and leaving a trail any idiot could follow, and for one simple reason – the risks of ambush or pursuit seemed considerably less serious than the risk of us getting stranded somewhere in this unpopulated tract of no man's land.

I wasn't that worried about food – those lessons from Brunei had certainly stuck in the memory, and with good reason. I'd eaten snails, grubs, beetles and spiders in my time, as well as the more standard fare of curried snake and stewed monkey. I had a fair notion of which jungle fruits, roots and leaves were edible, and I knew how to test the dubious ones, rubbing them, in order, on skin, lips, tongue and gums to test for a possible adverse reaction. If none came after the prescribed interval, which differed from plant to plant, you ate a tiny piece, and if that didn't do it then you scoffed whatever it was with reasonable confidence. So, even if it took us several days longer than I expected to reach Lake Kivu, I knew we wouldn't starve. And there was no shortage of water around us – rather the reverse.

There was no reason to die in the jungle, just as long as you didn't let the dark and the humidity and the alien immensity of the place get to you. It was a great place for inducing panic, as I'd found out in Brunei on a couple of occasions. The lack of an horizon, or any fixed reference point, was unnerving, and so was the whole feel of the place. The ecologists are always going on about the earth being one great organism, and the jungle certainly feels like one. It's like you're inside a living creature, stumbling around in its dark belly like Jonah in the whale. But whereas the whale doesn't seem to have given a toss what Jonah was up to inside him, I always got the feeling the jungle knew only too well that most humans were bad news.

Still, I told myself, as the path snaked up the densely forested flank of a small ridge and emerged beneath the open sky, I was coping with it a lot better now than I had fifteen years before. If my boots hadn't been almost sloshing with sweat I might even have been enjoying it.

I called a halt, not so much to admire the sea of trees which lapped at the shore of our small island, as to check how everyone was doing. Since I was planning on walking right through the next day, a few hours' rest was probably in order before dawn, but I was also hoping we could keep going until about two in the morning. No one seemed in danger of imminent collapse, but Rachel insisted that the adults take turns carrying the younger children. If not, she said, they'd be in trouble the following day.

We marched on, still following the path. Occasionally it turned a little to the north or south, but soon thereafter it would resume its slightly north of easterly direction. It was almost too much to hope for, but I found myself hoping nevertheless that we'd stumbled by sheer chance on the one track which would lead us straight to our pass across the mountains.

By two o'clock I reckoned we were about ten kilometres east of our starting point, which was better progress than I'd expected when we left the road. It began to rain as we set up camp, but by now everyone had acquired a certain proficiency when it came to erecting bashas, and within fifteen minutes of our choosing the site most people were lying down listening to the rain beating on their makeshift roofs. The four of us each took an hour on watch, huddling miserably in the dark some fifty metres from camp, staring out across a dark valley at a distant stretch of the path we'd climbed earlier. If the rebels were after us we'd receive ample warning.

I'd taken the last watch for myself, and was studying our map by the first light of dawn when Rachel arrived with a welcome mug of tea. She didn't go back immediately, instead squatting beside me and staring out across the mist-laden valley. 'It's beautiful, isn't it?' she said.

I grunted a reluctant affirmation.

'I was just thinking,' she went on, 'that if we do have a cure for AIDS it's a kind of poetic justice that we've had to fight our way out of the jungle with it.'

'Why?' I asked, knowing she wanted me to.

She smiled, and if I hadn't been a happily married man I might have fallen in love with her on the spot. 'Because AIDS, like Ebola and the other lethal viruses we've seen break out over the last few decades, is part of the jungle's defence system.'

'That sounds almost mystical.'

She shook her head. 'No, it's evolution. The rain forest is a living thing – or a tissue of living things, it doesn't really matter which – and, like all living things, it will fight for its own survival. These viruses may have been here for millions of years, but it's the human exploitation of the forest which has let them loose – the problem supplying its own solution. And this is only a small part of what's happening in the world. Look at how many diseases are making a comeback, with new strains resistant to anything we can throw at them.' She smiled again, a little more sadly. 'People talk about humanity destroying the global environment, but I'm not at all sure we'll be allowed to.'

'But aren't hundreds of species already disappearing each day?'

'Oh yes. We're being given lots to rope to hang ourselves with. But I don't mean to sound utterly pessimistic – after all, if we do have a cure for AIDS, that's a sign the rain forest is giving us another chance, isn't it? It's like a practical demonstration, as if it's saying: "Look, see what I can offer you if you'll just let me alone. Cures for cancer, cures for God knows what." There's a rosy periwinkle over there' – she pointed at a red-flowered plant a few metres away – 'and it was almost fifty years ago that they discovered two of the alkaloids from its leaves were cancer inhibitors. There's a plant called ouabain that some tribes around Kima used to use for arrow poison – now, parts of the plant are used to treat heart conditions and rheumatoid arthritis. The poisonous seeds of the calabar bean were once used to determine a person's guilt – they thought anyone who survived force-feeding must be innocent – and now we use extracts from the same seeds to treat glaucoma and high blood pressure. The rain forest – this one and the ones in South America and South-east Asia – is just an enormous pharmacy waiting to be labelled, but we're cutting it down and burning it down at such a rate that most of it will be gone in our lifetime. And for what? Just profits for a few logging corporations and a few acres of easily exhausted soil for poor farmers. It's completely insane.'

It certainly sounded it. 'Do you think you do have a cure for AIDS?' I asked.

She shrugged. 'The test results looked really good in monkeys, but it's really too early to say. The moss we were using in the serum grows throughout the African rain forest, so there wouldn't be any problem with supplies.'

* * *

The light was improving rapidly, brightening the patches of mist which clung to the floors of the distant valleys and pointing up the changes in the jungle around us. We were about twelve hundred metres up now, and though the canopy was just as dense, the trees were both shorter and broader than these lower down. There were ferns everywhere and, at least here on the open edge of a valley, a profusion of flowering trees and shrubs. It seemed less grand but more colourful, and somehow less foreign than the dark majesty of the lowland jungle.

There were also, as we discovered on our walk back to the camp, non-human tracks on the path. Neither Nyembo nor Imaculée knew what they were, but Camille did. 'They are forest elephants,' the boy told us hesitantly. 'It will be their way to the grassland higher up,' he added.

If we'd continued in their tracks we might well have met some on their way back down, but soon after leaving camp we were forced to choose between the path and our intended direction. Choosing the second was made easier by the relatively open terrain – patches of jungle were now alternating with small areas of grassland – and it was a couple of hours before we had reason to regret the choice. Glimpses of the mountains had become increasingly frequent, the land suddenly seemed to turn upwards, and we spent the better part of two hours scrambling in and out of small valleys, clawing our way up mud slides and forcing passages through almost impenetrable thickets of vegetation. It was still hot and humid, and soon a persistent drizzle was falling, like an endless lukewarm shower. I was supposedly leading the way, but Camille had apparently decided he could do a better job, and was now scrambling hither and thither across the slopes in front of me, seeking out the easiest path.

It was exhausting, debilitating and depressing, and by noon just about everyone seemed to be on their last legs. When I called a halt people simply dropped whatever they were carrying and sank to the ground with such heartfelt sighs of relief that I decided a siesta was needed. I felt in rougher shape than usual myself, even though I was accustomed to long treks over difficult terrain with a fearsome weight on my back. The four of us were also wearing appropriate footwear, which made a big difference, whereas all the other Europeans were by this time suffering with blisters of varying severity.

But, hard-hearted to the last, I had everyone back on their feet by two o'clock, and for the next three hours we continued our slow progress. I was considering stopping for the night while there was still enough light for pitching camp when it suddenly became clear that the jungle was coming to an end. The hint of light up ahead brightened with every step until I could actually see the last trees silhouetted against a wide expanse of yellow-green nothingness.

I halted the party and went forward, accompanied

by the uninvited Camille. From the edge of the trees we could see rolling hills of grass lapping at the foot of distant jungle-covered slopes which rose precipitously into the blue sky. Behind these heights others rose in steep progression, and in that moment I felt more than a little daunted by the prospect of coaxing a party of exhausted women and children up and over such an obstacle.

I must have heard the buzzing sound, but either I was too busy thinking about the climb in front of me or I'd just grown used to crediting the jungle with each and every unusual noise. It was only when Camille grabbed hold of my arm that I realized he was shouting at me, and pointing. A kilometre or so away to the north a helicopter was speeding towards us.

I threw myself on the ground, pulling Camille down after me, and we wriggled back into the shelter of the trees. The chopper was a French Puma, one of the SA 330L series built in the sixties, many of which had been sold on to the French Government's African allies in the eighties. It flew straight across our field of vision, not much than a hundred metres above the waving grass, and the man in the co-pilot's seat seemed to be training his binoculars right in our direction. If he saw anything he gave no sign, and the sound of the helicopter slowly faded into the south.

The rebels hadn't mounted a jungle pursuit, but they sure as hell hadn't forgotten about us. I looked again at the wall of mountains, and wondered what would be waiting on the other side.

Back inside the forest the others, having heard the chopper come and go, had begun setting up camp. I went round asking all the adults how they were doing, then checked on the state of the kids with Rachel and Imaculée. None of the adults claimed they couldn't possibly walk another metre, but then I hadn't expected any of them would. All of them were hurting, and some more than others. Barry and Rubina were both having trouble with their feet, Andy with his breathing – he'd apparently suffered from asthma as a teenager. Nell and Rachel just seemed dog-tired, while Imaculée looked like someone who'd been walking for months, which, of course, she had. The children were also exhausted, but otherwise seemed little the worse for their forced march, and the younger girl, Sylvie, actually looked in better shape than when we'd started.

I have to admit that at that moment I had doubts about our making it over the mountains. This lot probably had one day's stiff climb in them, but I was afraid that if we hadn't got within spitting distance of the top by this time the next day, we'd be in real trouble. Up shit mountain without a funicular, as one veteran of G Squadron's Mountain Troop was fond of saying.

But at least the condemned troop would eat a hearty dinner. We'd crossed a promising-looking stream about ten minutes before reaching our current position, and when Paul and Nyembo suggested a fishing expedition I happily agreed. The *chikwanges* had kept us going through the day, but they were hardly a treat for the taste buds.

The two men returned soon after dusk with four reasonable-sized fish of uncertain provenance. With assistance from the older girl, Console, Imaculée first cooked up a football-sized lump of manioc dough, then turned the fish into a yellowy sauce. When it was ready she showed us how to eat it, making a round indentation in a lump of the doughy manioc, spooning the sauce into the hole, then popping the whole thing into the mouth. Maybe it was just hunger, but it tasted delicious. We washed this feast down with sweet tea, and the sense of stolen bliss began to fade only when we became uncomfortably aware of the fact that it was growing a lot colder than we were used to.

Someone tentatively suggested a fire, and I decided that the boost to morale would more than outweigh any slight risk of our being spotted – I found it hard to believe that the rebels would be flying by night over terrain like this. Ten minutes later, with the wood crackling and the surrounding faces lit by the glow, I knew I'd been right. People were talking and laughing like they were on holiday, and the groan that greeted my news of a three a.m. start would have been recognized by any tour guide worth his salt. They might have been running for their lives, but for an hour or so they were able to forget the fact and give their bodies and souls a much-needed rest.

*   *   *

Breakfast in the middle of the night was a more glum affair, but we were ready to leave on time. Obligingly, the rain which had fallen for several hours stopped, and the first part of the day's journey was a treat, especially in the light of what was to follow. As we started across the open grassland, revelling in the unaccustomed freedom of movement, the sky quickly cleared, leaving the black mass of mountains in front of us crowned with brilliant stars. It was one of those nights when you can almost feel the earth turning beneath you, and the notion of a beneficent God doesn't seem quite as ludicrous as usual.

For the better part of three hours we advanced across the green slopes, sometimes uphill and sometimes downhill, but gradually climbing just the same. We trampled across stretches of short grass and tunnelled through patches of tall elephant grass, the mountains looming ever higher, until dawn paled the sky and it seemed as if the wall was almost leaning over us, vast and threatening. And then suddenly the grasslands were gone, and we were having to fight our way up the first of many steep and jungle-covered slopes.

Now that it was light I was grateful for the cover, but that was about all. The mountain slopes were anything but smooth – broken by gullies and gorges, strewn with rocks, carpeted with brambly undergrowth and packed with trees, they were a climber's nightmare. Such openings as there were in this tangled mess had usually deteriorated into mud slides, and we had to push and pull ourselves up these, grabbing trailing vines and tree trunks for support, cursing our lack of gloves. The trees seemed full of leaping monkeys who'd been waiting for a good laugh, and to cap it all it started to rain again.

Just finding the path upwards was hard, let alone climbing it, and after a couple of hours of this I found myself remembering Frodo and Sam going through something similar in *The Lord of the Rings*. Admittedly they'd been on their way to Mordor, but if recent history was any judge Rwanda's recent governments could have given the Dark Lord a run for his money. For the first time I wondered what sort of reception Imaculée was expecting across the border. She was a Hutu, after all. She had fled from the country once. Was she only going back because dying at home was preferable to dying by the roadside somewhere in Zaire?

Half an hour later, as we stopped for a rest and a brew-up in a dark copse overlooking the scene of our struggles, I asked her if she was heading for her old home and what she expected to find there.

She gave me the sort of look Ellen gives me when I ask a question no one can answer. 'I don't know,' she said. 'Many Hutus are going back, so I have to hope that there is forgiveness in my country, that we can make a new beginning. But I don't know,' she repeated. 'When we cross the border I will know.'

I nodded, and tried to convince myself that if that was good enough for her, then it should be good enough for me. But I couldn't. As long as we Europeans were accompanying her and the children, the locals would think twice about picking a fight, but once across the border our voluntary escort duty might last only a matter of hours. I had the feeling Her Majesty's Government would be in quite a hurry to remove us from the danger area, which in their minds would definitely include Rwanda.

I sat there with my mug of tea, conscious of the silent Camille sitting beside me, feeling distinctly powerless. I knew it wasn't my fault that Rwanda was full of ethnic-cleansing wannabes, and that Imaculée and the kids would have to take their chances once they got there. I couldn't guarantee their safety any more than I could guarantee that of all the other billions of children out there. Christ, you only had to watch the horrors on the TV news to know that these days no one could guarantee their own child's safety.

I shook my head, looked round at my sprawled companions and struggled to my feet. First we had to reach Rwanda, and by my reckoning we'd only ascended about two hundred and fifty metres in three hours. There was still an awful lot of climbing to do.

We wore out as the day wore on. For the next two hours it was more of the same, mud and brambles, rain and sweat, but then suddenly the terrain changed, and we found ourselves climbing through a more open forest of twisted trees and tangling roots, clambering up ridge after ridge as if we were ascending a giant staircase. There were still long slides and pits of cloying mud but there was little else in the way of obstacles, and the occasional glimpses behind us of cloud-filled valleys and the now-distant rain forest offered visible proof of our upward progress.

By mid-afternoon everyone was getting very tired, especially those who were taking turns carrying the children. Among the civilians only Nell seemed indefatigable, – we later learnt she'd been a long-distance runner at school – and her sense of humour was obviously still intact. We were just getting underway again after a rest stop when she swung past Sheff and me, Patrice on her back, turned her head and said, 'I always thought you lot were just superfit thugs, but you're not really fit at all, are you?'

Just one more hour, I decided, and if we weren't in sight of the top by then we'd make camp anyway. I was given hope by the fact that the forest was changing character again, showing a marked preponderance of bamboos. According to Gonzo this was the type which grew at between two thousand four hundred and two thousand six hundred metres – above the latter there were only alpine meadows.

It was certainly getting colder, and I realized I had no idea just how low the temperature was going to drop. We were only about a hundred and fifty kilometres south of the equator, and our nights in the lowland rain forest hadn't exactly been air-conditioned, so what difference would the altitude make? I found it hard to believe that we could freeze to death in Zaire, but then stranger things had happened.

One thing I did know – we'd need another early

start to get across the open meadows and back inside the shelter of trees before dawn arrived. Once we'd managed that, we could . . .

'Boss!' Sheff called, interrupting my rambling train of thought. 'They've had enough.'

I looked back down the line of zombies on the path behind me and instantly saw that he was right. 'We'll stop here,' I announced, half expecting everyone to sink instantly to their knees. On this stage of the journey at least, our enemies were all within.

Paul and Gonzo still seemed to have energy to spare, so I sent them on a forward recce, hoping they'd discover we weren't that far from open ground. In the meantime the rest of us wearily set up camp. We'd carried the bundles of cut bamboo poles a long way, and I decided that after this night's sleep we'd leave them behind. With any luck this would be our last night in the jungle, and on the other side of the mountains it wouldn't hurt to be travelling a bit lighter.

'You're going to miss all this,' Sheff said out of the blue, as we waited for water to boil on the hexy stove. He now had a week's growth of beard on his face, and looked as ragged as I felt.

'Only on really bad days,' I said, not altogether truthfully. 'I've been thinking fifteen years of playing soldiers is probably enough for anyone,' I added.

Sheff looked more thoughtful than usual. 'I doubt I'll last that long,' he said. 'A man has only so many mercy missions in him.'

I laughed. 'And what new employer will you bless with your efforts?'

He shrugged. 'I don't know. Something more to do with life, less to do with death.'

'We're trying to save lives now.'

'I know. But we've taken a few too.' He looked at me, and I had the strange feeling of seeing someone age, in the best sense, in front of my eyes. 'Don't get me wrong,' he said. 'We did what we had to and I've got no regrets. I don't feel guilty or anything. I just don't fancy the idea that one day my kids are going to ask me what it feels like to kill people. Know what I mean?'

'Yeah,' I assured him. I'd never quite thought of it in that way, but I knew at once what he meant. Uncle Stanley had once told me that the thing he most resented about his time in the war – the Second World War – was that he could never reconcile the man who'd been through all that with the man he'd been through the rest of his life. The man who'd been a soldier, and all those years he'd spent soldiering, had not been reclaimable. That man and those years had just been lost.

'Here come Gonzo and Paul,' Sheff said, breaking the silence that had fallen between us

They had good news. The forest came to an end about four hundred metres further up the slope, and beyond it there were only meadows and mountain peaks. I felt a surge of relief, and half expected a round of cheering from the assembled company, but they were all too tired to either take it in or care. We gave our bodies another feeding because we knew they needed it, but I don't think I was the only one hoping never to taste manioc again. And then we collapsed into our bashas for what I hoped was the last time.

13

That night I dreamt I was playing for West Ham in the European Cup Final, but then it had been a very long day. We were losing when I woke up soon after one-thirty, and try as I might I couldn't find any more sleep to slip in an equalizer. Eventually I just gave up and lay there with my eyes open, staring up at the gently swaying trees and the clear moonlit sky, thinking about Ellen and Louise.

A good night for walking, I thought. If everything went well we'd be out of Zaire by this time tomorrow. Admittedly we'd then be in Rwanda, but no plan was perfect. I grinned like an idiot in the dark and got up to start waking the others.

By two o'clock we were all standing round drinking tea and from time to time stretching our limbs like a bunch of runners about to settle into the blocks. A combination of the previous day's exertions and the cold damp had made everyone stiff, and it looked as though we'd be running mostly on adrenalin for the first couple of hours. No one was complaining though, and as far as I could tell every last one of them was as eager to see the back of Zaire as I was.

We set off in the familiar column, Camille and I in the lead. The forest seemed different now that I knew we were nearing its edge – the claustrophobic feeling had gone, and the play of shadows in its depths seemed more beautiful than threatening. Even inside the trees the light was good, and when we finally emerged into the promised meadow it was truly dazzling. The moon was only half full, but I didn't think I'd ever seen one brighter.

The sense of space was just as overwhelming. Jostling peaks filled the facing horizon, the endless roof of the forest stretched across the one behind, glistening with a billion points of moonlit moisture. This was another one for Uncle Stanley, I thought, another of those sights you didn't get to see in the course of a normal life. I thought back on what Sheff had said about missing it all, and decided he'd been only half right – you didn't have to be a soldier to see nights like this. The Regiment had given me extraordinary opportunities, but there was nothing to stop me finding more for myself.

Gonzo reckoned we were now two thousand six hundred metres above sea level, and the moonlit peaks of the chain which crossed our path rose another five hundred into the night. The wind was chilling, and nice view or not, I didn't want to spend any more time on this stretch of the world's roof than was strictly necessary. A decent map would have been helpful, but we'd now slipped off the edge of the map of the Kahuzi–Biega National Park, and the one we'd brought with us from England wasn't much more useful than a classroom globe. Our only hope was to head east and look for the cleft or pass which would lead us through to the other side.

This proved much easier imagined than done, and for almost two hours we seemed half lost in a maze of interconnecting valleys. Each hopeful-looking cleft would lead through into yet another valley, and above us the peaks seemed locked in a circle around us, as if we were going round and round in some mountain equivalent of a black hole. My compass told me we were still walking east, but I was beginning to think that the surrounding peaks were made of iron, and we were just following a magnet.

It was just after four-fifteen when we scrambled over the rim of another high pass, hiked through a twisting dry gorge, and suddenly emerged on to the mother of all OPs. The moon was down behind us by this time, but there was still enough light to make out the vast panorama which had just opened at our feet. Some fifteen hundred metres beneath us lay the expanse of Lake Kivu, its still waters mirroring the stars, and away to our left, beyond the end of the lake, a line of volcanoes were silhouetted against the sky. The rebel capital of Goma lay close to their feet, but there no was no sign of lights there, nor on the Rwandan lakeshore opposite. I knew these shores were heavily populated, at least by Zairean standards, but at that moment the

Great Rift Valley looked much as it must have done when mankind was born there all those thousands of years ago.

I turned to find Camille staring into the distance, and for once the emotions seemed close to the surface of his young face. He was looking at his home, and I thought he must be remembering things that had happened there, things that had been done to him and his family, and wondering if the people who'd done them were still waiting for another opportunity.

We started our descent, conscious of the need for speed with dawn only an hour and a half away. Now that the moon was down, the steeper slopes on this side of the range were also darker, but, buoyed by our sight of the finishing post, we made good progress, and by the time the first hint of light appeared above the distant mountains of Rwanda we were sheltering in a huge stand of eucalyptus trees some nine hundred metres above the lake. There we rested, ate the last of the *chikwanges* and drank tea, and waited for daylight to expose the details of the terrain which still lay below us.

The news, when it came, was good and bad. The eastern side was no mirror image of the western, and there was no thick jungle covering the lower slopes to offer us cover. On the contrary, there was a fair bit of agricultural land, most of it apparently farmed by the inhabitants of three visible villages. One of these, which sat right on the bay almost directly below us, was larger than the others, almost a small town. The

Goma–Bukavu road obviously ran through it and, more to the point as far as we were concerned, a small harbour was playing host to several boats.

'Any ideas?' I asked the other three, all of whom were sharing the temporary OP with me.

'How far is it across the lake?' Paul wondered out loud.

'About thirty kilometres,' Gonzo told him.

'It's the boat for us then,' Sheff said. 'Maybe more than one, judging by the size of most of them.'

'How long do you think it'll take us to get down there?' I asked, staring at the patchwork of farmland and forest.

'No more than a couple of hours,' Sheff said. 'But it might be an idea to get a bit closer now, so we don't have to do any more descending in the dark.'

'We could do most of it now,' Gonzo suggested. 'See that section of forest down there, above the village and a bit to the left? As far as I can see, there's tree cover all the way, and then we'll only be a few minutes away from the water.'

Ten minutes later we were on our way down, zigzagging across the slopes to take advantage of the trees. We were seen by two separate locals, but neither ran off screaming for help; they just made sure – like locals everywhere – that we weren't heading in their direction, and then went back to what they'd been doing. By eight o'clock we were ensconced in Gonzo's chosen piece of forest, another stand of mostly eucalyptus trees which clung to a steep slope above the

Goma–Bukavu road. Leaving the civilians to rest their weary limbs, the four of us found an OP just above the point where the road turned sharply downhill in the direction of the invisible village.

Through our first half-hour on watch nothing went by on wheels, but there was plenty of traffic on foot, most of it segregated by gender. The men, in pairs or larger groups, walked by as if they hadn't got a care in the world, while most of the women carried agricultural produce of some sort, presumably for sale in the village. This obviously wasn't a war zone, and as if to emphasize the fact a bus finally rattled in from the north, bursting at the windows with passengers. For a few moments I wondered whether the innocence of public transport might be a more sensible option for our party, but decided that even if we could squeeze seventeen of us on to a bus, the two-tone composition of our party was hardly inconspicuous. There might well be roadblocks, there was bound to be a police presence at the Bukavu bus station, and there'd still be the border to deal with.

'How about a recce?' Paul asked. 'Nyembo and I can just walk down like everyone else, take a look round, maybe check out the boats.'

It seemed like a good idea.

Nyembo was willing, and soon the rest of us were watching the two of them disappear round the first bend in the road. The Congolese had been incredibly helpful right from the beginning, but suddenly I found myself wondering whether he'd forgotten how to consider his own safety. I assumed he was coming to Rwanda with us, but I had no idea why he wanted to – he wasn't a Tutsi, he wasn't Rwandan. Maybe the Moirs had offered him work at their next jungle outpost, but if so I hadn't heard about it.

A couple of hours dragged by. It got hotter, but not jungle-hot – the climate here seemed more Mediterranean than tropical. A mid-morning shower was almost Irish in its lack of intensity, but the sky cleared soon afterwards, and the mountains across the lake swam into focus as if I was adjusting the view through binoculars.

It was almost midday when the twosome returned with some reassuring news. There were a few soldiers in the village, but if they were on duty they weren't taking it very seriously, just lolling around drinking beer and flirting with the women. And the boat situation was even better. Most of the bigger craft tied up at the dock were fishing boats from the time when Lake Kivu still had fish, their condition reflecting their recent lack of use, but there was one vessel which looked almost ideal. It was the sort of pleasure boat often used for river cruises, complete with sun awning and copious seating. This obviously hadn't been used for a while either – probably since the war interrupted the local tourist trade – but it was being repainted while we spoke, and according to the boastful owner its engine was in tip-top condition, ready to take the Americans and the Germans wherever they wanted to go.

'Don't they like Brits?' Sheff asked indignantly.

'They'll like them even less by tomorrow,' Gonzo told him.

I took a few hours' sleep in the afternoon, and it was almost dark when I woke up. Everyone knew what was planned, and now it was just a matter of waiting. One a.m. was our scheduled time of departure, late enough for the village to be comatose, early enough for us to make it across the lake in darkness.

I asked Nyembo if he was coming with us, and he looked at me as if he couldn't believe the question. When I gave him a puzzled look in return he just said that Imaculée and the children would be needing his protection.

I nodded wisely, realizing I must have missed something. But then Ellen was always telling me how unobservant I was.

It rained for a couple of hours before midnight, but the clouds cleared off with their usual alacrity, leaving us with the moon and some ideal sailing weather. Visibility was certainly not going to be a problem, either for us or the bad guys, and at the appointed hour we took a collective deep breath, scrambled down the wooded bank to the road and set off in procession behind Paul and Nyembo. After about half a kilometre we passed the first clay-built dwellings of the sleeping village, moving on downhill as silently as we could. My main fear was that one of the children would suddenly burst out crying, but they were all impeccably behaved, and soon we were filing past the few concrete boxes which represented the village centre, crossing the empty road and edging our way along the shoreline to the dock, where our chosen craft was bobbing in the gentle swell between the rotting hulks of two former fishing boats.

Its freshly painted name proclaimed it, in English, as the *Kivu Queen*, which suggested someone had done his homework. It was even roughly the same size as the boat which had carried Bogart and Hepburn downriver to their contretemps with the German gunboat on nearby Lake Tanganyika, which I hoped was a good omen. This whole mission had been a trip through various movies, so why not end with a classic?

Everyone got aboard before Paul went to work on the engine – if it fired we would be ready to go.

He fiddled for a long couple of minutes while we kept our eyes glued on the sleeping village, and I was just about to ask what the hell was keeping him when the engine coughed happily into life. It probably wasn't that loud, but, without much to compete with in the way of night noise, it sounded deafening. Almost immediately there was a banging sound from somewhere onshore, and we were only about thirty metres out from the dock when first one figure, then another, tumbled out of one of the concrete boxes, stopped for a second to work out what was going on, then ran shouting towards us. I thought about shooting them, but stealing their boat and killing them seemed a bit much, particularly since it would serve no purpose whatsoever – they'd already woken the whole village with their cries of outrage.

The two men did stop shouting after a while, but by that time a minor crowd had joined them on the dock, and I could almost feel the vibes of indignation and reproach pursuing us across the water. I only hoped the village lacked any means of contacting the local military HQ, wherever that might be. There had been no sign of telephone wires, but if our luck was out the soldiers would have a radio of some sort.

Once the jaws of the bay were behind us, Paul set the *Kivu Queen* on the north-easterly course needed to swing round the northern end of Idjiwi, the large dumb-bell-shaped island which sat in the middle of the lake. According to our map the border ran east of the island, about two-thirds of the way across, and as the minutes went by I began to feel increasingly sure that we'd make it. The lake was calm, the fuel tank was almost full, and the engine was pushing us forward at a reliable, if hardly dizzy, ten knots. As the forested northern tip of Idjiwi loomed ever closer we were reduced to tourists ourselves, just drinking in the majestic scenery which surrounded us.

Sheff, of course, was longing for a cigarette.

'You haven't seen one in four days,' I told him. 'The physical craving's gone. It's all in your mind now.'

'It always was,' he retorted. 'And anyway it wouldn't be fair. I want some credit when I stop – any fool can do it if he can't get hold of a cigarette.'

I shook my head with all the wisdom of an ex-smoker. 'Nell's a nurse,' I pointed out.

'Yeah,' he answered with a grin. 'She's been pining for a fag herself.'

It was at that moment that our ears picked up the sound of the helicopter. It was still a long way away, and for a few moments I tried to convince myself its flight had nothing to do with us. But then we saw it, a brightening star in the north-western sky, heading straight in our direction.

My first instinct was to order everyone under the seats, leaving two or three men upright to play the innocent boatmen. But what was the point – who would be out on the lake in a boat like this at two in the morning?

The helicopter – it was the same Puma I'd seen thirty-six hours before – was almost on us now, and with a deafening roar it flew almost directly over our heads, before making a tight turn to the left and approaching us again at a more oblique angle. I was half expecting a megaphone – something on the lines of 'come in Zulu Four . . . your time is up' – but I should have known better than to expect a presumption of innocence in such pragmatic times. What I saw instead was moonlight glimmering on a moving weapon and a split second later automatic fire was ripping through the boat. I heard the plunking sounds of bullets embedding themselves in wood, the alarming ferocity of bullets chewing up the plastic awning. I heard a sharp intake of breath and a sudden cry, but there was no time to worry about who'd been hit or how badly.

The chopper was turning once more, this time against the absurdly beautiful backdrop of a moonlit wall of volcanoes. I handed the last of our M72s to Paul and silently prayed that his luck hadn't run out. He positioned himself with one foot on the deck and one knee on the slatted seat which ran round the edge of the boat, and tried to make allowances for the gentle rocking.

As the Puma closed in on us again both Gonzo and Sheff opened up with their MP5s, but both bursts died a quick death as the depleted magazines ran dry, and whatever hits the chopper sustained made no obvious difference to its course or intentions. The man in the doorway opened fire once more, but Paul held his for what seemed an eternity, just half kneeling there, a figure of stillness as the bullets whipped past him. I didn't see his finger tighten on the trigger – just felt the whoosh of the rocket as it leapt from the stubby barrel, and then closed my eyes against the blinding flash of exploding fuel tanks. A wave of heat washed over us and the sky was full of smoke and debris. There was a succession of splashes, a moment of silence, and then a child began to cry.

Console had taken a bullet through her left forearm, Barry another through the fleshy part of his thigh, but they were the lucky ones. Knox-Brown had taken two bullets to the head, either one of which would have killed him.

Rachel was already looking after Console, and Nell was doing what was needed to prevent Barry from bleeding to death. 'Cover him up,' I told Sheff, nodding in Knox-Brown's direction, and then gave Gonzo a signal to take Paul's place at the helm. Paul was still staring out at the lake, as if he couldn't believe what had happened.

'Great shot,' I said quietly.

He blinked a couple of times, gave me a sheepish grin, then gently lobbed the spent M72 over the side.

We headed on, ears and eyes straining for a second visitor, but either the first had failed to call home or, as seemed more likely, the rebels had possessed only one helicopter.

It was about half-past three when we crossed the imaginary line in the water that marked the Rwandan border, and despite having my doubts as to how rigorously such niceties were observed in Central Africa, I couldn't help feeling a little safer.

'Any idea where we should land?' I asked Camille, not really expecting any answer, let alone the one I got.

'My town is over there,' he said slowly, pointing slightly south of east. 'And I must go there.'

He told us its name was Kibuye, that it was bigger than any of the Zairean towns he had seen, and that we could call the capital, Kigali, from the post office.

'Sounds great,' I said.

'As long as there's a fag shop,' Sheff murmured.

We pulled in alongside Kibuye's ramshackle pier just as the sun was breasting the wall of mountains which lay behind the town. The row of old colonial buildings fronting the lake offered evidence of past importance, and a few dust-begrimed cars still lined the rutted street which ran east through the town towards a V-shaped cleft in the mountains, but the overall impression was of neglect and decay. Killing or exiling about twenty per cent of the national population obviously hadn't done much for urban renewal.

Some of the locals were already up and about, and we drew long stares from those who went by on the lakeside road. None were in uniform, though, and none seemed disposed to come any closer than they had to.

If the town still boasted a post office it was unlikely to be open, but there didn't seem much point in just sitting around waiting. I checked that both Console and Barry were doing OK, then picked Gonzo, Nyembo and Camille to come with me. 'We'd better leave our guns behind,' I told Gonzo, and we removed the Brownings from our belts. The local military might be hostile, but I couldn't see us shooting our way across more ranges of mountains to Uganda or Tanzania – not with four loaded handguns, four empty MP5s and a cargo of wounded to look after.

We started up the main street, carefully smiling at the two men we passed, and quickly came to Camille's post office, a small concrete building with a limp Rwandan flag above the door. It was closed, and looked like it had been for some time. This impression was confirmed by a man in the neighbouring yard, who nervously went on to tell us that the foreign-run refugee centre operating out of the old Hôtel du Lac had a radio.

We retraced our steps to the lake, turned left, and walked about three hundred metres down the front. The Hôtel du Lac was now the 'Hôt d La,' and what little paint remained on its colonial-style veranda was flaking off in the breeze. The front doors were open, and the sound of a child crying drifted down the stairs as I rapped on the wood.

A Rwandan woman came into the lobby, took one look at us and disappeared again. A few seconds later a white woman emerged, and after a moment's hesitation strode purposefully forward. She was probably in her early thirties, dark-haired and very slim, with tired eyes that seemed almost too big for her face. 'What do you want?' she asked abruptly in French.

I explained the situation, that I was one of four British soldiers who had just arrived from Zaire with a medical team and some Hutu refugees, and that I'd heard there was a radio here. She listened patiently, the distrust slowly fading from her eyes, and finally offered a reluctant acquiescence. 'But I do not want soldiers in the hotel,' she insisted. 'The children here . . . some of them will be very frightened. I will speak to our people in Kigali and they can inform your embassy.'

I didn't argue. 'We'll wait outside,' I told her.

She nodded again, and as she turned away another child began wailing somewhere inside the building.

There was a day-old newspaper out on the veranda. The Zairean rebels were apparently closing in on

Kisangani, and it now seemed likely that Mobutu's long reign was over. 'Meet the new boss – same as the old boss,' I murmured to myself. There was no mention of rebel atrocities, but there was a paragraph about a group of French mercenaries who'd been forced into the jungle by a determined rebel attack. It was thought unlikely that they'd ever be seen again.

After about ten minutes the woman reappeared, this time leading a child by the hand. 'These are the men who knocked on the door,' she told the girl, who must have been about seven years old. 'See, they are not bad men,' she added. 'They have no guns or knives.'

The fear in the little girl's eyes made me ashamed of the whole fucking human race.

'I talked to Kigali,' the woman said. 'They'll call back in ten minutes. My name is Francine, by the way, and this is Flora.' She smiled for the first time, and the change in her face was almost miraculous.

'You can bring the other children here,' she said, turning back from the doorway. 'And the adults can wait outside.'

It seemed a better bet than sitting in a stolen boat at the bottom of Kibuye High Street. I sent Gonzo and Nyembo to collect the others, and stared across the blue lake at the mountains we had crossed.

I suddenly realized Camille was standing in front of me, extending his hand.

'I must go,' he said.

'Where?' I asked stupidly.

He didn't answer for a moment, just let his head

drop and stared at the wooden floor. 'I have done many terrible things,' he said finally, the words almost tumbling out of his mouth. 'Here . . . before . . .'

I looked at him. 'But you can't have been . . . ?'

He gave me a look of frustration, as if I was too stupid to understand. 'I was twelve years old, almost a man. I did terrible things, and if I stay with Imaculée and the others then they will suffer too for the things I did.'

I didn't know what to say. 'Does Imaculée know you are going?' I asked.

'No, but she will understand. She knows what I have done.'

At that moment Francine came back through the door, this time alone. 'Your people are sending transport for you,' she said. 'It should be here early this afternoon.'

'Thanks,' I said automatically.

We'd be going home, but Camille was already there. He was offering me his hand again, his eyes brimming with a desolation which no fifteen-year-old should know. I shook it, wished him good luck, then watched him walk away up the dusty road.

We might be going home with a vaccine for AIDS, but humans were still killing each other in numbers that any virus would envy, and as far I could tell no one was even looking for a cure.

OTHER TITLES IN SERIES FROM 22 BOOKS

Available now at newsagents and booksellers
or use the order form provided

continued overleaf . . .

ZULU FOUR

All at £4.99

All 22 Books are available at your bookshop, or can be ordered from:

22 Books
Mail Order Department
Little, Brown and Company
Brettenham House
Lancaster Place
London WC2E 7EN

Alternatively, you may fax your order to the above address. Fax number: 0171 911 8100.

Payments can be made by cheque or postal order, payable to Little, Brown and Company (UK), or by credit card (Visa/Access). Do not send cash or currency. UK, BFPO and Eire customers, please allow 75p per item for postage and packing, to a maximum of £7.50. Overseas customers, please allow £1 per item.

While every effort is made to keep prices low, it is sometimes necessary to increase cover prices at short notice. 22 Books reserves the right to show new retail prices on covers which may differ from those previously advertised in the books or elsewhere.

NAME ....

ADDRESS ....

....

....

☐ I enclose my remittance for £ _____
☐ I wish to pay by Access/Visa

Card number

☐☐☐☐ ☐☐☐☐ ☐☐☐☐ ☐☐☐☐

Card expiry date

☐☐ ☐☐

Please allow 28 days for delivery. Please tick box if you do not wish to receive any additional information ☐